IN TOO DEEP

JAYNE ANN KRENTZ

THORNDIKE
WINDSOR
PARAGON

This Large Print edition is published by Thorndike Press, Waterville, Maine USA and by AudioGo Ltd, Bath, England.

Thorndike Press, a part of Gale, Cengage Learning.

Thorndike Press® Large Print Basic.
The text of this Large Print edition is unabridged.
Other aspects of the book may vary from the original edition.
Set in 16 pt. Plantin.

LIBRARY OF CONGRESS CATALOGING-IN-PUBLICATION DATA

Krentz, Jayne Ann.
   In too deep / by Jayne Ann Krentz.
     p. cm. — (Thorndike Press large print basic) (The looking glass trilogy ; no. 1)
   ISBN-13: 978-1-4104-3427-2 (hardcover)
   ISBN-10: 1-4104-3427-3 (hardcover)
   1. Psychics—Fiction. 2. Arcane Society (Imaginary organization)—Fiction. 3. Large type books. I. Title.
PS3561.R4416 2011
813'.54—dc22   2010044614

BRITISH LIBRARY CATALOGUING-IN-PUBLICATION DATA AVAILABLE
Published in the U.S. in 2011 by arrangement with G. P. Putnam's Sons, a member of Penguin Group (USA) Inc.
Published in the U.K. in 2011 by arrangement with Little, Brown Book Group.
U.K. Hardcover: 978 1 445 85531 8 (Windsor Large Print)
U.K. Softcover: 978 1 445 85532 5 (Paragon Large Print)

Printed and bound in Great Britain by the MPG Books Group
1 2 3 4 5 6 7 15 14 13 12 11

For Frank,
with all my love.

PROLOGUE I

Fallon Jones: three years earlier . . .

Paranormal fire burned in the darkness. Auroras of psi splashed across the ether. The night sky above San Francisco was ablaze with light from across the spectrum. Fallon Jones gripped the condo balcony railing with both hands, fighting to anchor himself to reality. There were spectacular patterns wherever he looked: wondrous, astonishingly intricate webs of connections and links that illuminated the path back to the heart of the universe.

The dazzling radiance of the midnight world was compelling beyond anything he had ever experienced. He was certain that if he only looked closely enough, he would be able to distinguish the light from the dawn of creation, perhaps even grasp a fistful of the raw power of chaos that fueled the forces of life and death.

"Good night for a walk, isn't it?" Tucker

7

Austin said.

Fallon turned to look at the figure silhouetted in the opening of the sliding-glass doorway. There was something wrong. Tucker looked as if he stood on the other side of a waterfall. It was impossible to focus on him. He held something in his hand but Fallon could not make it out.

"What are you doing here?" Fallon asked. He was vaguely aware that he sounded drunk. But he was almost positive that he'd had only one glass of wine with dinner.

"We both know why I'm here." Tucker moved out of the doorway and went to stand at the railing a short distance away. He kept the object in his hand out of sight against his left leg. "The magic lantern really slammed your senses, didn't it? That's one of the interesting side effects of the device. The higher the level of talent, the greater the impact. You are literally off the charts on the Jones Scale. That makes the lantern the ideal weapon to destroy you without arousing any suspicions. By now you're lost out there on the paranormal plane. There's no coming back from this trip."

"You came here to kill me," Fallon said. A simple statement of fact, nothing more or less. It was good to know he was still able to think logically.

"I did warn you that one day your talent would be the death of you." Tucker sounded amused. "I'm not alone in that opinion, as I'm sure you're aware. Fortunately, a lot of people are convinced that a chaos theory-talent as powerful as you is doomed. And there have always been those rumors about the men in your family who inherit that aspect of the founder's talent. Everyone knows that Sylvester Jones was a paranoid whack-job at the end."

"Sylvester died more than four hundred years ago," Fallon said. "No one knows what really happened to him at the end. And rumors are, by definition, not facts."

"But as you have often pointed out, an interesting rumor always has more influence than a boring fact."

Fallon shook his head once and blinked a couple of times, trying to bring Tucker into focus. The small motion caused the universe to shift around him. The disorientation was so fierce now that he had to clench his hand around the balcony railing to stay on his feet.

"Why?" he asked. It was a foolish question. He knew the answer. But for some reason he wanted to hear Tucker put it into words. Then again, that had been the prob-

lem all along. He had wanted to believe
Tucker Austin.

"I'm afraid there's no other way out."
Tucker rested both elbows on the railing
and contemplated the night. "It's either you
or me this time. Survival of the fittest and
all that. The magic lantern has certain
hypnotic effects. In addition to creating
those fascinating hallucinations you're currently viewing, it makes you vulnerable to
suggestion. For example, you feel like taking a walk off this balcony, don't you?"

"No," Fallon said again. He tried to move,
but when he took a step he stumbled and
went down to his knees.

Tucker gestured toward the building
across the street. "You know what you
should do, Fallon? You should cross that
crystal bridge. Halfway over, you'll have a
terrific view of the heart of the universe.
How can you resist?"

Fallon tightened his grip on the railing
and hauled himself upright. He tried to
focus, but the crashing waves of the auroras
that lit up the night were too distracting.

"What bridge?" he asked.

"Right there." Tucker pointed. "It leads
from this balcony to the roof of the building
across the street. Just step over the railing
and you'll be on your way."

Fallon looked down. Strange machines moved on the street below. Lights glowed and flashed. *Cars,* some part of his brain whispered. *Get a grip. You're fourteen floors above the street.*

"Don't you see the bridge?" Tucker asked. "It leads to all the answers, Fallon. You just follow the crystal brick road to find the wizard."

Fallon concentrated. A crystal bridge materialized in the night. The transparent steps were infused with an internal light. He pulled harder on his talent. The bridge brightened and beckoned. But a tiny sliver of awareness sliced through the wonder of the scene.

"Think I've seen that bridge before," he said.

"Yeah?" For the first time Tucker sounded slightly disconcerted. "Where?"

"In the movies. Damn silly plot but the special effects were mildly entertaining."

Tucker chuckled. "Leave it to Fallon Jones to come up with a logical explanation for a perfectly good hallucination. Well, it was worth a shot. But if you won't do this the easy way, I guess we'll have to go with Plan B."

He moved suddenly, bringing up the object in his hand. Fallon tried to raise one

11

arm to block the blow, but his muscles would not obey. Instinctively he twisted aside, instead. He lost his balance and went down hard on the tiled floor.

The object Tucker wielded was a hammer. It struck inches away from Fallon's head. He heard the crack of the tiles. The entire balcony shuddered with the force of the blow.

Somewhere in the night a woman started screaming.

"You crazy son of a bitch," Tucker said. He raised the hammer for another blow. "You're supposed to be out of your head by now."

Fallon rolled away and reached for more talent. The hammer struck the floor of the balcony again.

He managed to scramble to his feet. The sparkling, iridescent night spun wildly around him.

Tucker charged him in a violent rush. The promise of imminent death sent another rush of adrenaline through Fallon, producing a few seconds of brilliant clarity.

He finally succeeded in getting a focus. For an instant the familiar features of the man he had considered a trusted friend were clearly visible in the light from the living room. Tucker's face was twisted with a

12

maddened rage. Fallon realized that he had never known the real Tucker until tonight.

The shock of being so terribly, horribly wrong brought another dose of clarity. People had died because of Tucker Austin, and Fallon knew that he was, in part, to blame. He summoned up the full, raging force of his talent, reached into the heart of chaos and seized a fistful of fire. He hurled the invisible currents of paranormal radiation into Tucker's aura. Not exactly Zeus with the lightning bolts but good enough to get the job done.

Tucker grunted once, clutched at his heart and instinctively reeled backward to escape the onslaught of energy. He fetched up hard against the balcony railing. He was a tall man. The barrier caught him at mid-thigh. The force of his momentum sent him over the edge.

He did not scream, because he was already dead. But Jenny's scream went on forever. Fallon knew he would hear it for the rest of his life.

PROLOGUE II

Isabella: one month ago . . .

She was not expecting the killers to come for her in the lingerie department.

She was always especially alert at night after work when she walked through the mall's deserted parking garage. She never entered the cheap motel room that she rented by the week without checking for the telltale paranormal fog indicating an intruder. When she shopped for groceries, she was careful to keep an eye on strangers who invaded her personal space, and she never, ever ordered in. No one had an excuse to knock on her door.

But for some reason Isabella had felt reasonably safe selling women's underwear in the discount department store for the past week. The sight of the two men loitering across the aisle in women's sportswear sent a frisson of electricity across the nape of her neck. When you were psychic, you paid attention to your intuition.

She heightened her talent cautiously, bracing for the unpleasant chill of awareness. She possessed the ability to perceive the unique energy generated by those who kept secrets. Everyone harbored countless mysteries, small and large, however, so it was a given that if there were people in the vicinity, there would be a lot of fog.

Her coworkers and the shoppers around her were abruptly surrounded by misty auras. She wrestled with her talent for a few seconds, concentrating on those two men. Although she was prepared, the sight of the hot, seething energy around the pair made her go cold to the bone. Definitely talents of some kind, probably hunters.

You're the one they're hunting, her intuition whispered. *Run.* Sure, like she could outrun two trained men who would be as quick and ruthless as a pair of wolves.

She struggled to maintain her outward composure. Panic would get her killed as surely as any gun or knife.

The middle-aged woman standing directly in front of her tossed three pairs of lacy thong panties onto the sales counter with a defiant air.

"I'll take these," she announced, daring Isabella to object.

The customer displayed all of the visible hallmarks of a woman who had just gone through a nasty divorce. Isabella did not need the psychic side of her nature to pick up on the cues: a pale white line where the wedding ring had been, eyes too wide and tight from a recent surgical lift, new haircut, fresh dye job, trendy, tight-fitting clothes. The woman's life had recently crashed and burned.

I know the feeling, Isabella thought. Sort of. The truth was, she had never actually had a real life. Still, for a while during the past six months she had come close, so close, to feeling normal. *Face it — you weren't born to be normal.*

She managed a polite smile and picked up the panties. "Great buy, aren't they?"

"Yes." The customer was somewhat mollified now that she was assured she wasn't going to be mocked for buying the thongs. "That's why I bought three pairs."

"Good idea. The price will go back up next week after the sale," Isabella said.

She watched the two men in women's sportswear out of the corner of her eye while she rang up the panties. The hair on the back of her neck was standing on end. Goose bumps covered her upper arms. A cold sweat formed between her shoulder blades. Her senses were screaming. Her pulse was pounding. *Get out of here. Now.*

Viewed in normal light there was nothing to mark the two hunters as anything other than what they appeared to be, bored shopping escorts waiting for their companions to come out of the dressing rooms. But Isabella noticed that customers in their vicinity edged away from them. The two were probably really cranked, preparing to close in on their prey. As a result they were giving off so much energy that even people without any measurable talent sensed the threat on a subliminal level.

"Excuse me, I'm in a hurry here," the woman on the other side of the counter snapped.

"Sorry." Isabella smiled apologetically. "Cash register is a little slow today."

She pushed the credit card slip and a pen across the counter. The woman scrawled her name and grabbed the shopping bag containing the thongs.

Isabella forced herself to smile at the next customer in line, a young mother with a baby in a stroller.

"Can I help you?" Isabella asked. *Run.*

"I want to buy this." The customer put a pale blue nightgown on the counter and leaned down to pick up the small plush toy

18

the baby had tossed out of the stroller.

"This is such a pretty color," Isabella remarked, falling back on the one day of training the department store had given her at the start of her employment. *Always compliment the customer's good taste.* She folded the nightgown in the precise way she had been instructed and reached for a sheet of tissue. "Such a beautiful shade of blue."

The woman straightened, brightening immediately.

"Yes," she said. "It's my favorite. Good price, too."

"You were smart to get here early for the sale." Isabella started to wrap some tissue around the nightgown and paused, frowning. "Hmm."

"What's wrong?"

"There's a small spot on this gown," Isabella said.

Alarmed, the woman leaned over the counter. "Where?"

"Right here." Isabella whisked up the nightgown, careful to hold it so that the customer could not see the mythical spot.

"It's the last one in blue in my size," the woman wailed.

"Don't worry, I think I've got one more in the back room, same color and size. I'll only be a moment."

Nightgown in hand, Isabella turned and went quickly toward the discreet door directly behind the counter.

She knew the hunter-talents saw her go through the door into the stockroom, but with luck they would not realize that she had spotted them. Even if they were suspicious, they were unlikely to follow her. One of the clerks would be sure to call Security.

She dropped the nightgown onto a table and started toward the door that opened onto the emergency stairwell. Darlene, one of her coworkers, emerged from between two rows of floor-to-ceiling shelving crammed with boxes of undergarments. She had a stack of lacy bras in her hand.

"Annie, are you okay?" Darlene asked, frowning in concern. "You look like you're not feeling well."

"I'm fine, thanks," Isabella said.

She had used the name and ID of a non-existent woman named Ann Carstairs to get the job in the department store. There was only one individual on the face of the earth who knew her real name. In the past week she'd been forced to face the possibility that that person, her grandmother, might be dead. *If no one knows your real name do you even exist?* she wondered.

That's it, she thought. *Stop right there.*

Negative thinking will get you nowhere. Until it was proven otherwise, she was going to go with the assumption that her grandmother was alive. Meanwhile, her job was to keep herself breathing. That meant avoiding the two hunter-talents.

"You look a little shaky," Darlene said.

"Low on caffeine," Isabella replied. "I'm going on break. Thought I'd use the stairs to the coffee room. I need the exercise."

"Huh." Darlene hurried toward the door to the sales floor. "Seems to me we get plenty of exercise during a sale. My feet are killing me. I'm going to be exhausted by the time we get off work tonight."

"Me, too," Isabella said. "Would you mind taking the blue nightgown out to the counter? There's a customer waiting for it. Tell her there was no spot, after all. Just a trick of the light."

"No problem."

"Thanks."

She waited until Darlene disappeared out onto the sales floor, and then she opened the stairwell door.

More fog swirled on the concrete staircase, but unlike the energy that enveloped the hunter-talents, this stuff glowed with a cold fire. It was the kind of fog she had learned to associate with impending death.

"Oh, crap, not now," she whispered.

She was running for her life. She did not need any distractions.

She started down the stairs, determined to ignore the atmosphere of the stairwell. But there was no ignoring the seething fog cascading down the steps. It was so very cold.

She stopped and looked up. The fog came from the rooftop of the three-story mall, one floor above. The part of her that had been dealing with her talent since her thirteenth year screamed at her to follow the luminous trail. There was something at the top of the emergency stairwell that needed to be found immediately. Time was of the essence.

The thought of getting cornered on the roof by the two hunters held no appeal. But the odds were good that the pair would assume that she would flee down into the mall garage or out onto the street. Going up might be an excellent strategy.

Okay, she was rationalizing. Still, there was a slender thread of logic involved. The bottom line was that she had to find whatever was waiting to be discovered on the mall roof and she had to find it quickly.

The emergency stairwell was a highly efficient echo chamber. The sound of footsteps carried from top to bottom. If the hunters realized that she was not coming back out onto the sales floor, they would surely guess that she had escaped via the emergency stairs. If they decided to risk following her into the stairwell, they would hear her climbing up toward the roof.

She slipped out of her flats, clutched them in one hand, and went quickly up the stairs in her stocking feet. At least she was dressed for flight, she thought. She always wore trousers and flats or boots to work, always dressed to run for her life.

She had been living on the edge for ten days. Lately she had begun to wonder how much longer she could keep up the unrelenting vigilance. The fact that Julian Garrett's men had found her so easily tonight was a sure sign that her life in hiding was taking a toll on her senses. She could not go on like this much longer.

Start thinking like that and you might as well jump off the roof when you get there.

At least it would all be over. If her grandmother was dead, there was no one left who was linked to her by bonds of blood. Ten days ago, she had been forced to sever the workplace friendships she had forged at Lucan Protection Services. Now she was profoundly alone in a way that most people

23

could never imagine. In a world where everyone possessed an identity, she was utterly anonymous. In a very real sense she did not exist.

So why go on?

Rage kicked in, generating heat and energy and another burst of adrenaline. She dashed up the stairwell. She did have something, she thought. She had an enemy. His name was Julian Garrett. She would not let the bastards win so easily.

Always nice to have a goal.

She made it up the final flight of stairs, breathless now, and opened the door. Warily, she stepped outside into the balmy Arizona night. The lights of Phoenix, Scottsdale and the neighboring communities glittered and winked below. A nearly full moon bathed the scene in silver.

The vast expanse of the roof was dotted here and there by the looming shapes of several tons of HVAC equipment. It took a lot of air-conditioning for a mall to survive summer and winter in the desert.

She hesitated, trying to concentrate on the possibilities that might be available if the hunters followed her to the top of the mall. She could see at least three other stairwell entrances that opened onto the roof.

24

But the river of icy fog did not lead toward one of the potential escape routes. It illuminated a path to the edge of the roof. At the end of the trail of freezing mist a woman stood silhouetted against the city lights.

Isabella slipped into her shoes and went slowly toward the woman.

"Hi," she said. Her heart was pounding, but she managed to keep her voice calm and soothing. "Are you okay?"

The woman gasped and turned quickly. "Who are you?"

"This week I'm Annie. What's your name?"

"Sandra. What are you doing here?"

"I don't know. You tell me."

"What's that supposed to mean?" Sandra sounded angry now.

"You're thinking of jumping off this roof, aren't you?"

"Don't come any closer."

"Okay." Isabella stopped. "I'd really like to help you, but we're going to have to make this fast. I don't have a lot of time."

"Got another appointment?" Sandra's tone was utterly flat now. "Don't let me keep you."

"The thing is there are a couple of guys downstairs who want to kidnap me."

"What on earth are you talking about?"

Isabella inched closer. She was still too far away from Sandra to do what needed to be done.

"They're hunting for me as we speak. It won't take them long to realize that I'm not coming out of the stockroom. It would be good if I could get off this roof before they find me."

"Two men are hunting you?" Sandra's voice rose in disbelief. "Is this some kind of sick joke?"

"I wish."

"You're serious, aren't you?"

"Very."

"You're probably on drugs. Did you stiff your dealer? Look, I don't want to get involved, okay? I've got my own problems."

"No, honest," Isabella said. "This has nothing to do with drugs. Ten days ago I stumbled into a very dangerous conspiracy. Someone set me up to take the fall. The real conspirators think I know too much. I'm afraid they may have murdered my grandmother because I told her about the scheme. And now they're trying to kill me. Oh, damn, I really don't have time for this conversation."

"Are you some kind of nutcase? One of those conspiracy freaks?"

"That opinion has been floated occasionally." Isabella edged closer. Almost there. Another couple of feet and she would be able to touch Sandra. All she needed was physical contact.

"Stop," Sandra said. "Don't come any closer. I mean it."

Muffled footsteps sounded inside the nearby stairwell.

"I think we just ran out of time," Isabella said. "Here they come."

"Who?" Bewildered and distracted, Sandra turned her head toward the stairwell.

"The killers," Isabella replied.

She pounced. Seizing Sandra's wrist, she found a focus and pulsed some energy.

Sandra's face became expressionless. She stared off into the distance.

Isabella yanked her behind the massive metal housing that shrouded the HVAC equipment. She pushed her down onto the rooftop. "Stay here. Don't move and don't say a word until I tell you it's safe to come out."

Sandra did not respond. Isabella pulsed a little more energy and then released Sandra's arm. The woman sat very still, her back against the metal housing, and gazed out into the night.

The door of the stairwell slammed open. Isabella knew that there was no point trying to hide on the rooftop. The killers would conduct a thorough search.

She moved out from behind the HVAC tower and looked at the figure that had just emerged from the stairwell. The hunter-talent didn't see her at first. Moonlight and neon glinted on the small pistol in his hand.

"Hi," Isabella said. She waved.

He turned toward her with preternatural speed, gun elevated.

"Got her," he called over his shoulder.

His companion emerged from the same opening. He, too, gripped a gun.

"Did you really think we wouldn't find you?" the first man said. "You're coming with us."

"I'm a little busy at the moment," Isabella said.

"No shit," the second man said. "So are we. Wasted over a week trying to find you. The boss is not happy."

He moved forward and seized Isabella's arm.

The contact acted like a psychic electrical contact, making it possible for her to pulse energy directly into his aura.

She got a focus and sent out a small blast of disruptive psi.

"Get lost," she said softly.

The gunman went still for a few seconds.

Then he turned and started to walk toward the edge of the roof.

His companion stared. "What the hell? Hey, Rawlins, where are you going?"

Isabella took a step toward the stairwell doorway.

"Don't move," the man snarled. He lunged forward, grabbed her wrist and turned back to his companion. "Rawlins, have you gone crazy? Come back here."

Rawlins continued toward the edge of the roof as though captivated by the clusters of lights sprinkled across the desert.

"Rawlins," the second man shouted. He sounded on the verge of panic. "You're gonna go off the damn roof, man. Come back." He put the barrel of the pistol against Isabella's head. "What did you do to him, you little bitch?"

"I just told him to get lost," she said. She got the fix and pulsed energy into his aura. "Same thing I'm telling you. Take a hike."

The gunman froze for a beat or two and then he lowered the gun. She took the weapon from his unresisting hand. He turned and started to follow Rawlins toward the edge of the mall roof.

"Oh, good grief," Isabella said. "I'll admit, I'm tempted to let you both walk off this roof, but it would probably cause more trouble than it's worth."

She put down the gun, hurried forward and stepped in front of Rawlins. She touched him lightly. "Wrong way. Come with me."

He stopped obediently, his face a complete blank. She took the gun from him and set it down. Then she took his wrist in one hand and grabbed the other man's arm. She guided them both toward the stairwell. When they reached the doorway, she urged them inside.

"Go down the stairs, leave the building and keep walking," she ordered. "Cross the streets only at the crosswalks. Wait for the green light."

Sometimes the hypnotic suggestions worked; sometimes they didn't.

Rawlins started down the stairs. The second man followed.

There was no way to know how long the trancelike state would last. She simply did not have enough practical experience. It was an aspect of her talent that did not allow for a great deal of experimentation. But with luck she would have time to get out of the mall and disappear. Again.

She went back to where Sandra sat, took hold of her wrist and pulsed a little energy.

Sandra blinked and came back to her senses.

"I know you," she said, frowning. "You're the nutcase who thinks people are trying to kill her."

"Right, let's go." Isabella guided her toward another stairwell. "I hate to rush you, but I'm in a hurry here."

"I'm not going anywhere with you. You're crazy."

"Hey, I'm not the one who was about to jump off the roof."

"I'm not crazy," Sandra said, annoyed. "I'm depressed."

"Whatever, you're coming with me."

"Where are you taking me?"

"To the nearest hospital emergency room. You can explain everything to someone who will know what to do. I'm not a shrink."

Sandra paused at the doorway of the stairwell. She looked back out at the edge of the roof.

"I don't want to jump anymore."

"Glad to hear that." Isabella drew her down into the stairwell.

"But if you hadn't come along when you did, I wouldn't have had a chance to change my mind."

"Always a good idea to give yourself time to reconsider the really big decisions."

31

"I've been planning to jump for weeks and suddenly I changed my mind." Sandra frowned. "Why would I do that?"

"Because you're smart and stronger than you think."

"No, it was something about you that made me decide not to jump. Something in the atmosphere around you."

"You're the one who made the call. Don't ever forget that."

They went down the stairs to the parking garage. Isabella stuffed Sandra into the beat-up junker she had bought for cash ten days earlier and drove to the hospital. She escorted Sandra into the emergency room and stayed with her until an orderly came to take her into a treatment room.

Sandra paused in the doorway and looked back. "Will I see you again, Annie?"

"No," Isabella said.

"Are you an angel?"

"Nope, just a garden-variety conspiracy theorist who thinks some people are out to silence her."

Sandra studied her intently. "I remember the footsteps on the emergency stairs. I remember you telling me to stay quiet and not move. And I saw a gun lying on the mall roof. Be careful, Annie."

"Thanks," Isabella said. She smiled. "I

will. You do the same, okay?"

"Okay," Sandra said.

She followed the orderly down a white corridor.

Isabella went back outside to the hospital parking lot. She would have to leave the car behind. They had found her at the mall. She had to assume they had a description of the junker.

She opened the trunk, took out the small backpack she kept inside and closed the lid. She slung the strap of the pack over one shoulder and walked through the garage toward the street.

She knew where she was going now. The events of the evening had left her no choice. To get to her destination she would use the one form of transportation that did not leave a paper or computer trail.

She would hitchhike to Scargill Cove.

1

"This is the perfect case for me to cut my teeth on here at Jones & Jones," Isabella said. "You know that as well as I do. You're just being difficult, Mr. Jones."

"I'm told that's a good working description of what I do," Fallon said. "Evidently I have some expertise in being difficult. And stop calling me Mr. Jones. The name is Fallon, damn it. You didn't start with the Mr. Jones thing until you went to work here. When you were pouring coffee for me at the Sunshine, it was Fallon."

"All right." Isabella paused a beat and then she smiled. "Fallon. Now, about my new case."

As always her smile and her energy seemed to light up the whole office. He had been struggling to comprehend the para-physics involved, but thus far he'd gotten nowhere. In theory, a smile was merely a facial expression, the result of small changes in the position of tiny little muscles and nerves. It should not have the kind of power that Isabella wielded with her smile.

There was no scientific way to explain how her personal aura could create a sense of well-being for others in her vicinity, either; no logical reason why her force field helped him clarify and organize his thoughts.

"Your so-called case," he said deliberately, "falls into the category of Lost Dogs and Haunted Houses. We try not to encourage that sort of business here at Jones & Jones. This happens to be a real investigation agency."

"Norma Spaulding just wants us to check out that old house she's trying to sell and declare it ghost-free."

"There are no such things as ghosts."

"I know that, you know that and so does Norma," Isabella said patiently. "She doesn't actually believe the place is haunted. She just wants to put the rumors to rest. She says the gossip about weird stuff going on at the house is killing sales. She thinks that getting a clean bill of health from a genuine psychic detective agency will take care of the problem."

He lounged back in his chair and stacked his booted feet on the corner of his desk.

The desk, like the glass-fronted bookcases and the Egyptian-motif wall sconces, had been among the furnishings of the Los Angeles office of Jones & Jones when it opened for business back in the 1920s. Before that the West Coast office of J&J had been located in San Francisco. Unlike the London office, the West Coast office had been moved a number of times since it was established in the late 1800s. The directors tended to be a restless lot.

In the 1960s Cedric Jones, one in a long line of Joneses to inherit the business, had moved the headquarters to Scargill Cove for a time. The office had been moved yet again twenty-five years ago when Gresham Jones had taken charge. Gresham's wife, Alice, had flatly refused to live in the remote little village on the Northern California coast. At that point, J&J had returned to Los Angeles, where it operated out of Arcane Society headquarters.

But when Fallon had inherited the business, he had found Cedric's notes about the Cove and the unique energy in the area. Intrigued, he had come to the little community to check out the location and discovered that Cedric was right. Something about the energy of the Cove suited the business. It also suited him, Fallon thought.

He had unlocked the door of J&J and walked into a room that had been trapped in a time warp. Beneath three decades of dust, everything, right down to the desk and the wall sconces, was just as Gresham had left it when he had closed the office to move back to L.A.

In addition to the art deco furnishings, there was a scattering of other antiques reflecting the history of J&J. They included the Victorian-era clock on the desk, an old umbrella stand and a wrought iron coatrack. The only things Fallon had added were the computer and a new, industrial-sized coffee machine.

He contemplated his new assistant, trying for what had to be the millionth time to get a fix on the mystery that was Isabella Valdez.

Outside rain fell steadily. The Pacific Ocean was the color of tempered steel and the waves churned down in the Cove. But here in his small, second-floor office all was bright and relentlessly positive. Under other circumstances he would have found all the warm, cheerful energy irritating in the extreme, but for some reason things were different with Isabella.

She was sitting at the other desk, the new one that she had ordered from an online antiques reproduction store her first day on the job at J&J. It had taken two people — that would be the delivery guy and himself, he reflected — to muscle the heavy wooden Victorian-style desk and the chair that went with it up the narrow stairs to the second floor of the building. Isabella had supervised. He had to concede that she had a flair for organization.

But it wasn't her office management skills that disturbed and intrigued him. It was the fact that she had no problems with his talent. She acted as if there were nothing unusual about his psychic nature. That made her unique in his considerable experience. The core of his talent involved an intuitive grasp of patterns within chaos. It was a messy, complicated ability that he himself did not understand. Others often found his ability unnerving.

Within the Arcane Society there had always been rumors about powerful chaos theory-talents, especially those that popped up now and again in the Jones line. He was well aware that there were those who whispered that he was doomed to fall deeper and deeper into a web of dark conspiracy constructs of his own making. Some speculated that there would come a time when he would no longer be able to distinguish the boundary between fantasy and reality: the classic definition of madness.

If they knew the full extent of what he could do with his talent, the whisperers would be appalled, he thought. But he was a Jones. He knew how to keep secrets. He was pretty sure Isabella Valdez knew how to keep them, too. Always nice to have something in common with a woman who aroused all the basic instincts in a man. That, of course, was one of the big complications in his life these days. He had been fascinated with Isabella from the moment he had met her.

The other baffling aspect of Isabella's personality was that she did not have a problem with his moods or a temperament that required a lot of time spent walking alone on the beach down in the Cove. She simply accepted him as he was.

He understood the physical attraction. Isabella lacked the generic perfection that made so many female movie stars and fashion models look as if they had popped out of the same mold. But her strong, striking features and mysterious golden brown eyes had riveted him from the start.

She wore her shoulder-length dark hair in a severe, no-nonsense twist that highlighted the sharply sculpted angles of her chin, nose and cheekbones. She was curvy in all the right places but he had yet to see her in a skirt or dress. Her daily uniform invariably consisted of jeans or dark trousers, a long-sleeved shirt that she wore with the sleeves rolled up, and low boots or flats. She carried a backpack instead of a purse. The backpack was not a fashion statement. It was sturdy and functional, and it was filled with stuff.

It was as if Isabella was always dressed to go for a hike. *Or maybe dressed to run?* The thought had floated through his head on more than one occasion during the past month.

He was quite certain that she was a strong intuitive talent of some kind, although she seemed reluctant to discuss the exact nature of her ability. Fair enough. She did not press him about his talent, either. In addition, she had no problem with the concept of working for an investigation agency that specialized in the paranormal. In fact, she acted as if she'd had some experience in that line. That was not a huge surprise. A lot of powerful intuitives found themselves in the investigation or security business. If they didn't follow that career path, they sometimes wound up as shrinks or storefront psychics.

When he had pointed out that Jones & Jones was closely affiliated with an organization devoted to research into the paranormal, she had simply shrugged. She had then proceeded to inform him that every office, even one run by a psychic detective, required sound, efficient management.

"I realize that you are a bit obsessed with control," she said. "But I believe we have established that the time has come for you to learn to prioritize and delegate. You should be devoting your talents to investigation, not to keeping your office organized."

He had no clear recollection of having actually hired her. True, he had been toying with the notion of employing someone to help him get a handle on the heaps of papers, books and computer printouts that littered the small office. Even the thought of having someone around to make sure he did not run out of coffee had become an increasingly attractive notion. But he had not gotten to the point of advertising the position. For one thing, he had no idea how or where to go about the business of finding the kind of office assistant he needed.

But Isabella had taken the matter out of his hands. She had quit her job as a waitress at the Sunshine Café across the street, walked into J&J and announced that she was his new assistant.

The transformation of the headquarters of the West Coast office of Jones & Jones had happened within a matter of days. Where once controlled chaos had reigned, there was now efficiency and order. Isabella had even managed to unearth the small kitchen off the main room of the office.

The only problem in the arrangement as far as he could see was that, having accomplished her initial objectives, Isabella now wanted to do some real investigation work.

"Norma is willing to pay us for our time," Isabella said. "The house is only a few miles from here. Why not let me check it out?"

"There's nothing to check out," Fallon said. "Norma is new to the local real estate scene. She'll soon figure out that the reason she can't sell the old Zander mansion isn't because of the rumors. It's because the place is more than a hundred years old. Every potential buyer who walks through the front door realizes immediately that it would be a nightmare to remodel the house and bring it up to code."

"Norma thinks it's the mansion's reputation that is killing the deals. She's convinced that if she can advertise that she had the place certified as ghost-free by a real psychic investigation agency she could sell it."

"This is a joke, not a legitimate case. It's bad for the image of J&J."

"J&J is so low profile it doesn't have an image," Isabella said in a tone of sweet reason. "Why not take the easy money? I'll spend an afternoon at the house and report to Norma that all the ghosts have been dispatched. She'll write a check that will go straight to our bottom line."

"Arcane keeps J&J on retainer," Fallon pointed out. "We get plenty of other business from members of the Society. We don't have to go after the Lost Dogs and Haunted Houses trade. And on the rare occasion when we do take on that kind of job, we hand it off to one of our contract agents who doesn't mind the work."

"Norma's office is over in Willow Creek. She says the Zander house is about three miles from there somewhere out on the bluffs. There are no other J&J agents available for a radius of nearly a hundred miles. We're all she's got."

"Forget it," Fallon said. "I need you here."

"This will only take an afternoon. I think we should develop new revenue streams."

He wasn't into the zone. Nevertheless, his intuition went *ping,* sounding a lot like his computer when a new bit of data arrived.

"You were a waitress before you took this job," he said thoughtfully. "Don't tell me you picked up the term *revenue stream* in the food-and-beverage business?"

She ignored that. "You said yourself that the Governing Council or whatever it is that runs the Arcane Society is starting to whine about the costs of the recent operations against that Nightshade conspiracy you're chasing. It would be sound policy for J&J to find other sources of income in case our budget gets cut by the Council."

"The Council can grumble all it wants. Zack is the Master of the Society and he understands what's at stake. He'll see to it that I get the funding I need."

"Fine." Isabella gave him another radiant smile. "Then I'll take Norma Spaulding's payment as a commission for my work. I could use the money, given the lousy salary you're paying me."

He felt like a deer in the headlights when she used that smile on him. It was more dangerous than the crystal gun that had turned up in the Hawaii case. His finely tuned brain seemed to short-circuit when she glowed the way she was glowing now.

"You're the one who told me how much to pay you," he said, grasping at straws. "If you wanted more money, why didn't you ask for it?"

"Because I needed the job," she said smoothly. "I didn't want to scare you by asking for what I'm really worth."

"I don't scare that easily."

"Are you kidding?" She chuckled. "You should have seen the look on your face when the new desk and chair arrived."

"If I flinched, it wasn't because of the price of the damn furniture," he said.

"I know." Her tone gentled. "It was the shock of realizing that you were going to be sharing your working space with me. I understand."

"What the hell is that supposed to mean?"

"You're accustomed to being alone," she said. "By now you've probably convinced yourself that you need solitude in order to do your work. And it's true, up to a point. But you don't require as much of it as you think you do. You've built a fortress around yourself. That's not good."

"Now you're analyzing me? I sure as hell didn't hire you to do that."

"You're right. You don't pay me nearly enough for that kind of work. Do you have any idea how much a psychologist charges per hour these days? And good luck even finding one who understands those of us who are psychic. Most respectable shrinks would take one look at you and conclude that you're crazy."

He went cold and still.

"Oh, for pity's sake," Isabella said. She made a face. "Don't look at me like that. You're not crazy. Not even close. I wouldn't work for you if I thought you were. Now let's get back to the Zander house case."

He exhaled slowly. "Fine. Your case, your commission. But don't spend too much time on it. Like I said, I'm not paying you to chase ghosts."

"Right." She got to her feet and plucked her yellow raincoat off the Victorian wrought iron coatrack. "Norma told me that there is a key box on the Zander house. She gave me the code to open it. I'll drive out to the mansion now, check it out and pronounce it a ghost-free zone."

"Have fun."

Isabella flew out the door, taking all the light and energy that had illuminated the office with her.

He contemplated the closed door for a long time.

I need you here at the office. I need you.

He listened to her light footsteps on the stairs. After a moment he got up and went to the window. Isabella appeared on the street. She paused long enough to hoist her

47

umbrella against the rain and then hurried along Scargill Cove's twisted little main street to Toomey's Treasures. Toomey's window was filled with a lot of New Agey, so-called metaphysical tools, chimes, tarot cards, crystals and exotic oils.

Instead of going up the outside stairs to the rooms she had rented above the shop, Isabella disappeared around back. A short time later she emerged behind the wheel of a little yellow and white Mini Cooper. She had bought the car from Bud Yeager, who operated the Cove's sole gas station and garage. No one knew where Yeager had obtained the vehicle. In the Cove you did not ask those kinds of questions. Fallon braced one hand against the windowsill and watched Isabella drive out of town toward the road that would take her to the old highway.

She had not arrived in Scargill Cove in a car. She had appeared, as if by magic, late one night, carrying only the backpack. That was not so unusual in the Cove. The tiny community had always been a magnet for misfits, drifters and others who did not fit in with mainstream society. But most people moved on. The Cove was not for everyone. Something about the energy of the place, Fallon thought.

The aura of power that shimmered around Isabella Valdez had sent up a lot of red flags. He did not like coincidences. Having another strong talent move into town and take a job at the café directly across the street from J&J had struck him as highly suspicious. The fact that he had been blindsided by the sudden and acute physical attraction he had experienced had been even more disturbing. He had not been able to explain away the sensation by reminding himself that he had been living a celibate life far too long.

His first thought was that Isabella was a Nightshade spy. When he researched her online, he found a very neat, very tidy bio that, as far as he was concerned, only added to the mystery. Nobody had such a pristine personal history. According to what few records existed, she had been raised outside the Arcane community by a single mother who had died when Isabella was in her sophomore year in college. Her father had been killed in a traffic accident shortly before she was born. She had no siblings or close relatives. Until her arrival in the Cove, she had made her living in a series of low-level jobs, the kind that did not leave a lot of footprints in government databases or corporate personnel files.

Hungry for answers and the need to make certain that Isabella was not a Nightshade operative, he had brought Grace and Luther, his best aura-talent agents, all the way from Hawaii, just to take a look. They had detected no signs of the formula in Isabella's energy field. Grace's verdict was that the town's newest resident was just one more lost soul who had found her way to a community that specialized in lost souls.

But Fallon knew that there was more to Isabella's story. Sooner or later he would get the answers. For now he was left with his questions.

And an inexplicable need to keep Isabella close and safe.

2

The old Zander place definitely fit the classic image of a haunted house, Isabella thought. A three-story stone monstrosity from the early 1900s, it hunkered like some great, brooding gargoyle on the cliffs above a skeletal beach.

She brought the Mini Cooper to a halt in the drive and contemplated the weathered mansion. She was still not certain why she had felt compelled to take the case. Fallon was right. J&J was a for-real psychic investigation agency. The firm had enough to do handling the weird Nightshade conspiracy that obsessed Fallon, as well as the routine jobs commissioned by members of the Arcane Society. The agency did not need to take on Lost Dogs and Haunted Houses cases.

But her intuition had kicked in after talking to Norma Spaulding on the phone. The familiar shiver of awareness and the compulsion to find that which was hidden had only grown more fierce in the past twenty-four hours. Now, looking at the old house, she knew that there was something important inside, something that needed to be found.

A shiver of awareness ghosted her nerves. She slipped into her other senses. The house was enveloped in screaming cold fog. Ice crystals shimmered in the mist.

The paranormal light that swirled around the mansion was very different from the fog she had perceived in Scargill Cove a month ago when she had walked into town late on a rainy night. The driver of the truck who had picked her up outside Point Arena had driven her north on Highway One, past Mendocino, had let her out at a gas station. She had walked the rest of the way to the Cove, following the faint sheen of energy.

It had been a long hike, but the closer she got to the tiny town tucked away in the forgotten little cove, the brighter the eerie fog had become. It told her that she was going in the right direction. It was after midnight when she finally reached the heart of the community.

The town had been enveloped in the other kind of fog, the damp, gray stuff that rolled in off the ocean. Every window, save one, was dark. The single window that was illuminated was on the second floor of a building directly across from the café. The light in that window glowed with the luminous aura of a computer screen. The paranormal fog that wreathed the upper level of the building was infused with power and heat. It was a place filled with secrets.

She walked close and aimed her flashlight at the name on the front door. JONES & JONES.

She switched off the flashlight and stood there in the fogbound street for a long time wondering if she should knock. Before she could make up her mind, a thin, scragglylooking man strode briskly toward her out of the shadows of a narrow alley. He did not have a flashlight, but he moved as if he had no difficulty seeing in the dark. His hair and beard were long and unkempt. He wore a heavy, black all-weather coat and a pair of hiking boots. Everything about him spelled *homeless man* but the coat and the boots looked surprisingly new.

Her senses were still heightened. She could see that the man was enveloped in a lot of fog but she did not sense any threat.

"You're n-new here," he said. His voice was hoarse and he stammered a little as if he was not in the habit of speech. "You'll be w-wanting the inn. They'll have a room for you. C-come with me. I'll take you there."

"Thank you," she said.

She allowed him to lead her to the darkened inn. She rang the bell. A light went on in the hall, and a short time later two women in their midfifties, dressed in robes and slippers, opened the door. They smiled when they saw Isabella standing on the porch.

"Yes, of course, we've got a room," one of them said.

"It's January," the second one explained. "We rarely have any guests at this time of year. Come on in."

Isabella turned to thank the stranger in the long black coat, but he was gone.

"Something wrong?" the first woman asked, stepping back to let Isabella into the hall.

"There was a man," Isabella said. "He brought me here."

"Oh, that must have been Walker," the woman said. "He's what you might call our night watchman here in the Cove. My name is Violet, by the way. This is Patty. Come on upstairs and I'll show you to your room. You must be exhausted."

"Shouldn't I register?" Isabella asked.

"We're not real big on the formalities here in the Cove," Patty explained. "You can register in the morning."

Half an hour later, Isabella had crawled into a cozy bed and pulled a down quilt up over her shoulders. For the first time in weeks she slept through the night.

The following day no one remembered to ask her to register as a guest at the inn. She handed over enough cash to cover the first week and then, on Patty's advice, went down the street to see about the gig at the Sunshine. Marge Fuller, the proprietor of the small café, immediately put her to work waiting tables and helping out in the kitchen. There were no pesky applications or tax forms to fill out. Isabella knew then that Scargill Cove was her kind of town.

Fallon Jones had walked through the front door of the café that same morning and sat down at the counter to order coffee. When she emerged from the kitchen, she had seen him talking to Marge Fuller. A thrill swept through her, igniting all of her senses.

Everything about Fallon Jones whispered of power. He wore the fierce energy like a dark cloak but something in the atmosphere around him told her that he was living on the edge of exhaustion.

A dark, ice-cold fever burned in Fallon Jones. With her senses cranked up, she could see the glacial heat in his eyes. The para-fog swirled around him, indicating deep secrets and mysteries.

He had the hard, unyielding face of a man who lived life on his own terms. He was big, too, tall, broad-shouldered and solid as a boulder. She had never been attracted to physically overpowering men. She stood five-foot-three and three-quarters in her bare feet and she had always preferred males who did not tower over her. Usually when she was around men Fallon's size, her instinct was to put some distance between herself and a creature who could pin her down with one hand.

But with Fallon she felt none of the usual wariness. Instead, she was amazed to discover that when she was near him, she experienced an oddly sensual feminine recklessness. A part of her wanted to challenge him, probably because of the self-discipline that emanated from him in waves. She sensed that his formidable control was his way of handling his equally formidable talent.

All the evidence indicated that he lived an austere, almost ascetic existence, but she was quite certain that he was no monk. There was an inferno burning just beneath the surface. In spite of the way Fallon aroused both her normal and paranormal senses, old habits prevailed. She needed to know what it was that fueled the volcano before she leaped into the fires.

She pushed the thoughts of Fallon Jones aside and sat quietly behind the wheel, studying the Zander mansion through the rain-glazed windshield. If there had ever been any gardens around the big house, they had long ago disintegrated under more than a century's worth of Pacific storms. The grime-darkened windows would surely limit light inside even on a sunny day.

Fallon had a point. Pronouncing the Zander mansion specter-free was probably not going to be enough to convince anyone in his or her right mind to buy such an enormous money pit. But she was committed now. She had assured Norma Spaulding that J&J would take the job.

She closed down her other senses, opened the car door, slung her pack over one shoulder and raised her umbrella. A blast of wind-driven rain caught her squarely in the face.

She fought her way across the drive and up the cracked stone steps. When she reached the shelter of the wide front porch, she collapsed the umbrella and punched the code into the key box. The key tumbled into her gloved hand.

The door opened with a suitably ominous squeak of rusty hinges. She stepped into the shadowy foyer and took the small flashlight out of her pack. Norma had warned that the electricity had been turned off eons ago.

She stood the dripping umbrella in a corner and heightened her talent again. Given the amount of energy that enveloped the old house, she had been expecting to find something of interest inside: an old will, perhaps, or an envelope filled with long-forgotten stock certificates. Maybe even a few pieces of valuable jewelry. But the sight of the glowing river of obsidian-dark mist that roared through the house caught her completely off guard. Shards of black ice fluoresced in the vapor.

She pulled herself together, took a deep breath and followed the terrible luminescence down a shadowy hall. The mist disappeared under a door. She opened the door and looked down a flight of stone steps. A terrible sea of energy flooded the basement.

She hurried back to the foyer, grabbed her umbrella and went outside. She opened the phone that Fallon had given her the first day on the job. The list of contacts was quite short. There was only one number.

Fallon picked up midway through the first ring.

"What the hell is wrong?" he asked. "Flat tire? Out of gas? I knew I shouldn't have let you drive out there in this weather."

"I need backup."

"Huh. Don't tell me you found a ghost."

"There's something here to find," she said. "Not sure what yet, but I don't think it's going to be anything good."

"What makes you say that?"

"There's a basement involved."

3

She waited for him in the car, doors locked, key in the ignition. She was ready to speed off to safety if necessary. But no one burst out of the house wielding a meat cleaver. The mansion loomed, bleak and dripping with ominous energy.

Her pulse was still beating too fast and the hair on the nape of her neck hadn't settled down by the time the black SUV pulled into the drive. She glanced at her watch. It had taken Fallon less than ten minutes to reach her, driving through pouring rain on a narrow, winding road.

He got out of the big vehicle and walked toward her. The hood of his black rain jacket was pulled up over his face partially concealing his features, but she could tell that he looked even more grim than usual, and when she revved up her senses, she saw a little heat in his eyes.

She opened the driver's-side door and

extricated herself from behind the wheel, fumbling again with the umbrella and her pack. Fallon took the umbrella from her, snapped it open and held it up to shield her from the elements while she got herself organized.

"You do realize that agents who get spooked by a haunted house don't make J&J look good," he said.

"You ever see one of those slasher horror films?" she asked. "The kind in which the too-stupid-to-live perky blond teenager goes down into the dark basement and gets hacked to pieces by a serial killer in a mask?"

"Can't say that I have."

They started toward the stone steps. Getting to the front porch was much easier with Fallon holding the umbrella and using his big frame to protect her from the worst of the squall. There were some advantages to size, she reflected.

"Let's just say I didn't want to star in the role of the perky blond teen," she said.

"You're not blond," he pointed out. "And you're not a teenager."

"But at least I'm perky, right?"

He gave that some thought. "I don't think that's the right word."

"Has anyone ever told you that you have a tendency to be extremely literal, boss?"

"Yes," he said. "Usually at the same time that I'm being told I don't have a sense of humor."

"Nonsense. Of course you have a sense of humor."

"I do?" He seemed genuinely surprised to hear that.

"It's just a little offbeat, that's all."

"Like my talent?" His voice went flat.

"Like your talent," she agreed. "It's not as if I'm exactly normal, myself. Which is probably why I'm working for J&J."

She opened the door. Fallon collapsed the umbrella and stood quietly for a moment, contemplating the darkened foyer. She sensed energy shiver in the atmosphere around him and knew that he had heightened his talent. She did the same. Once again, icy mists pulsed and seethed in the entry hall.

"What do you see?" Fallon asked.

"A lot of energy that is infused with some really dark ultralight. Looks like fog."

"Huh."

"It's hard to explain," she said. "All I can tell you is that when I'm in my zone, I see the residue of energy laid down by people with something to hide. Most of the time I ignore it because everyone has secrets. But occasionally I detect the sort of currents that tell me there is a secret that needs to be found. And before you ask, I can't explain that part, either. As the old saying goes, I know it when I see it."

He nodded once, satisfied. "You're a kind of finder-talent."

"Yes."

"Any idea what the fog in here is telling you?"

"No." Another frisson of awareness chilled her. "But like I said, the answer is in the basement, and I don't think that it's going to be good."

"The house feels empty."

"I agree." You could always tell, she thought. Empty houses gave off their own unique vibes. "But something feels wrong."

"Let's take a look at the basement," Fallon suggested.

"Okay." She took out her flashlight and switched it on again. "Electricity is off."

"No surprise there."

He moved into the foyer and reached inside his jacket. She was startled when she saw the gun appear in his hand.

"Wow," she said. "You brought your gun."

"You made me nervous when you called and said you needed backup."

"Oh. Sorry. I really don't think there's an immediate threat. As you said, the house feels empty. But I hate finding dead bodies by myself."

"And that's what you're expecting?"

"I've seen this kind of fog before."

She followed him into the foyer, her senses wide open.

He took a flashlight out of the pocket of his coat and switched it on. "Which way?"

"I forgot you can't see the energy." She aimed the beam of the flashlight directly in front of him. "Turn left. The basement door is halfway down that hall."

He glanced at the floorboards. "Lot of footprints in the dust."

"Don't forget, Norma Spaulding has been in here. She also said that there were indications that transients had camped out in the house from time to time."

"Probably the source of the rumors about the place being haunted." He stopped in front of the basement door. "Is this the right door?"

"Yes."

Fallon opened the door. They both looked down the concrete steps.

"Still feels empty," Fallon said.

Isabella moved closer to the opening and studied the cold light roiling and surging below. The sense of urgency that had set her nerves on edge climbed higher.

"We need to find whatever it is down there that needs finding," she said, resigned. "Crap. I hate this part."

He studied the scene below. "Interesting."

She glanced sharply at him. "What?"

"A wooden floor."

"What about it?"

"Looks new."

"Maybe one of the previous owners finished off the basement," she suggested.

"I did a quick search of the property records after you left the office today. No one has lived in this house for over forty years. That floor was put in recently."

"Okay, I'm not arguing the point." She tried to ignore the fact that she was shivering. "The good news is that I don't see any bodies down there."

"Wait here. I'm going to take a closer look."

"No, I'll come with you."

He looked at her. "Are you sure you want to do that?"

It wouldn't be the first time she had followed the currents of fog to a bad end.

"When I get this far, I need to find the answer," she said.

He surprised her with one of his rare smiles. "Same here."

"Two of a kind," she said, keeping her

voice light.

He seemed briefly startled by the comment, as if it had never occurred to him that he might have something in common with another human being. But he did not say anything.

She followed him down the steps. When they reached the bottom, they stood knee-deep in the sea of fog. The paranormal cold was so bone-chilling now that even Fallon sensed it.

"You're right," he said. "Lots of bad energy down here."

She studied the glacial whirlpool in the center of the room. "I think most of the really terrible stuff is coming from under the floorboards."

He raked the windowless room with the beam of his flashlight. "What about the armoire in the corner?"

She studied the old-fashioned wooden wardrobe. The doors were closed but a lot of fog shivered around it.

"Definitely something in there," she said. "But it's different from the stuff that's coming up from under the floor."

He started to prowl the room with the flashlight. "No dust down here. Someone keeps this room clean."

She sniffed the air. "I can smell some kind

66

of strong detergent or disinfectant. Damn, I knew it. This is going to be one of those body-in-the-basement scenarios."

"Starting to feel that way." He looked at her. "Not your first, I take it?"

"No. Unfortunately, with my kind of talent I get this kind of thing occasionally. Goes with the territory. When do we call the local cops?"

"As soon as we know for sure that we've got something to show them," Fallon said. "Without hard evidence, we'd just be asking for trouble."

"I guess J&J can't just pick up the phone and tell the local authorities that one of the firm's agents has had a psychic vision telling her that there's a body in the old Zander house."

"Regular law enforcement tends to take a dim view of people who claim to have paranormal powers. Can't blame the cops. Lot of fake mediums and phony psychics out there. They've given our end of the investigation profession a bad name."

"I know."

"I'll check the armoire first." He started toward the wardrobe.

"Fallon," she said. "Wait."

He stopped and looked back at her.

"Do you hear a clock?" she asked.

He went silent. They both listened to the steady, stately ticking of an old-fashioned antique clock.

"It's coming from inside the armoire," Fallon said. "I didn't hear it a few seconds ago. It just started up."

"Sounds like the clock on your desk in the office," she said. "The old one that you said was a Victorian-era antique."

"Yes," he said. "It does."

He opened the door of the armoire and aimed the flashlight inside. Isabella held her breath, half expecting a body to fall out.

But the only object in view was a large, ornate mantel clock. It sat on a shelf. The beam of the flashlight glinted on the brass pendulum and gilt trim.

Isabella stilled. "Please don't tell me that we're going to have to decide whether to cut the blue wire or the red wire."

"No." Fallon examined the clock and the interior of the wardrobe with the flashlight. "No wires. It's not attached to anything. It's just a clock. Looks Victorian, like mine."

"Old-fashioned clocks like that have to be wound every week or so. The fact that it's ticking indicates that someone comes down here on a regular basis."

"But we didn't hear it when we first entered the basement," Fallon said. He aimed the flashlight at the back of the clock, clearly fascinated now. "I'll be damned. It's one of Mrs. Bridewell's inventions. I can see the alchemical symbol she used as her signature. How in hell did the device end up here?"

"Who is Mrs. Bridewell? Never mind, you can explain later. Why did it start ticking?"

"Our presence activated it. Which makes this a red-wire-blue-wire scenario after all." He came toward her swiftly and grabbed her arm in one of his big, powerful hands. "Out. Now."

"What's going to happen?"

"I have no idea," Fallon said. "But it won't be good."

They got as far as the bottom step before the flashlights failed, plunging the basement into midnight. The faint twilight that filled the doorway at the top of the stairs darkened rapidly.

"What's going on?" Isabella asked softly.

"The clock." Fallon drew her to a halt halfway up the steps and lowered his voice. "It's doing this. Generating some kind of energy that is eating all the normal light in the house. Filling the place with night."

The relentless ticking continued.

"I don't get that, but I agree we definitely need to leave," she said.

"Too late." Fallon's voice was very low now. He spoke directly into her ear. "We're going back down. Hang on to the railing. If you fall on these stairs, you could break your neck."

She seized the metal banister and probed cautiously for the edge of each concrete step with the toe of her shoe. Simultaneously she pushed her talent a little higher. The para-fog did not illuminate objects the way normal light did, but the seething psi whirlpool in the center of the space and the dark light around the armoire were clearly visible. The luminescence provided a general sense of direction.

She sensed Fallon heightening his own talent and wondered how the basement appeared to him. He seemed remarkably sure-footed on the steps. It occurred to her that with his unusual ability, he had probably created a very clear mental construct of their surroundings.

"Why are we going back down?" she breathed.

"Because we are no longer alone in the house," he said.

The floorboards squeaked overhead. Fallon was right. The house was no longer giving off empty vibes.

"Something tells me that is not a prospective buyer," Fallon said.

"But the darkness extends to the floor above. I saw it filling the hallway. It must be like midnight up there now. How can he navigate?"

"Probably because he is some kind of talent."

Fallon must have turned his head toward her then, because she could suddenly perceive the dark heat in his eyes.

"You can see in this night?" she whispered.

"I come from a long line of hunter-talents. Good night vision runs in the family. Whatever happens, keep silent. I'll handle this."

They reached the last step. Fallon drew her through the cold sea of energy and brought her to a halt. The absolute night was disorienting, but when she put out her hand, she realized that they were standing under the staircase.

They listened to the footsteps overhead. The long, sure strides were definitely those of a man, Isabella thought. He was moving like someone who could see in the dark.

The intruder was coming down the hall toward the basement entrance. A moment later she sensed the presence in the open doorway at the top of the staircase. She knew from Fallon's great stillness that he, too, was aware of the stalker.

71

The intruder started down into the basement.

"Welcome to my little game," the man said. Unwholesome good cheer reverberated through the words. "I've never used local players. Too risky. But when I heard that the silly new real estate agent in town had hired an investigator to clear out the ghosts in the old Zander place, I knew I would have to change the rules for this round."

The hunter paused midway down the steps.

"Then, again, you aren't exactly local, are you? The office of Jones & Jones is over in Scargill Cove. So, I guess I'm not bending the rules all that much after all. Let's see now, you're hiding either under the stairs or behind the armoire. There is no other option in this room. Keeps the scoring simple. I'll try the armoire first."

Isabella sensed the hunter's sudden movement on the staircase. At first she thought that he was rushing down toward the armoire. But in the next instant she heard the jarring thump of running shoes on the floor directly in front of her. The hunter had vaulted over the railing.

"Fooled you," the stalker said happily. "I chose the stairs. Bonus points for me. My name is Nightman, by the way. Think of me as an avatar."

A pair of eyes hot with madness and psi burned in the mist from a distance of less than two yards. The preternatural speed, balance and agility with which the intruder had moved, as well as the intense energy in the atmosphere, told Isabella that the intruder was a true hunter-talent.

"Well, well, well," Nightman said, "I can sense a little energy in the atmosphere. Maybe you two aren't complete frauds, after all, huh?"

"No," Fallon said. "We're the real deal."

"Once in a while I pick up a player who has a little talent," Nightman said. "Adds spice to the game. Tell you what, I'll do you first, Mr. Private Eye. Save the lady for some fun later. After you and I are finished, I'll take her upstairs and let her run. It's so much fun to watch them try to find a door or a window in the darkness."

"Where did you get the clock?" Fallon asked as if it were a matter of idle curiosity.

"Interesting gadget, isn't it?" Nightman chuckled. "I found it in an old tunnel under the floor in this room a few months ago. I was checking out the place to see if it would be a good platform for my games. The innards of the clock were in pretty good shape considering that it had been sitting in a damp cave for quite a while. It was stored in a weird glass box. I cleaned it up and got it working. Imagine my surprise when I discovered what it could do."

"It generates night," Fallon said.

"Sure does." Nightman laughed. "I have to tell you, it makes my little live-action video game very interesting for all concerned."

"What turns off the clock?" Fallon asked, still speaking in tones of academic interest.

"It runs down after about three hours," Nightman said. "Then it has to be rewound. It's motion-sensitive, though. When I'm in the mood for a game, I pick up some junkie whore on the streets of Oakland or San Francisco and bring her here. I set the clock, explain the rules and turn the player loose in the house. We play until I get bored."

"The bodies go under the floorboards here in the basement, right?" Fallon asked.

"There's a tunnel down below. Probably an old smuggling route. This stretch of coastline is riddled with caves."

Isabella could not stand to remain quiet any longer.

"You must have really freaked when you found out that Norma Spaulding had hired

Jones & Jones to investigate this place," she said.

The hunter's vicious eyes switched to her. "I'm afraid I'll have to do something about Norma. Can't let her actually sell this place, not after I've put so much creative effort into my game."

"How do you plan to explain the fact that we're both missing?" she asked.

"Nothing to explain." There was a shrug in Nightman's voice. "There won't be any bodies to find. I'll drive your cars to one of the roadside lookouts and leave them there. No one's going to look too hard for a couple of missing psychic detectives from Scargill Cove. Everyone knows the town is populated by crazies and losers."

"What kind of weirdo loser picks a name like Nightman for his avatar?" Isabella demanded. She was pretty sure she heard Fallon heave a small sigh but she ignored him. "Or didn't you know Nightman was what they used to call the guy who cleaned out the cesspools and emptied the privies in eighteenth-century England?"

"That's a *lie.*" Nightman's voice rose in shrill rage. "You're laughing now, but wait until I start using my knife on you."

"New rules tonight," Fallon said.

Isabella felt energy flare fiercely in the unnatural night. She heard a choking gasp and knew that it came from Nightman.

The killer uttered a strangled scream. His eyes got hotter, this time with the energy of terror and comprehension of his impending death.

"No," he wheezed. "I'm the winner. I'm always the winner. You can't do this to me. It's my game."

There was a dull thud as his body hit the floorboards. The hot psi dimmed in his eyes and vanished altogether.

The clock continued to tick into the sharp silence that descended on the basement.

"Fallon?" Isabella whispered.

"Game over," he said. His eyes were still hot.

She felt him move away from under the staircase and realized that he was crouching beside the fallen man.

"Dead?" she asked.

"I couldn't let him live." Fallon's voice was flat on the surface but underneath there was a soul-deep weariness. "He was too strong. A hunter-talent of some kind. If the cops had tried to arrest him, it would have taken him about five minutes to escape and disappear."

"Don't get me wrong, I wasn't complaining. But what do we do now? There's no way we can explain that clock to the police."

"We're not going to explain it to the cops. We'll take it with us. They won't need it to find the bodies and figure out what was going on here."

She heard a rustling sound and realized that he was going through the killer's clothes.

"We'll have to find a way to stop that clock before you drive it back to Scargill Cove," she said. "It's generating too much energy, enough to fill this entire house. You might be able to see where you're going, but the driver of any car that you pass will be temporarily blinded."

"It's just a damn clock," Fallon said. "Got to be a way to stop it. Mrs. Bridewell's curiosities all incorporated traditional mechanical escapements."

She shuddered. "I can't wait to hear more about this Mrs. Bridewell."

"I'll tell you later. The point is that, paranormal aspects aside, the clock's mechanism is very similar to the one in my office."

She sensed his movement when he got to his feet. He crossed through the strange night, a dark shadow silhouetted against the eerie mist. There was a squeak of small hinges and a cranking sound. The ticking stopped abruptly.

The flashlights reignited, spearing beams of light across the basement. At the top of the stairs, the entrance was once again filled with normal shadows.

"That worked," Isabella said.

"Which means this really is one of her infernal devices, not some new variation," Fallon said. "That's the good news."

"Why is it good news?"

"I wasn't looking forward to hunting down a modern-day inventor who had decided to create a high-tech version of some of Bridewell's gadgets. The originals are bad enough. The question now is, how did the clock get into this house? But we'll deal with that later."

He aimed his flashlight at the body on the floor. Isabella looked at the crumpled figure of Nightman. The killer's face was set in a death mask of stark horror. He looked to be in his midthirties, sandy-haired and lithe in build. He was dressed in dark green work pants and a matching shirt. The logo on the pocket of the shirt spelled out the name of a construction firm based in Willow Creek.

She looked away. "He told us he found the clock in a cave beneath this basement."

Fallon swept the light across the floorboards. "Before we call the cops, I want to

78

make sure the evidence is there."

She speared her flashlight at the section of the flooring that was in the heart of the whirlpool of energy. "Try that section."

He walked to the circle of light created by her flashlight, crouched and began probing with his gloved fingers.

"Here we go," he said. "A trapdoor."

She went toward him, watching as he opened a wide, square section of the flooring. They aimed their flashlights into the darkness below. A metal ladder disappeared into the depths. Isabella leaned forward slightly, trying to get a better view of the object near the foot of the ladder.

"What's that?" she asked.

"Looks like a body bag," Fallon said.

Isabella straightened quickly. "Norma Spaulding is never going to sell this house now."

"Real estate has always been a tough market in this part of California." Fallon reached for his phone.

Isabella cleared her throat. "One thing before you call the cops."

"Don't worry, you won't be here when they arrive. You're leaving now."

"Right, thanks." She exhaled slowly. "But there's a complication. Norma knows that I was the one who promised to check out the house for ghosts."

"As far as everyone involved is concerned, including Norma Spaulding, I got an intuitive flash of impending disaster and decided that I would handle the Zander house case personally. I sent you back to the office before I found the bodies. Now go. Get out of here."

"Right," she repeated. She turned and hurried up the stairs. When she reached the doorway, she paused and looked back at him.

"An intuitive flash of impending disaster?" she said.

"I'm supposed to be psychic, remember?"

"Of course."

"Where did you pick up that factoid about the meaning of the word *nightman?*"

"I had what you might call an eclectic education."

"Homeschooled?"

"Yes. Plus, I read a lot."

"When this is over, maybe it's time you told me who or what you're hiding from," Fallon said quietly.

"I should have known better than to take a job as an assistant to a psychic detective."

4

"We still don't have any leads, Mr. Lucan," Julian Garrett said. "Turned over every stone we could find in Phoenix. It's like she never existed except during the short time she worked at that department store."

"It's been damn near a month," Max Lucan said.

"I'm aware of that, sir."

Max got up from his desk and went to stand at the window of his office. Absently he touched the black granite pedestal that stood nearby. The pedestal held the bronze statue of a seated cat. The creature had a gold ring in one ear.

The statue was Egyptian. Like the other antiquities displayed in the room, it was authentic. It had been created sometime around 600 B.C. But it was not the age of the bronze that intrigued Max. It was the power that the artist had somehow infused into the metal. After all these centuries, the energy in the figure still whispered to him.

"How could a little finder-talent drop off the radar so easily?" he asked.

"Beats the hell out of me," Julian said.

"Rawlins and Burley still haven't recovered their memories?"

"No, sir, and I think we should assume they never will. Evidently the finder-talent put them into some sort of fugue state. They remember locating her in that mall store, but the next thing either of them remembers is waking up in front of a restaurant three miles away."

Max felt the hair on the back of his neck stir. He knew it was because he was missing some important pieces of the puzzle. "Interesting that Rawlins and Burley didn't get run down by a car, walking blind like that through Phoenix traffic at night."

"They can't account for that, either," Julian said. "They had to cross a lot of streets in the process of getting as far as the restaurant. Damn lucky, I guess."

"I think it's more likely there are a few things we don't know about the finder-talent," Max said. He could hardly blame her. He kept his own unique ability secret, too. As far as most people were concerned, he was just very, very good at tracing stolen antiquities and providing security for museum collections. "I wonder what else she kept from us while she was here."

"We need to find her, sir."

"I'm aware of that," Max said.

He watched the sunlight flash on the yachts in the harbor. Lucan Protection Services occupied two floors of a gleaming new office building in one of the most exclusive enclaves on California's Gold Coast. Not that his clients were ever impressed with the view or the refined sophistication of the décor of his company's headquarters. The majority of the collectors who commissioned the services of his firm were wealthy and well traveled. They frequently owned handfuls of residences in locales ranging from the Caribbean to New York to Paris. It took more than a view and expensive interior design to impress them. Nevertheless, Max thought, you could not run a business like Lucan out of a storefront in a strip mall. Appearances mattered in the world in which he operated.

I'm missing something here.

"Tell me again what went wrong in Phoenix?" he said.

Julian ran through the details again but there was nothing new.

"Obviously she made my men when they found her in that department store," he

83

concluded. "From what they could piece together later, she escaped through the emergency stairwell. Her car was gone from the mall garage. It turned up later in a parking lot outside a hospital emergency room. All indications are that she never did return to the motel where she was staying."

"In other words, she went to work that night ready to run if necessary."

"Yes, sir."

"Just like she ran from Lucan when we found the files on her computer."

"Yes, sir."

"She's damn good at getting lost." Max pondered that for a moment. "Any news on Caitlin Phillips?"

"No, sir. She's still missing, too," Julian said. "We need to assume that she's dead."

Max tightened his grip on the edge of the granite pedestal. "Someone has been dealing para-weapons out of Department A for nearly a year, and now two women have vanished. The broker handling the arms deals was shot to death, a dangerous artifact has gone missing and I've got a black-ops agency breathing down my neck. This is not good for Lucan's corporate image, Garrett."

"I understand, sir. Believe me, I'm working the case night and day."

Max turned around to face him. "No one

gets away with using the resources of my company to deal black market weapons."

"Yes, sir."

"Find the women and find that damn artifact."

5

There was a take-out container sitting on top of the garbage can in the alley behind the Sunshine. Walker picked it up and was pleased to note that the fried chicken, mashed potatoes and peas inside were still warm. It was his lucky night.

Just like last night, he thought. He had a vague recollection of having gotten lucky the night before that, as well, but his memory was somewhat unreliable when it came to the unimportant stuff. Sometimes it took everything he had to stay focused on his mission.

He hunkered down, bracing his back against the wooden wall of the café, and methodically consumed the chicken dinner. Really, it was a shame the way people threw away good food. All the starving kids in the world and yet folks in the Cove tossed out perfectly edible stuff like chicken and mashed potatoes and peas every night.

Same deal with muffins and coffee in the mornings. Damn shame.

He finished the meal and got to his feet. He went back to the garbage can, lifted the lid and deposited the empty take-out container inside.

Adjusting the hood of the long, heavy coat to shield his face from the rain, he resumed his patrol. The pressure in his head had been building again lately. That was not good. It meant something bad was going to happen.

He had discovered the warm, waterproof coat and the boots sitting on top of another trash container in the Cove. He was pretty sure that particular can was located in the alley behind the PI's office.

The PI was important to Scargill Cove, but Walker wasn't sure why, not yet, at any rate. He knew what he knew and that was enough. He had gotten the same whispery sense of certainty again when Isabella Valdez arrived in town. He had watched her walk into the Cove that night and known that she belonged there. Just like Jones.

Walker walked behind the row of darkened shops and turned right at the corner. The familiar route took him past the Scar. It was early, not quite seven o'clock. The tavern was still busy. He could hear the voices of the regulars inside. Elvis music drifted out into the night. He paid no attention. Everything was normal in this sector. His job was to keep an eye out for things that were wrong or out of place.

There had already been a couple of very disturbing developments today. Several hours ago Isabella had driven out of town. Jones had followed not long after. Walker had been very relieved when Isabella had returned, but it alarmed him that Jones had not yet come back to town.

He looked in the windows of the bookshop. It had closed recently following the death of the proprietor, a guy named Fitch. The bookseller had keeled over one day down in the basement. Heart attack, the authorities said. But Walker had known from the start that Fitch was bad news, an outsider who did not belong in the Cove. No loss.

He walked some more and checked out the windows of Isabella's apartment above Toomey's Treasures. The shades were closed but the lights were on. She was safe inside for the night. That was good. That was the way it should be.

Walker heard the low growl of Jones's SUV in the street. The PI was back in town. The pressure in Walker's head eased.

Jones parked the big vehicle behind the building that housed the Jones & Jones office. Walker waited in a darkened doorway, hands crammed into his pockets. He watched the upstairs window of the agency, waiting for the lights to go on inside. The lights were almost always on in J&J.

But the lights did not come on tonight. Instead, Fallon Jones emerged on the street and started toward Isabella's apartment. He carried his computer in one hand and a bulky object wrapped in a blanket under one arm. He walked right past the doorway where Walker stood. Most folks would not have been aware that Walker was there, but Jones always seemed to sense his presence, always acknowledged him.

"Evening, Walker," Fallon Jones said.

Walker did not respond. He was too stunned. He did not know what Jones was carrying in the blanket, but he recognized the traces of energy emanating from the object.

The pressure in his head abruptly got stronger, becoming almost intolerable. He resumed his rounds in a desperate effort to ease the pain while he tried to decide how to handle the catastrophe that had just struck the Cove.

6

"Her name was Millicent Bridewell," Fallon said. "She was a brilliant inventor and a trained clockmaker who lived during the Victorian era. She was also a powerful talent with a very unusual gift for accessing the paranormal properties of glass. All of her inventions include glass of some kind."

"Like the face of the clock?" Isabella asked.

"Yes." Fallon looked at the blanket-wrapped clock sitting on the floor of Isabella's apartment. "Glass is still a big mystery to the Arcane experts. It's unique in that it has properties of both liquids and solids. Generally speaking, paranormal energy passing through glass has unpredictable effects. But Bridewell figured out how to control the results. She used her talents to create a large number of what she called her clockwork curiosities. They were actually weapons."

"How many did she make?" Isabella asked.

"No one knows for certain. She operated a legitimate shop that featured beautiful clockwork curiosities. Essentially, her creations were elegant toys for wealthy collectors. But she also ran a side business that catered to a different clientele."

"What kind of clientele would that be?"

"Folks who wanted other folks such as inconvenient spouses or business partners permanently removed."

"Got it," Isabella said. "In other words Mrs. Bridewell ran a murder-for-hire business."

"Well, in fairness to Mrs. B, she always insisted that the customer had to actually commit the murder. She considered herself an artist, after all, not a professional killer."

"But she supplied the murder weapon," Isabella said.

"Which was disguised as a charming example of the clockmaker's art. The victim never saw it coming until it was too late."

Fallon took a swallow of the whiskey Isabella had poured for him and let himself sink into the lumpy sofa. A great weariness was seeping into his bones, but it was not the kind of drowsiness that would promote sleep. The whiskey was taking off some of the edge, but it couldn't touch the deep places. He would not get any real rest tonight. Just as well — he needed to think.

He watched Isabella through half-closed eyes. She was moving around in the minuscule kitchenette, putting together a meal. Her motions were economical, efficient, graceful. He was not hungry, but whatever she was making was starting to smell good.

He had been surprised when she had suggested that he come to her apartment for dinner after he finished with the county cops. *We both need to decompress,* she said. He wasn't accustomed to decompressing with anyone else, but it had suddenly seemed like an excellent idea.

Isabella's apartment was a warm, cheerful space filled with thriving green plants and cast-off furniture. The former tenant had disappeared one night, leaving no forwarding address, not an uncommon event in the Cove. Ralph Toomey owned the shabby rooms above his shop. He had offered them to Isabella and told her she could have the previous occupant's furniture as well.

She had taken the apartment but declined the furniture. Fallon had helped Toomey haul a battered table, a couple of wobbly chairs, an unattractively stained mattress and rusty bedsprings to the town dump.

On the final expedition to the dump, a plastic baggie full of marijuana had fallen out of one ripped cushion.

"Always wondered how he managed to pay the rent," Toomey remarked, pocketing the baggie. "Guy had no visible means of support. Figured he was in the business."

"Probably explains why he disappeared in a hurry," Fallon said.

Scargill Cove was on the fringes of the Emerald Triangle, a tricounty region in Northern California. In these parts it was freely acknowledged that marijuana was the largest cash crop, an economic engine that supported a multitude of businesses from gardening supply stores to gas stations. It also brought with it the usual law enforcement problems.

Toomey contemplated the stained mattress that they had tossed over the cliff into the ravine that served as the Cove's dump.

"You know," he said, "Isabella fits right in at the Cove. It's like she belongs here with the rest of us or something."

One more lost soul in a town where lost souls constituted the majority of the citizenry, Fallon thought.

When the apartment had been emptied out, Isabella, together with Marge from the café, Harriet Stokes, proprietor of Stokes's

Grocery, and the innkeepers, Violet and Patty, scrubbed the place from top to bottom. The cleaning had been followed by a fresh coat of sunny gold paint.

After the paint had dried, several people in the Cove had offered Isabella replacements for the furnishings and kitchen equipment that had been tossed. She had accepted each used item with glowing pleasure, as if it were a treasured house-warming gift or a valuable antique. The table and chairs and the heavy crockery had come from Marge. The secondhand sofa and the end table were courtesy of Violet and Patty. The Elvis lamps were a gift from Oliver and Fran Hitchcock, owners of the Scar.

The only new furniture in the place was the bed. Everyone in town had witnessed its arrival. The big van bearing the logo of a discount mattress store had blocked the street for half an hour while the new mattress and box springs were unloaded.

Fallon had watched the operation from the window of his office. Keen detective that he was, he had observed that the mattress was a traditional double. Unfortunately, that information was inconclusive. It did not tell him what he really wanted to know. Single people often used double beds.

On the other hand, the size of the mattress could indicate that there was a man in Isabella's life. If so, the guy had not yet put in an appearance. On the whole, though, the evidence appeared to indicate that Isabella was alone.

Like me, Fallon thought.

The weariness was getting heavier, weighing him down. He had used a lot of energy to take down the killer. Energy was energy, and when you pulled on your reserves, you had to allow time to recover. But he knew that the soul-deep exhaustion that was sinking into him was more than just the result of having pushed his para-senses to the max. It was not the first time he had killed and it might not be the last but coming to terms with the psychic damage was not getting easier. He knew it never would.

"More whiskey?" Isabella asked, coming toward him with the bottle.

He looked down at the glass he cradled in his hands and was surprised to see that it was empty.

"Yes," he said. "Thanks."

She poured out another healthy measure and went back into the kitchenette, where she splashed a little more into her own glass. She knocked back the whiskey with a dashing air and promptly went into a small coughing spasm.

He got up, crossed the room and thumped her lightly between the shoulder blades.

"Thanks," she managed. She took a deep breath. "Whew. Bad day at Black Rock."

"You okay?" he asked.

"Yeah, sure. I'm a J&J agent. I can handle the whiskey."

"I'm surprised you keep a bottle around," he said. "Thought women liked white wine and pink cocktail drinks."

"Shows how much you know."

"Yeah, it does, doesn't it?"

He looked at the bottle. It was nearly full. He'd heard her crack the seal earlier when she'd opened it and knew that his glass was the first she had poured from it. He wondered how she knew the brand he preferred, and then it dawned on him that she had probably seen the bottle he kept in the bottom drawer of his desk.

What were the odds that she drank the same brand? he wondered. About zero, given all available evidence. That left one tantalizing possibility. She had purchased this particular bottle of whiskey with the express purpose of serving him a drink from it. Something inside him warmed at the thought.

"Isabella."

"Hmm?" She looked at him with her wonderful eyes.

"I think I'm going to kiss you," he said.

"Want some advice?"

"Sure."

"Don't think about it too much," she said. "Just do it."

He set his glass down on the counter, took hers from her hand and put it down as well. He pulled her into his arms and kissed her.

For an instant, she did not respond. A heartbeat later the atmosphere around them exploded with blazing energy. Isabella put her arms around his neck and kissed him back with a fierce, feminine hunger that set his senses on fire.

She might as well have picked up a sledgehammer and used it to shatter the crystalline prison cell in which he had lived most of his adult life. He was suddenly free, wholly consumed by a fever unlike anything he had ever experienced.

"Isabella." He could barely shape the word. It was as if he were invoking magic. He framed her face in his hands, astonishment and wonder unfurling somewhere inside him. *"Isabella."*

Her mysterious eyes widened briefly, as though she, too, was amazed by what was happening.

97

"It's okay," she said. "I won't break."

"I might."

She smiled again and kissed him just under his jaw.

"No," she said, sounding very certain. "You won't. Nothing could break you, Fallon Jones."

He could not seem to find his breath. The hair on the back of his neck stirred. He tightened his arms around Isabella, pinned her to him and kissed her mouth and then her throat. She responded with a soft cry and an electric passion. She was so delicate and sleek and feminine. He was afraid of crushing her.

He picked her up in his arms.

"Wait," she said urgently. "The soup."

He waited while she reached down to turn off the burner. Then he carried her swiftly down the short hall into the small bedroom. He set her on her feet beside the bed. When he started to undress her, he fumbled the business because his hands were trembling.

"It's been a long time for me," he warned.

"For me, too," she said. "But I'm sure we'll figure it out."

The sound of his own laughter startled him. Delight gleamed in Isabella's eyes. She reached up to take down her hair and then she unbuckled his belt.

They undressed each other in a haze of hot, shuddering excitement. Finally Isabella stood before him wearing only her panties. He looked at her, overcome by a sense of wonder. He cupped the gentle swell of one of her breasts in his hand and drew his thumb across the tight little nipple.

"You're so beautiful," he said.

"No," she said. "But you make me feel beautiful." She flattened her palms on his bare chest and slid her fingers up to close around his shoulders. "You, however, are absolutely gorgeous."

He knew he was probably turning red, but he did not care.

"Sounds like we have a mutual admiration society going here," he said.

"Works for me."

He fell with her onto the bed, careful to make certain that he landed on the bottom. She sprawled on top of him and kissed him with an abandon that enthralled him. He felt her warm, damp mouth on his throat and then his shoulder. She started to go lower.

In an effort to get a grip on what was left of his self-control, he rolled Isabella under him, anchoring her there. In response her eyes became luminous. He could have sworn that the energy level in the bedroom kicked up a few more degrees. The place was so hot now, he half expected bolts of real lightning to appear.

He wanted to take his time, to make everything perfect for her, to imprint himself on her so that she would never forget him. But when he moved his hand down over her belly and slipped his fingers under the waistband of her panties, he discovered the liquid heat between her thighs. The scent of her arousal drove him to the edge. He groaned. The knowledge that she was so hot and wet for him undermined what little was left of his control. He was a man in the grip of a raging fever, and he had never felt more alive.

When he probed she made a soft, low sound and twisted beneath him. Her nails sank into his back. He raised his head and looked down at her.

"I want you," he said.

He knew that his voice sounded stark and savage with the force of his need. He was afraid that he might frighten her. But she wrapped herself around him and opened her thighs so that he could settle between her legs.

He seized the invitation and thrust into her. She was snug and tight and he was desperate not to hurt her. He longed to please her but the need to join with her in the most intimate, elemental way was paramount tonight. The small muscles of her passage resisted at first but he pushed steadily deeper until she sighed and closed around him, accepting him completely.

He dragged his mouth across hers as if he could somehow seal the bond between them with a kiss.

"Remember me," he grated.

"Always."

Then he began to move within her, seeking the rhythms that pleased her. She clutched at his shoulders. Her head tilted back on the pillow. She closed her eyes.

He felt the tension gathering in her. She started to tremble in his arms. He sensed the first small contractions sweeping through her lower body.

"Fallon," she gasped.

Everything inside him went rigid. For a timeless moment he hung there with her on the edge of the abyss. The searing intimacy was the most profound sensation he had ever experienced.

The storm broke. And then he was flying with Isabella into the dazzling energy that fueled the heart of chaos.

7

He awoke to the sweet-and-sour aroma of the ginger-scented soup. He could hear Isabella moving about in the kitchen. He hauled his arm up over his face and looked at his watch. An hour had passed since he had carried Isabella into the bedroom and made love to her as though the future of the world depended on it. Maybe his own future had depended on it, he thought. One thing was certain. He felt a hell of a lot better than he had an hour ago. Almost human again.

He climbed out of bed and went into the bathroom. When he saw the man in the mirror, his sense of well-being faded rapidly. It was replaced with dread. *She'll want to talk about it,* he thought. He was not good with conversations of that sort.

He washed up, dressed and went back into the front room, determined to do what a man had to do. Isabella was waiting for him.

She had put on a fresh shirt and a pair of trousers. She looked a little flushed and her eyes seemed brighter than usual but she made no comment on the fact that he had just emerged from her bedroom.

"Dinner's ready," she announced. She ladled the soup into two bowls. "Have a seat."

It dawned on him that she was acting as if nothing of significance had happened between them. He'd been worried about having the conversation, but now he was more alarmed by the fact that she didn't seem interested in discussing what had occurred on her new double bed. Maybe the sex was what she had meant when she talked about decompressing together. He did not want to think that was all it had been for her.

Warily, he sat down at the table. "Smells good."

"It's my grandmother's recipe. She used to make it for me whenever I got a cold or felt ill. Vegetable stock, ginger, garlic, soy sauce, vinegar, water chestnuts, tofu, red bell peppers and then, at the very end, you drizzle in some beaten eggs. The eggs come out looking like little noodles."

When she put the steaming bowl in front of him, he discovered that he did have an appetite, after all. In fact, he was suddenly starving. He picked up the spoon and started to eat. Nothing had tasted so good in a very long time. The sense of well-being flooded back. Nothing like sex and home cooking to put the world to rights.

Isabella sat down across from him. She looked pleased to see him eating with enthusiasm. "I understand that this Mrs. Bridewell could manipulate the paranormal properties of glass, but that clock isn't generating any energy now."

"It has to be wound up first," he said.

She pursed her lips, thinking. "But winding up a clock is a mechanical action. How does that produce paranormal power to activate the special properties of the glass?"

He liked the way Isabella's brain worked.

"Good question," he said. "That, as it happens, was Bridewell's real genius. She found a way to use mechanical energy to ignite paranormal energy that was otherwise locked in stasis."

"Like using a mechanically generated spark to ignite the pilot light in a gas fireplace?"

"Right. According to the J&J notes on the case, Mrs. B. also supplied the client with a small mirror that could be used to switch off the curiosity."

"So the customer didn't accidentally zap

himself?"

"That was evidently the idea. The deactivating devices were not ordinary mirrors, however. The glass involved, like the glass in the killer toys, possessed unique properties that have never been duplicated. To my knowledge, none of the small deactivation mirrors survived. There are no examples in any of the Arcane museums."

"Holy cow. I'd like to read the file on that case one of these days."

It was the first time she'd shown any curiosity about the history of the agency, he thought. Progress of a sort.

"Sure," he said. "Remind me tomorrow. You can tell me what you're running from then, too."

"Not tonight?"

"I'm too tired to concentrate tonight."

"Okay," she said.

They were both quiet for a while.

"So Kevin Conner Andrews, alias Nightman, turned out to be an upstanding citizen." Isabella said after a time. "Sterling employment record at the construction company. No criminal record. Everyone thought he was such a nice, normal guy. Blah, blah, blah."

"They always say that. The fact that he was local and in the construction business does explain how he knew about the basement in the old Zander house. Explains the new floor, as well."

"Yes. Want some more soup?"

"Yes," he said.

She got up, refilled his bowl and came back to the table.

"Think the cops are done with J&J?" she asked.

"Pretty much," he said. "The detective might come back for another statement from me, but everything I gave him was the truth, at least up to a point. Norma Spaulding hired us to check out the rumors of ghosts in the old Zander mansion. I went there to take a look. Found the dumping ground in the basement and was confronted by the killer, who must have been watching the house."

"Said killer attacks you in the basement and dies of sudden cardiac arrest."

"It happens, even to men Andrews's age. The authorities may spring for an autopsy but they won't find anything more. And I doubt they'll go that far, not when there's so much evidence."

She looked at him. "You mean the bodies?"

"Not just the bodies. Andrews took pictures. The cops found them in his house."

"Geez."

"Sudden deaths happen, even to killers," he stated. "The cops know that no shots were fired and there's no sign of a struggle. There's no way they're going to go with a theory of the crime that involves death by paranormal forces, so cardiac arrest is all they've got."

"Sounds like you've had experience in situations like this."

"Some," he admitted. "I don't think there's anything to worry about. The detective in charge just cracked the biggest case of his career. He'll be too busy giving interviews to the media to wonder why a serial killer in his prime keeled over and toppled down a flight of basement stairs. As far as he's concerned, the incident saved the county the cost of a trial."

"But it wasn't an *incident*," Isabella said quietly. "You had to kill a man."

"Yes."

She watched him with her knowing eyes. "That sort of thing, no matter how justified, causes some major psychic trauma."

"Not as major as the trauma that Andrews went through."

"He deserved it. Do you want to talk about the psychic trauma thing?"

"I don't think talking about it will do

anyone, including me, any good."

"Okay," she said.

"That's it? You're not going to lecture me about the dangers of ignoring the consequences of serious psychic trauma?"

"Not tonight."

Half an hour later, after consuming two bowls of soup and another glass of whiskey, Fallon Jones fell profoundly asleep on her sofa.

Moving quietly, she turned off the lights and took a spare blanket out of the hall closet. She covered Fallon with the blanket and then stood for a time in the shadows, looking at him. He was too big for the sofa, too big for the tiny apartment. But for some reason it felt right to have him here in her space, surrounded by her plants and the precious used furniture, lamps and dishes that her new neighbors had given her.

Fallon Jones and the secondhand treasures that filled the small apartment anchored her now. She belonged here in Scargill Cove.

8

The smell of freshly brewed coffee and the unfamiliar sounds of someone moving about in his kitchen awakened him. The cramped, stiff feeling told him that he had fallen asleep on the office sofa again.

He opened his eyes and looked out the window at the dark sky of a foggy winter dawn. It was raining but his office seemed much cozier than usual.

Something wrong with the view, Jones. You're a hotshot detective. Figure it out.

Not his office. Not his kitchen. Not even his sofa.

Memory kicked in. He'd had decompression sex with Isabella, eaten her homemade soup and then proceeded to fall asleep on her sofa.

Hell of a way to impress a woman, Jones.

It was an awkward scenario but he felt surprisingly good, rested. He glanced at the table. The clock was still there, wrapped in its blanket, silent and still.

"Good morning," Isabella said.

He turned his head and saw her. And instantly got hard. She was in the kitchen, looking as if she had just stepped out of a shower. Dressed in a robe and slippers, her hair caught back in a ponytail, her face still bare of makeup, she was the most erotic sight he had ever seen.

He tried to think of something intelligent to say and came up empty.

"Morning," he managed.

"How did you sleep?" She cracked an egg into a bowl. "The sofa is a little on the small side for a man of your size, but you were sound asleep. I didn't want to wake you."

Feeling like a great, clumsy mastodon, he lumbered to his feet.

"Sorry about this," he said gruffly. "Not sure what the hell happened."

She looked amused. "You were exhausted. You went to sleep after dinner. That's it. No big deal."

"Didn't think I'd be able to sleep at all."

"You've been pushing yourself and your talent too hard for too long. Yesterday you drew on the last of your reserves when you took down Andrews. Last night your body signaled that it had had enough. It more or less forced you to give yourself a chance to recover."

That wasn't the full answer, he thought. He'd experienced the aftermath of violence before and it had kept him awake for a couple of days. It was Isabella's good energy that had made it possible for him to get some much-needed rest last night. But he did not know how he knew that, much less how to explain it to her.

"I'll have breakfast ready when you come out of the bathroom," Isabella said.

Grateful for the opportunity to have a chance to figure out how to handle the situation, he headed down the hall. Once again he contemplated the man with the thousand-year-old eyes gazing back at him in the mirror.

The damage was done. There was nothing he could do now to stop the gossip.

"You really screwed up," he said to the man in the mirror.

When he emerged from the bathroom fifteen minutes later Isabella handed him a warm mug.

He drank some of the coffee and studied the rapidly lightening sky.

"I'd apologize," he said. "But it won't do any good."

"What are you talking about?" Isabella asked.

"This is one very small town," he said. "When I leave here this morning to go back to my place, someone is sure to see me."

She opened the door of the ancient refrigerator. "So?"

"So, by noon, everyone in the Cove will know that I spent the night here."

She closed the refrigerator and set a dish of butter on the counter. "So?"

His usually reliable brain seemed to have locked up like a computer that had been hit by a stealthy cyberattack. It took him a second to realize that he was actually feeling a condition that could be classified as confusion. He never got confused. He tried raising his talent a few notches to see if he could achieve a clearer view of the situation, but it didn't help. If anything he was more confounded than ever.

"It doesn't worry you that everyone will know I slept here?" he asked.

"Of course not." She dropped two slices of bread into the old-fashioned chrome toaster. "It was a rough day at the office. We had a couple of drinks and a meal to unwind and you fell asleep on my sofa. It happens."

"It's never happened to me. Not like that. And we didn't just have a meal and a few drinks, damn it. We had sex."

She raised her brows. "You're worried

about your reputation?"

"The problem," he said, groping for the right words, "is that after today the entire population of the Cove will know that we had sex."

"Who cares?"

He drank some more coffee, hoping the hit of caffeine would help him untangle the strange bewilderment that was fogging up his senses. Isabella did not seem to mind the possibility that people would know that they had spent the night together. Why was he worrying about it? Enlightenment did not come.

"It's my reputation you're worrying about, isn't it?" Isabella said. "It is very sweet of you to be so concerned. It's not necessary, but it is sweet."

"Yeah, that's me," he said into his mug. "Sweet."

"There are so few true gentlemen left in the world."

"Uh-huh." He sensed that things were going downhill fast, but he could not think of a way to stop the runaway train.

A rush of tiny springs followed by small popping sounds interrupted his fugue state. In the kitchenette, two slices of toast leaped high into the air.

"The toast," Isabella yelped.

113

She managed to snag one slice out of midair, but the other landed on the counter.

"Oh, good," she said. She smiled her brilliant smile. "They didn't fall on the floor this time. Of course, those of us with a strong background in the food-and-beverage business do have this two-second rule that is generally applied in such situations. But I hate to apply it in front of guests."

"Who gave you the toaster?" he asked.

"Henry and Vera. They said they found it in one of the cabins at the old Sea Breeze Motor Lodge."

The Sea Breeze had been abandoned for decades. A few years back, using a somewhat dubious legal claim of squatter's rights, Henry and Vera Emerson had moved in and proceeded to make it their home. To date no one had challenged them. Given the very large dogs they kept on the premises, it was unlikely that anyone in his right mind would try to evict Henry and Vera without the backing of a small army. Thus far no one with an army had shown up.

"You know," Fallon said, "now that you've got a steady job, you could probably afford a new toaster."

"Probably." She slathered butter on the toast. "But I like this one. It has a cool vintage look, don't you think?"

114

"Probably because it is vintage. Must be more than fifty years old. Amazing that it still works."

"It needed a little tuning up, but Henry got it running again."

"I can see that. Not every toaster can put a couple of slices into orbit."

"Nope." She looked pleased. "Mine is one of a kind."

It occurred to him that he had not given her a housewarming gift.

He sat down at the wooden table and examined the two neatly arranged place settings. The knife, fork and spoon were in proper order. The napkin was neatly folded. There was a tiny flower in a miniature bud vase positioned between the two place mats. He felt as if he had stepped into another dimension.

"So," he said. "When are you going to tell me how you wound up in Scargill Cove?"

"Later," she said. "At the office. Breakfast first. It's the most important meal of the day."

She fed him a heaping plate of eggs scrambled with ricotta cheese, a pile of toast and a fresh, juicy pear, hoping that the old adage was true and that the way to a man's heart really was through his stomach. A

115

large man like Fallon Jones needed his food.

He left after his third mug of coffee, taking the clock with him. She stood at her window and watched him walk through the fog — the damp kind off the ocean — to the office of Jones & Jones.

She had seen him kill. He was certainly not the first extremely dangerous man she had known. But he was different. Fallon Jones was that rarity in the modern world, a man who lived by a code, a man who cared about old-fashioned things like honor and a woman's reputation.

The Sunshine Café was open. She knew that the regulars would be at the counter, eating Marge's delicious homemade muffins and drinking coffee. They would see Fallon come down the street and go into his office. By noon everyone in town would know that he had spent the night with her.

She smiled to herself. "Fine by me."

9

"Mr. J-Jones?"

Fallon paused at the top of the stairs, the key in the lock of the office door, and looked down at Walker.

Walker rarely entered any building except his own cabin.

"What can I do for you, Walker?" Fallon asked.

If Walker had a last name, no one in town was aware of it. He was the closest thing that Scargill Cove had to a homeless man but he was not, strictly speaking, homeless. He had a cabin out on the bluffs where he took short naps during the day. All the evidence indicated that Walker did not need a lot of sleep. He was a man with a job to do. Patrolling Scargill Cove was his calling, and he was faithful to the task.

He bathed in the hot springs out at the Point. He wore his clothes until they became tattered and frayed. When he needed new garments, someone in town would leave whatever was necessary on top of a garbage can. Walker would only take items that he found in the trash. He refused flat-out gifts of any kind. *I don't take charity* was part of his code and he lived by it.

He got plenty to eat. Marge at the Sunshine always left an evening meal out for him at night and fresh muffins and coffee in the mornings. In between times Walker foraged in the trash behind Stokes's Grocery. Although he seemed physically healthy, he never gained any weight. Fallon figured that was because Walker was nearly always in motion. He walked the streets of Scargill Cove all night long, regardless of the weather.

"Got to t-talk to you, Mr. Jones."

Walker hardly ever spoke. When he did, it was always in very short sentences. Most people in the Cove assumed that Walker had done some hard drugs when he was a young man. They said he had gone out on a very bad trip and never found his way back home. Fallon wasn't so sure of that diagnosis. He sensed that Walker was some kind of talent. Something had happened here in the Cove decades ago that had launched him on his relentless patrols.

Fallon turned the key in the lock and

opened the door. "Come on inside. I'll make some coffee."

Walker said nothing but he climbed the stairs and entered the office. He stood in the doorway for a minute, looking around uncertainly.

Fallon set the blanket-covered clock on a table and shrugged out of his jacket.

"Have a seat, Walker," he said, indicating Isabella's chair. It was the only chair in the room other than his own. There had never been much need for a client chair. J&J got very little in the way of walk-in business. Mostly the firm was a single-client agency and that client was the Arcane Society. The services of J&J were available to all members of the Society, but when those calls came in, Fallon usually handed off the work to other investigation firms operated by sensitives in the Arcane community.

Walker hesitated and then lowered himself gingerly onto the chair, as if he was unaccustomed to sitting in one. He stared hard at the blanket-covered clock, fascination and dread drawing his taut face even tighter around the bones. He started to rock.

Fallon poured water into the coffee machine. "Something wrong, Walker?"

"It needs to go back," Walker said urgently. "It sh-shouldn't be here."

"What needs to go back?"

"Whatever is under that b-blanket. It needs to go back."

Fallon had been about to shovel the ground coffee into the machine. He stopped, put the package on the table and contemplated Walker.

"Do you know what is under the blanket, Walker?"

Walker shook his head. He rocked harder. His eyes never left the blanket. "No, Mr. Jones. I just know it needs to go b-back. It should be with the other things in the vault."

Fallon forgot about the coffee altogether. He jacked up his talent a little. A multidimensional spiderweb appeared in his mind. For the moment several of the strands remained concealed in the dark night of chaos energy. But that would change as bits and pieces of data came in. Each item of information would land somewhere on the web, get stuck and light up. Relationships, connections, links and associations would gradually illuminate the delicate design. Eventually he would see the answers he needed.

He looked at Walker.

"What other things?" he asked.

Walker finally dragged his hollow eyes away from the clock. "The alien weapons."

Another small section of the web lit up.

The muffled sound of Isabella's light footsteps interrupted Fallon's thoughts before he could examine the new strand of light. The door opened.

Isabella came into the room on the wings of good energy. At the sight of Walker sitting in her chair, she paused in surprise. But she recovered immediately and gave him her glowing smile.

"Good morning, Walker," she said.

Walker seemed to relax. He stopped rocking. "Hello, Miss Valdez."

Fallon looked at Isabella. "Meet our new client."

Isabella did not even blink. She started to unbutton her coat. "What's the problem, Walker?"

Walker looked at the clock again. "That thing. It's dangerous. It has to go b-back into the vault."

Isabella gave Fallon a questioning look. He knew what she was thinking. If Walker had somehow sensed the energy in the clock, then he most certainly had a measurable amount of talent.

Isabella hung up her coat. "Why don't you start at the beginning, Walker?"

Walker's face crumpled in dazed panic. He started to rock violently. He had no clue how to locate the beginning, Fallon realized.

Isabella, too, understood immediately.

"Better yet," she said, "why don't you show us the location of the vault?"

Fallon was certain that would lead to another blind alley. But to his amazement, Walker's expression became focused once again. He surged to his feet.

"Okay," he said. "But we have to be very c-careful. The Queen is on guard."

10

Isabella opened her senses when Fallon pulled into the cracked, weed-studded parking lot of the Sea Breeze Motor Lodge. There was the usual amount of paranormal fog in front of the main lodge, but she saw nothing out of the ordinary.

"At least the energy here doesn't look like the stuff at the Zander house," she said.

"Good to know," Fallon said. He looked at Walker who was sitting in the rear seat, rocking gently. "You're sure the vault is here, Walker?" he said.

"Y-yes." Walker rocked harder. He rarely rode in motor vehicles. They made him even more anxious than normal.

The dogs appeared, coalescing out of the mist like a pack of wolves. They charged the SUV, barking furiously. Isabella sat quietly with Fallon and Walker, waiting. Not one attempted to open a door. Everyone in Scargill Cove knew the drill. If you visited

Henry and Vera, you stayed in the car, the windows rolled up, until someone called off the beasts. On the rare occasions when some hapless tourist, laboring under the mistaken impression that the lodge was still a functioning motel, pulled into the lodge, Henry and Vera remained inside until the people gave up and moved on.

Fallon glanced at the illuminated windows of the office.

"Looks like Henry and Vera are home," he said.

"They usually are," Isabella said. "Sometimes I do wonder what they do in that place all day long, day after day."

Fallon smiled. "You mean, you don't know?"

"No." She gave him a sharp look. "Do you?"

"Sure. I'm a detective, remember?"

In the rear seat Walker spoke up. "They g-guard the v-vault. That's their job. I do patrol at night. They s-secure the vault. Marge and the others keep watch during the day."

Isabella turned in the seat to look at him. "Marge and other people in town are involved in this thing?"

Walker gave her a jerky nod. "That was the plan back at the start. We've followed the plan. But s-something went wrong. We have to put things right. Alien technology is very d-dangerous."

The front door of the office swung open. A bulky, bearded figure in denim overalls and a red-and-black plaid flannel shirt lumbered out into the fog. He glowered at the dogs through a pair of old-fashioned gold-framed spectacles.

"Poppy, Orchid, Clyde, Samson, the rest of you, that's enough," Henry called. "They're friends."

The barking subsided immediately. The six dogs stood waiting, ears pricked, eyes cold and watchful.

Isabella was the first one to open the door.

"Hello, Poppy," she said to the big shepherd mix. "You look lovely today."

Overcome with delight, Poppy rushed forward, tongue lolling, to greet her. Isabella rubbed her ears. Poppy swooned. Orchid, Clyde, Samson and the rest crowded in eagerly. Isabella patted them all.

Fallon opened his door and got out. "Don't know what it is with you and those dogs."

"I like dogs," Isabella said. She gave Poppy one last pat. "I'm thinking of getting one of my own." A dog would make it official, she thought. A dog would mean that she had settled here in Scargill Cove, that she had found a home.

Henry peered at her. "How's the toaster working?"

"Great," Isabella said. "It's the best toaster I've ever owned."

Out of the corner of her eye she saw Fallon's brows climb but he made no comment.

Henry grunted, satisfied. "Don't make 'em like they used to." He looked at Walker and Fallon. "I take it this is about the things in the vault?"

"How did you know?" Fallon asked.

Henry angled his head at Walker. "Only one reason Walker would get into a vehicle. What's up?"

Walker got out of the SUV, jittering a little. "They found s-something, Henry. Something that belongs in the vault. I could feel it, you know?"

Henry gave Fallon a long, considering look. "Is this connected to the Zander house business?"

"You figured that out in a hurry," Fallon said. He went around to the back of the SUV, opened the rear door and removed the blanket-wrapped clock.

"Heard about the bodies buried under the basement," Henry said, watching him. "It was all over the evening news last night. They said they found the killer's body, too. Heart attack."

"Yes," Fallon said.

"Real neat and tidy ending," Henry said. "Vera and I like that kind of ending." He squinted at the object in Fallon's hands. "What did you find?"

"A clock," Isabella said. "Not an ordinary clock, though."

Walker twitched. "It's one of the alien weapons stored down in the vault, Henry."

Henry frowned. "It sure as hell didn't come out of there since Vera and I have been watching the place. Must have been re-moved before we locked it down all those years ago."

"The Zander house killer told me that he found the clock in a glass box hidden in a cavern beneath the basement of the man-sion," Fallon said. "Got a feeling the clock had been hidden for quite a while."

Henry looked interested. "You and the killer had a chat before he croaked?"

"Guys like that have to brag," Fallon explained. "Guess he wanted to impress me."

"Uh-huh." Henry grew thoughtful. "And after he finished with his bragging, he had his heart attack. Hell of a coincidence."

"It happens," Fallon said.

"Nope," Henry said. "No coincidences. Not when it comes to anything that came out of that vault."

Isabella moved to stand beside Fallon. "We understand that Walker sees things through his own private prism, but please don't tell us that you really believe that aliens from another galaxy visited Scargill Cove and left some baggage behind."

"Not aliens," Henry said. "They told us they worked for a small research company, but everyone around here knew that was probably a cover. The black-ops folks use a lot of private contractors when they want to keep a low profile."

"Right," Isabella said. "Everyone knows that."

Fallon winced, but he did not comment.

Henry contemplated her, and then he studied Fallon for a few seconds. Isabella could see him making a decision.

"You two are locals now," Henry said. "You've got a right to know what happened here twenty-two years ago. Come on inside. Vera is making coffee. Tea for you, Isabella. We'll tell you what we know, but I gotta warn you up front, it isn't a whole lot."

11

Walker trooped into the lodge and took a seat on a window bench. He wrapped his arms around his waist and rocked quietly.

Isabella scooped a pile of books off the cushion of an old-fashioned, padded leather armchair and sat down. Fallon grabbed one of the two wooden chairs at the small dining table, reversed it and sat down astride it. He put the clock, still covered in the blanket, on the floor beside his left boot and folded his arms on the back of the chair.

The interior of the lodge reminded him of his own office or at least the way it had looked until Isabella had swept in and taken charge. Every available surface was cluttered with books, magazines and printouts. There were a computer and a printer on the dining room table.

A fire burned in the big fireplace. Two rows of framed portraits hung on the wall above the mantel. Each featured a young man or woman. Some were in caps and gowns. Others wore military uniforms. One of the women stood, smiling proudly, in the doorway of a restaurant. Fallon knew that the name of the restaurant was her own.

Over the decades a number of runaways and homeless kids had wandered into Scargill Cove. Most did not hang around for long, but those who did were quietly taken in, sheltered and educated. Vera and Henry were the town's unofficial schoolmasters. The framed photographs were portraits of the Cove's graduates.

Out of the corner of his eye, Fallon saw Isabella glance briefly at the top page of a ream-thick stack of paper positioned on the arm of her chair. Her eyes widened a little and then she smiled. He was coming to know that particular smile. It meant that she had just solved some small mystery.

He winked. She laughed.

Vera, a good-looking, strong-boned, full-bodied woman in her mid-fifties came out of the kitchen carrying four mugs by the handles. Her graying-brown hair was tied back in a ponytail. She wore a long, loose-fitting dress of green and purple that fell to her ankles. Faded tattoos peeked out from beneath the sleeves of the dress. In spite of the chill of the day, she had a pair of flip-flops on her feet.

"Hello, Isabella, Fallon," she said, her voice pleasantly husky. "Nice to see you both. You, too, Walker."

She made no comment about the strangeness of seeing Walker indoors.

Isabella tapped the printout sitting on the arm of the chair. "You are Vera Hastings, the writer, aren't you? You do the suspense series featuring the vampire and the witch. I love those books."

Vera chuckled. "Thanks. Actually Henry and I are Vera Hastings. He does the vampire. I do the witch."

"Those novels are terrific," Isabella enthused. "I loved the one in which the vampire had to drink the witch's blood because he was dying, and her blood made him drunk."

Fallon decided it was time to step in and regain control of the conversation. "About the clock."

"The clock?" Vera echoed.

"The one in the blanket," Fallon said.

Walker jittered. "It came from the vault."

With a worried expression, Vera studied the blanket-covered clock next to Fallon's boot. "You're right, Walker. Whatever is under that blanket must have come from the vault."

Walker rocked harder. "You can feel it. Like me."

"Yes," Vera said. She set the mugs on the table. "Well, it was bound to happen sooner or later, wasn't it? We always knew that someday whatever is in that vault would cause more trouble."

Henry came out of the kitchen, a pot of coffee in one meaty hand, a pot of tea in the other. "We just never got around to figuring out what we'd do about it when the trouble came down."

"Because we didn't have any great ideas," Vera said. She looked at Fallon. "Have you told anyone else in town about finding that . . . thing, whatever it is, under the blanket?"

"Not yet," Fallon said. "Walker sensed it while I was taking it upstairs to my office. He made it clear that we needed to talk to you and Henry right away. I figured he knew what he was talking about."

"Yes," she said. "When it comes to objects in the vault, Walker knows at least as much as any of us. Maybe more."

Henry filled the mugs. Vera handed them around. Walker refused his, sticking to the no-charity code. Vera left the coffee sitting on the windowsill nearby. After a while, Walker picked up the mug as if he'd just happened to find it the way he found the other life necessities that came his way.

Fallon leaned down and raised the blanket.

Vera and Henry looked at the clock. They both appeared baffled.

"It's just a clock," Henry said, frowning.

"It's actually a clockwork device that generates energy that interferes with light waves in the visible spectrum," Fallon said. "Wind it up and when it starts to tick everything goes dark for a radius of several yards."

Henry whistled softly. "Son of a bitch." He looked up suddenly, eyes narrowed. "Looks old."

"It is old," Fallon said. "Late nineteenth century."

Vera eyed the clock. "Are you telling us that it was designed and built in the Victorian era?"

"Yes," Fallon said.

Henry shook his head. "What you're describing is cutting-edge technology. If it came out of the vault, it must have been designed and built in a high-tech lab." He glanced uneasily at Vera. "Like the other things down there."

"No," Fallon said. "It came out of the workshop of a very ingenious, very dangerous inventor who lived in the Victorian era. Mrs. Millicent Bridewell. Trust me."

"But the kind of technology involved in such a device would have to be state-of-the-art," Henry said. "Hell, beyond state-of-the-art. I don't care how brilliant your Victorian-era inventor was, she would not have had access to the kind of advanced materials and algorithms required to design and build a machine that can neutralize visible light waves."

"Mrs. Bridewell's clockwork curiosities, as she called them, were not based on software programs or cutting-edge manufacturing techniques," Fallon said.

Vera looked uneasy. "What are you saying?"

"The design of this clock is based on the principles of para-physics."

Vera and Henry exchanged looks. Henry cleared his throat and turned back to Fallon.

"Are you telling us that the clock generates some kind of paranormal energy?" he asked.

"Yes," Fallon said. "Vera and Walker are obviously somewhat sensitive to that kind of energy. That's why they can feel the psi infused into the clock."

Vera looked wary. She glanced at Walker. "It's just our intuition."

"That's what people say when they sense something they can't explain," Isabella said gently.

"She's right," Fallon said. "Most people are reluctant to acknowledge the psychic side of their natures, but they're usually okay with the concept of intuition. Scargill Cove is a nexus, a hot spot, psychically speaking, which probably explains how the clock, and whatever else is in the vault, got here."

They were all looking at him now, including Isabella.

Vera tapped one finger against the side of her mug. "Do you mean the Cove is a vortex? They say there are some in various places around the world. Sedona, for example."

"Similar principle," Fallon said. "But a nexus is more powerful."

Henry appeared reluctantly fascinated. "You want to explain that?"

No, Fallon thought. *I don't want to waste the time.* But he had a feeling that things would move more rapidly if he took a few minutes to go through it.

"There are different kinds of nexus points," he said. "Those like Scargill Cove occur where there's a natural confluence of several kinds of powerful currents. This stretch of coastline happens to be a place where the forces generated by strong ocean currents combine with currents from the earth's magnetic field and the energy of geothermal heat flowing deep underground."

Henry frowned. "What geothermal heat? We're not sitting on top of a volcano."

"The hot springs in the cave out on the Point," Vera said suddenly. "They're the result of geothermal energy in the area."

Henry reflected for a moment. "All right, I get that there are some powerful geophysical currents running through this area, but how does that translate into paranormal energy?"

"The paranormal and the normal exist on a continuum," Fallon said. "There's no hard, fast line that divides the two. Think of the light spectrum. There's plenty of energy just beyond the visible range. Some birds and animals can see it and there are instruments that can detect it."

"Well, sure," Henry said. He squinted through his spectacles. "But paranormal energy?"

Fallon felt himself getting a little impatient now. Isabella gave him a tiny, quelling frown. He decided to take the hint. He needed Vera's and Henry's cooperation.

"Someday we'll have the kind of instruments needed to detect psi, too," he said. "But take it from me, power is power and there's a hell of a lot of it running through the earth. In places like the Cove, where you've got a tremendous amount of geophysical energy flowing into a nexus, the currents are so strong that they register on human senses. Not everyone who comes to town is consciously aware of the confluence of forces here, but I think most pick up on it on some deep level. It bothers a lot of folks."

"Probably explains our low tourism numbers," Vera said dryly.

"Yes," Fallon agreed. He watched her very steadily. "The thing is, some people are attracted to nexus points, even if they aren't aware of the pull of the place."

"People like us?" Vera asked quietly.

"Yes," Fallon said. "People like us."

He noticed that Isabella was smiling a little again.

"That's right," she said. "People like us."

Henry's expression sharpened. "You say you think this nexus theory explains why the black-ops people set up the lab here? They wanted to tap in to some currents of power in the area?"

Fallon got the little buzz of adrenaline that he always experienced when the answers started coming. Out on the grid more sectors brightened.

"Tell me about this black-ops lab," he said.

12

Vera and Henry looked at each other. Walker rocked on in silence.

Vera took a deep breath. "Something very weird happened here twenty-two years ago."

"That would have been during the period when J&J was operating out of L.A.," Fallon said.

"There was no Jones & Jones in the Cove in those days," Henry said. "That's for sure. Wasn't much of anything, come to that. But for about a month someone ran a secret weapons research program here, at least that's what we all assumed was going on. If the weapons were paranormal in nature, it would certainly explain a few things."

"Certainly wouldn't be the first time the government has conducted secret paranormal experiments," Isabella said.

Henry snorted. "Might just be the first time they were successful, though. Don't think they liked the results. After the accident they left in one hell of a hurry, at least the survivors did. No one ever came back for the weapons."

Fallon heightened his senses a little. "Tell me what you know, Henry. It's important."

"Yeah, I can see that," Henry said.

He settled back in one of the big armchairs near the fireplace. "Might as well start at the beginning. Twenty-two years ago when Vera and I and Walker and the others arrived, Scargill Cove was a boarded-up ghost town. The whole damn place had been abandoned, including this lodge. There were twenty-five of us at the start." He glanced at Walker for confirmation. "Twenty-five in the beginning, right, Walker?"

"Twenty-five," Walker said urgently. He rocked harder.

Henry nodded. "We called ourselves the Seekers. We fell under the spell of a real asshole of a guru named Gordon Lasher. Don't ask me why we thought he was so smart and so enlightened. To give the man his due, he was incredibly charismatic."

"He was the perfect con man and we were young and dumb," Vera said. "We fell for his pitch. Gave him every dime we had. A few of the Seekers had some real money. Trust funds and inheritances. He took it all."

140

"Several people wised up or got bored and split after the first couple of months," Henry added. "Lost a couple of others the hard way."

"The hard way?" Isabella asked.

"Sam took his own life," Vera said. Her eyes were shadowed. "Lucy got stoned and drove her car off the Point."

Isabella took a sip of tea. "You were all members of a commune?"

Henry chuckled. "I believe the politically correct term is intentional community. What can I say? We were young and determined to find an enlightened path."

"America has a long tradition of intentional communities," Fallon said. "Goes all the way back to those folks who got off the boat in Plymouth."

"True," Henry agreed. "Well, here in the Cove we were into meditation, self-sufficient eco-living, serious philosophical inquiry and, oh, yeah, free love."

Vera rolled her eyes. "In hindsight I think it is safe to say that as far as the Asshole and the other men were concerned, it was the free love that was the big attraction."

"Which was probably what destroyed your community," Fallon said.

Everyone except Walker stared at him as if he had just spoken in tongues.

141

He shrugged. "Sex is the most powerful force in any social group. It has to be controlled and regulated in some manner or else it tears the fabric of the community apart. It's a fact that when a commune or intentional community disintegrates, it's invariably because of the sexual dynamics."

"Sure was fun while it lasted, though," Henry said somewhat wistfully. He winked at Vera.

"But it only lasted about six months," Vera said crisply. "The Seekers discovered what every other intentional community learns the hard way. Human emotions trump Utopian ideals every damn time."

" 'Hearts full of passion, jealousy and hate,' " Isabella quoted softly.

"Yeah," Henry said. "Fallon's right. Turns out the free love thing is one of those interesting concepts that just doesn't work out in the real world. Anyhow, six months into what we called the Grand Experiment, we met at the Scar and officially dissolved the community. Not that there was much left to dissolve by that time. The Asshole was already gone. One of the women went with him."

Walker stiffened. "Rachel."

Vera nodded. "That's right, Walker. Rachel Stewart went with him."

"Tell me about the vault," Fallon said.

"Right," Henry said. "The vault. Well, it's all connected, you see. The black-ops people showed up about a month before Gordon Lasher and Rachel left. There were three of them. They weren't interested in the Cove. All they wanted was this lodge. It was empty at the time."

"What was it about the Sea Breeze that attracted them?" Isabella asked.

Walker rocked. "The vault."

Henry put down his coffee mug. "Like Walker says, they wanted the vault. Come with me. I'll show you."

Fallon set his mug aside and got to his feet. Isabella rose, too. Together with Vera and Walker they followed Henry through the kitchen and out the back door into the yard.

Fallon sensed Isabella heightening her talent. She halted abruptly beside him. He heard her take a sharp breath.

"See anything?" he asked quietly.

"Oh, yes," she said in low tones. "There is some serious fog out here. I've never noticed it before because I've never been behind the lodge."

"We don't bring a lot of people back here," Henry explained.

"Why not?" Fallon asked

Henry pointed to a large, circular steel plate set into the ground. The steel had to be three inches thick, Fallon thought. It was secured with a heavy chain and a lock.

"What in the world?" Isabella asked. "It looks like a large manhole cover."

"It's the entrance to what we call the vault," Vera said. "But it's actually an old bomb shelter. It must have been constructed sometime back in the late nineteen-fifties or early sixties. In those days a lot of folks believed that a full-on atomic war between the U.S. and what used to be the U.S.S.R. was pretty much inevitable."

"The real paranoids like the man who owned the lodge at the time built private bunkers underground in their backyards," Henry explained. "Stocked 'em with enough supplies to last a year."

Fallon studied the steel plate. "The hatch doesn't look that old."

"It isn't," Henry said. "The black-ops folks took out the old hatch and installed this one twenty-two years ago when they took over the lodge for a time. Guess they wanted something more substantial."

Fallon gave that some thought. "Most of the people who built shelters kept quiet about it. When the bombs started falling, they didn't want to have to fight off their friends and neighbors, who would all try to get into the shelter."

"Right." Henry squinted again. "You're wondering how the black-ops people knew about this shelter in the first place, aren't you?"

"The question does come to mind."

"I don't have an answer," Henry said. "All we can tell you is that they must have known that the shelter was here. Moved right on in as if they owned the place."

Isabella narrowed her eyes. "Sure sounds like someone set up a clandestine government lab here."

"A secret lab, yes," Fallon agreed. "But I doubt that it was connected to any of the standard issue intelligence agencies. They've got plenty of underground research facilities of their own. They wouldn't need to buy an old motor lodge with a bomb shelter out back."

Isabella beetled her brows. "I'm not so sure about that. Looks like a perfect cover to me. Just the kind of thing a black-ops project would use. And you said yourself this stretch of the coastline is a nexus. They probably knew that."

He looked at her. "I'm supposed to be the conspiracy theorist in this agency."

She smiled. "Learn from the best is my motto."

He decided the only thing he could do with that was ignore it. "Whatever the hell was going on here, I'm ninety-eight-point-five percent certain it was not a secret government lab."

"Hmm." She considered that for a couple of beats. "A private research lab, maybe?"

"I think so, yes," Fallon said.

"Under contract to one of the intelligence agencies?" she prompted hopefully.

"No." He tried to quell her with a warning look. "Just some private researchers who somehow got their hands on one or more of Mrs. Bridewell's curiosities."

"Ah," Isabella said. "So we're talking mad scientists. What about the funding?"

He abandoned the attempt to introduce a degree of logic into the discussion. "What funding, damn it?"

"Who financed this small, private lab?" she asked with an air of sweet reason. "Labs take money. Lots of it."

"I don't know who financed the project," he admitted. "But I doubt that it was the government."

Isabella was disappointed, but this time she stayed silent.

Fallon turned back to Henry. "You said

146

this lab was only in operation for about a month?"

Henry scratched his ear. "That's all. Right, Walker?"

Walker nodded in his jerky fashion. "And then s-something real bad happened down there."

"Tell me about that part," Fallon said to Henry.

Henry heaved a massive shrug. "Who the hell knows? Whatever it was, it killed one of the three researchers. They hauled the body out of the shelter, threw it into the back of a van and drove off. Like I said, no one ever returned."

"Did they take anything with them in addition to the body?" Fallon asked.

Vera and Henry turned to Walker.

"Book," Walker said, voice ringing with certainty. He jiggled anxiously. "One of them had a book. Black cover."

"Sounds like a lab notebook," Fallon said.

"Like I said, they took off in a hurry," Henry said. "At that point we figured everyone in the Cove was probably walking six feet under."

Isabella stared at him. "You thought you were going to die?"

Henry grimaced. "Hell, as far as we knew it was a secret weapons research lab and something had gone real wrong. What else were we supposed to think? Figured we'd all been irradiated or poisoned."

"Of course," Isabella said, nodding in sympathy. "Those are certainly the first two possibilities that would come to my mind."

Fallon looked at Henry. "What did you do?"

"In another life I was trained as an engineer," Henry said. "I drove to San Francisco and bought a radiation detector and some basic soil, water and air-quality test equipment. Brought the instruments back here. Ran every test I could think of. There was no detectable radiation. No traces of any poisonous gas leaking out from under the ground."

"So you decided to go down and take a look, didn't you?" Fallon asked.

"Yeah." Henry shook his head. "Guess it was the engineer in me. I had to know what we were dealing with."

"A-alien technology," Walker rasped.

"I agree with Vera and Henry," Isabella said to Walker. "This looks more like a black-ops group conducting research on paranormal weapons."

Walker pondered that. "Alien paranormal weapons."

"Well, that's certainly a possibility," Isabella allowed.

With a valiant effort, Fallon possessed himself in patience. "What happened when you opened the shelter, Henry?"

"Hard to describe." Henry stared down at the thick steel hatch with a troubled expression.

Vera took up the tale. "He made everyone move several yards back before he raised the hatch."

Henry did not take his eyes off the steel lid. "Some kind of energy poured out. Felt like a strong wind but nothing moved. It didn't ruffle the leaves or my shirt or my hair. But it was intense and very disturbing."

"We all felt it," Vera said, "even though the rest of us were standing some distance away."

"Sounds like paranormal radiation of some kind," Fallon said.

"I couldn't handle the wind, whatever it was," Henry continued. "But the Asshole was still around at the time. He didn't seem bothered by it. Neither did Rachel Stewart. The radiation didn't seem to affect Walker, either. So those three went down into the shelter."

"What happened?" Isabella asked.

"When they came back up, Walker seemed

to be his usual self."

They all looked at Walker, who rocked harder in response to the attention.

"I take it he was always like he is now?" Isabella asked quietly.

"Yes," Vera said. "Just the same. But Rachel and Gordon Lasher were terribly excited when they came up the ladder, especially Lasher. He was shivering and he could hardly speak."

"When he calmed down, he told us that he'd seen a lot of lab equipment down there," Henry explained. "He told us that there were signs of a violent explosion but that the place was so hot with some kind of energy that no one else should risk going down."

"He said we should let the shelter cool down for a few weeks or months before anyone went back into it," Vera said.

"By then I couldn't stand the guy," Henry added. "But I agreed with him."

"But the shelter has never cooled down, has it?" Fallon asked. "Paranormal radiation tends to hang around for a while."

"Yeah, I noticed that," Henry said. "The Asshole took off with Rachel a couple of days later. That was the last we saw of either of them. A few weeks after that I decided to try going down into the shelter. I made it as far as the bottom of the ladder. That's the last I remember."

"What happened?" Isabella asked.

"Damned if I know," Henry said. "I passed out."

Walker rocked harder. "The Q-Queen."

"When I came to, I was lying flat on my back on the ground up here," Henry said. "Vera and Walker were standing around looking down at me."

"How did you get out?" Fallon asked.

"Walker was with us when Henry opened the hatch," Vera said. "Henry went down alone and disappeared. We called out to him but there was no response. I couldn't get through the energy wind no matter how hard I tried. But Walker climbed down and brought Henry back out."

"Figure Walker probably saved my life," Henry said.

Isabella smiled at Walker. "You were a hero."

Walker rocked and looked confused.

"Yes, Walker was a hero," Vera agreed. "Afterward everyone who was left in town got together to talk about the situation. We concluded that we could not allow whatever was down there in the shelter to fall into the wrong hands. We also needed to make sure that no children or thrill seekers fell into the shelter."

"We get a few drifters through the Cove from time to time, as you know," Henry added. "Didn't want to take a chance that some of them might try to go down, either."

Fallon nodded. "So you locked it down."

"Figured if the government wasn't going to take responsibility for protecting people from whatever was down there, we would have to do the job," Vera concluded. "And that's what we've done for the past twenty-two years."

"Good plan," Fallon said. "Heavy paranormal radiation can have unpredictable effects. And if there are more of Mrs. Bridewell's nasty little toys in the shelter, we're dealing with some very dangerous weapons." He studied the heavy lock on the steel hatch. "I take it you have the key to this thing?"

"Sure." Henry reached deep into the pocket of his overalls and removed a large key. "I keep it with me all the time."

"I'll go down," Fallon said, "assuming I can get past the energy winds." He looked at Isabella. "If anything goes wrong, make sure this hatch gets closed and locked again immediately. Then call Zack Jones. You have the number."

"I think I should go down with you," Isabella said.

He said the first thing that came into his head. "No."

"You're not being logical here, Fallon," she said calmly. "You don't know what you're going to find in the shelter. You might need backup like I did yesterday, remember?"

"Not the sort of thing I'm likely to forget."

"I'm good at finding things," she insisted. "And there is something down there that needs to be found."

Fallon gave it about three seconds' worth of thought, but he only needed a fraction of one second to reach the bottom line. She was right. Her talent might prove useful. He pulled a card out of his pocket and handed it to Henry.

"I'll go first and check the place out. When I give the all clear, Isabella will follow me. Anything goes wrong, seal the shelter again and call that number. Do it real fast."

Henry studied the card. "Who am I calling?"

"Zack Jones. Master of the Arcane Society. My agency's biggest client. Don't worry, Zack will take charge. He always does. It's a damned irritating habit."

13

Isabella stood with Walker and Vera. They watched Fallon and Henry open the shelter. The lock gave easily enough, but the men had to use a couple of crowbars to pry up the hatch.

"Don't know what they made this thing out of," Henry said. "Some kind of high-tech steel. But given time, anything will corrode in this climate."

The lid rose ponderously with a grinding squeak and a dull groan. Energy leaked out. Isabella felt the hair on the nape of her neck stir. Icy shivers of awareness slithered across her senses in warning.

The steel hatch rose higher. A storm of paranormal wind roared out of the dark opening. It was unlike anything Isabella had ever experienced. She felt as if she were standing in the teeth of a hurricane, but nothing around her was affected by the strange gale. The grass did not bend beneath the force of the howling energy. No leaves rustled. Her hair and clothes did not flutter.

But her senses responded with an all-consuming awareness. Adrenaline splashed through her veins. An intoxicating excitement rose within her. She was suddenly jacked. She looked at Fallon and knew by the heat in his eyes that he was experiencing a similar reaction to the heavy radiation.

"Shit." Henry dropped the crowbar and staggered back. "See what I mean?"

"Yes," Fallon said. He aimed a flashlight into the opening and got the intense, thoughtful expression Isabella was coming to know well. "Lot of energy down there, all right. Must have been one hell of an explosion. The nexus currents in the area would have intensified the effects."

Vera edged farther away. The dogs hung back, heads lowered. Poppy growled. Walker stayed where he was, but his agitation increased visibly. He rocked madly on his heels and wrapped his arms around himself.

"Alien weapons," Walker said. "The Queen g-guards them."

Isabella braced herself and struggled to focus her talent. When she went into her zone, she saw heavy waves of psi fog crashing out of the shelter hatch.

"Lasher and Rachel must have been fairly

155

strong talents of some kind," she said quietly to Fallon. "That's why they were able to go down there."

"Probably explains why Lasher chose the Cove to found his community of Seekers in the first place," Fallon said. "Consciously or unconsciously, he sensed the nexus currents here and was drawn to them."

He stirred the darkness with the beam of his flashlight. Isabella saw a ladder leading down into the shadows. The light glinted on the corner of a rusted metal lab bench. Shards of broken glass glittered in the depths. There was also a scattering of yellowed papers and what looked like a couple of notebooks.

"They pulled out in a hurry," she said. "No telling what they left down there."

"The Queen," Walker muttered. "Watch out for the Q-queen."

"I will," Fallon promised.

He disappeared over the edge and descended into the shadows. It occurred to Isabella, not for the first time, that for a big man Fallon Jones moved with an easy, masculine grace that conveyed an impression of both power and control.

"Ladder's in good shape," he called up a short time later. "And the energy level down here isn't any stronger than it is at the opening of the hatch. Come on down, Isabella."

She stuck her flashlight into the pocket of her jacket, stepped over the edge, found her footing on the ladder and descended cautiously. It was like going down into an invisible whirlpool. The energy whipped and flashed around her.

When her foot touched the bottom rung of the ladder, Fallon's strong hand closed around her arm.

"You okay?" he asked.

"Yes, but I have to say I've never experienced anything like this. Any sign of Walker's Queen?"

"Not yet."

"That's royalty for you. Always the last to arrive." She took out her flashlight and switched it on. "Of course it would help if we knew exactly what he was talking about."

"Whatever it was, Walker took it seriously, so we will, too," Fallon said. "Watch your step — there's a lot of broken glass in here."

She crouched and picked up one of the larger shards. "Very thick glass, too."

Fallon took it from her and held it up to the beam of his flashlight. "Looks like the kind they use in banks. Bullet-resistant. Exactly the type of glass that researchers familiar with laws of para-physics would use to deal with the energy generated by

Bridewell's curiosities. The best way to disrupt psi that is infused in glass is with a glass barrier."

Together they swept the concrete chamber with their flashlights. Broken lab equipment, overturned metal benches and scraps of paper gave mute testimony to the violence of whatever had occurred in the shelter twenty-two years earlier.

"This place is larger than I would have expected," Isabella said. "It's as big as a double-wide. There's even a second room off this one. I was expecting a tiny, cramped space."

"The folks who built bomb shelters planned to live in them for several months or even a year while they waited for the radiation levels to go down on the surface," Fallon said. "They wanted all the comforts of home."

She shuddered. "I can't imagine camping out down here while all of my friends and neighbors were dying of radiation poisoning on the surface."

"Guess you had to be there to get into the mind-set."

"Guess so. Well, safe to say that something chaotic certainly happened in here. But aside from the broken glass, there are no signs of a normal explosion. No fire damage. The papers and notebooks aren't even charred."

"There was a violent release of energy, but it all came from the paranormal end of the spectrum." Fallon broke off abruptly. "Huh."

Isabella glanced at him and saw that he was aiming his flashlight at the doorway that opened into the other chamber.

"What?" she asked.

But he was already heading toward the second room.

She started to hurry after him, but a faint scratching sound in one dark corner distracted her. She jumped and flicked the light beam in the direction of the noise. Something moved in the shadows.

"Crap," she whispered. "Rats."

"That's not a surprise," Fallon said. He did not look back. "We're underground and this space has been abandoned for years."

"I'm not interested in logical explanations, boss. We're talking about rats."

"They'll run from the light."

"Oh, yeah? I don't see any signs of this sucker running away."

"Wonder how he got in here," Fallon mused. "The place is supposed to be sealed."

"Rats can get into anything."

The scratchy noise got louder. An old-fashioned clockwork doll waddled stiffly out of the darkness. Isabella watched it with a sinking feeling. The doll stood almost three feet tall. It was dressed in what had once been an elaborately worked gown in the late-Victorian style of fashionable mourning. The dress was tattered and frayed, but it had obviously been made of expensive materials and trim.

The doll was mostly bald, but what was left of its hair was parted in the middle and pulled back into a tight chignon. A miniature crown, studied with small, ominous crystals, was perched on top of the porcelain skull.

"I think the Queen has arrived," Isabella whispered. "It's Victoria. She's dressed in black from head to foot. They say that after Prince Albert's death she wore mourning for the rest of her reign."

"It's motion-sensitive, like the clock," Fallon said. "That's a hallmark of Bridewell's work."

"How can it function after all these years?"

"We'll worry about that later."

Energy heightened abruptly in the atmosphere. The doll trundled toward Isabella with unnerving accuracy.

"Looks like she's got a fix on you," Fallon said.

"I can sense it. She's starting to generate some kind of energy. Reminds me of the psi that emanated from the clock just before everything went dark."

"Move," Fallon ordered. "Fast. Force her to get another fix."

Isabella tried to step out of the Queen's path, but her muscles refused to obey. She opened her mouth to tell Fallon that she could not move only to discover that she could not speak. Her mind began to grow cloudy. A terrifying numbness crept through her blood.

She concentrated fiercely on focusing her own talent. She knew how to disorient human psi but this was a doll, a clockwork robot. Nevertheless, the energy that had been infused into the thing originally was human in origin, she reminded herself.

She caught the telltale wavelengths of the paranormal energy emanating from the doll's cold glass eyes and sent out the counteracting currents. The sense of numbness eased. She took a deep breath and managed to step to the side.

There was an eerie clicking in the shadows. The eyes of the doll rattled in their sockets as the machine sought a new fix.

Fallon moved swiftly, coming up behind the Queen.

Sensing his movements, the doll turned, creaking in her high-button shoes, searching for the new target.

Fallon brought the heavy flashlight down on the robot's head in a sharp, savage blow. Porcelain cracked. The queen toppled backward and crashed to the floor, face turned toward the concrete ceiling. The glass eyes continued to skitter wildly in their sockets, seeking a target. The wooden limbs jerked and twitched, but the device could not right itself.

The light shifted at the entrance to the shelter.

"Everything okay down there?" Henry called. "We heard some loud noises."

"Just ran into the Queen," Fallon called back. "But things are under control."

Careful to keep out of range of the robot's eyes, Fallon flipped the clockwork figure facedown on the concrete. The energy pulsing through the eyes was spent harmlessly on the floor. The doll's head and limbs continued to twist and clatter and shiver.

Isabella watched Fallon open up the entire back of the doll, gown, miniature corset and wooden frame. In the beam of the flashlights the elaborate gears of the clockwork mechanism continued to move.

"There should be a lot more corrosion," Fallon said. "I can understand the paranormal energy in the glass eyes surviving all these years. Once infused into an object, a heavy dose of psi will emit radiation for centuries. But like Henry said, sooner or later, metal always corrodes, especially in a climate like this."

"Same story with the clock," Isabella said. "The killer told us that all he had to do was give it some oil and wind it up."

Fallon reached into the body of the doll and did something to one of the gears. The Queen went limp and still.

Isabella looked down at the lifeless robot. "We are not amused."

Fallon smiled briefly. "Couldn't resist, could you?"

"Sorry, no. How often do you get to use a line like that?"

"Rarely." He took a closer look at the guts of the device. "Most of the mechanism is late-nineteenth-century, but someone repaired it and installed some modern parts and fittings."

"Recently?"

"No. I'm thinking the repair work was done twenty-two years ago."

"Like the clock?" Isabella asked.

"Yes."

"That's what was going on here. Those three men brought some of Mrs. Bridewell's inventions here to the Cove and tried to get them functional again."

"Yes, but that's not the most interesting aspect of this situation," Fallon said. He looked down at his hand. In the light Isabella saw a faint sheen on his fingers.

"Freshly oiled?" she whispered.

"Yes." Fallon got to his feet and aimed the flashlight at the footprints on the concrete floor. "The guy who left those prints must be the maintenance man."

"But how is he coming and going? Unless Henry and Vera are lying to us about having kept the shelter locked all this time."

"I don't think so," Fallon said. "There's another, more likely possibility. I think I feel a slight draft coming from the other room. Let's take a look."

They walked through the doorway into the adjoining chamber. Isabella froze.

"Good grief," she whispered.

In the twin beams of the flashlights she could see a row of what looked like small coffins elevated on metal stands.

"Take a deep breath," Fallon said. "They aren't coffins."

She started breathing again. "Sure. I knew

164

that. It's just that at first glance they looked pretty freaky."

"You expected freaky?" Fallon aimed the light at what appeared to be a mound of trash. "Does that qualify?"

She saw the skull first. It was human. The rest of the skeleton came into view amid tattered remnants of clothing and a pair of boots. A ring glinted on one finger bone.

"Crap," she said. "Another body."

Fallon went to the skeleton and crouched beside it. He reached into the scattered bones, plucked out a wallet and flipped it open.

"Gordon Lasher," he said. "Looks like we now know what happened to the Asshole."

"He told everyone he was leaving town and then he snuck back here. I'll bet he sensed the power in the clockwork gadgets and planned to steal them. Looks like the Queen got him. Serves him right."

"I don't think the Queen was responsible." Fallon aimed the flashlight at an object that lay on the floor next to the skull. "This wasn't death by paranormal means. Looks more like good old-fashioned blunt force trauma."

"He fell?"

"No." Fallon reached down and picked up a crowbar. "Someone whacked him on the

165

back of the head with this."

"How can you tell all that?"

"Crack in the skull and the body fell facedown," Fallon said absently. "It's not rocket science."

"Oh, right. But that means that there was someone else down here with him."

"Yes," Fallon said. "It does indicate exactly that."

"Henry and Vera told us that Lasher ran off with a woman named Rachel Stewart. Both of them were able to tolerate the psi down here. I'll bet they came together to steal the curiosities. Rachel must have decided that Lasher really was an asshole after all and that she didn't need him anymore. She bashed him in the head with the crowbar."

"I'd say the probability of that scenario is about seventy-four percent."

"Only seventy-four?"

"Yes." Fallon swept the rest of the chamber with his flashlight. "Here we go, there's our second entrance."

Isabella studied the steel door built into the concrete wall. "It's a door but it doesn't go up to the surface."

Fallon went forward, gripped the handle and pulled on the door. It opened with only a few faint squeaks of the hinges. A great darkness lay beyond. Chilly, damp air flowed into the chamber. Isabella heard the muffled rumble of the ocean in the distance.

"A cave," Fallon said. "It leads out to a cove or a beach."

"That door opened fairly easily," Isabella said. "The salt air should have done a lot more damage by now."

"Whoever has been keeping the Queen in functioning order all these years uses this entrance," Fallon said.

"Why do you suppose the original owner built a second entrance?"

"Think about it. If you were down here waiting for the bombs to fall, not knowing what was happening on the surface, wouldn't you want a second escape route in case the first one got blocked?"

"Good point," she said.

He closed the cavern door, walked to the first elongated box and wiped off a layer of grime with one gloved hand.

"More bullet-resistant glass," he said. "They used these boxes to store the curiosities."

Isabella went to stand beside him. The glass box was empty.

"Looks about the right size for the Queen," she said. She glanced down the row of stands and cases. "There's no box on one of the stands. I'll bet that was the one that held the clock. The killer said that when he found the device in the tunnel beneath the Zander house basement, it was in a glass box."

They went to the third case in the row. Fallon wiped off more grime.

Isabella saw a wood-and-bronze clockwork dragon with eerie glass eyes. She moved to the next box. It contained an ornate miniature carriage and two small wooden horses. The glass windows of the vehicle glinted darkly. The third case held a toy-sized merry-go-round decorated with small mythical beasts. The last box held a Victorian-era camera.

"If we assume that the Queen was in the empty case and that the clock was stolen together with its glass box, all of the curiosities that were originally stored here are accounted for," Fallon said.

"You sound relieved."

"Trust me, I am," Fallon said.

"But who comes down here on a regular basis to keep the Queen in working order?"

"Someone who can handle the psi in this place and who also feels a duty to protect the artifacts."

"Walker," she said softly. "But that means he knows about the second entrance. Why didn't he mention it?"

"Walker operates in his own universe and employs his own kind of logic," Fallon said. "It's our fault. We didn't ask the right question."

"I think that, in his mind, he has turned over the responsibility of protecting the inventions to J&J. He probably assumes that you know everything he knows."

"Yes."

Isabella looked at the skeleton. "What do we do with the body?"

"Nothing until we get the inventions out of here. Gordon Lasher has been here for twenty-two years. He can wait a while longer."

14

They emerged from the shelter a short time later, closing the hatch to cut off the disturbing psi wind. Isabella fondled the dogs while Fallon told Henry and Vera what they had found and explained his plans to bring in an Arcane team to remove the remaining curiosities.

Henry squinted at Walker. "Let me get this straight. Vera and I have been guarding the front door of that shelter for twenty-two years while you've been coming and going through the back door?"

Walker was bewildered by the question. "Have to k-keep the Queen working. Takes oil."

"Why didn't you tell us there was another entrance to the shelter?" Vera asked calmly.

Walker looked confused. "No one knew about it."

"Except you and Rachel and the Asshole," Henry said, disgusted.

"J-just me, now," Walker said earnestly. "Gordon Lasher is dead. Rachel never came back. I kept the secret."

Henry grimaced. "Wonder how many other people discovered the second entrance during the past twenty-two years."

"I don't think that anyone else knows it exists," Fallon said. "As far as we could tell, all of the devices are accounted for. Walker's footprints are the only new ones down there."

Walker rocked. "No one knows about the tunnel d-door. Except me. And Rachel. But Rachel never came back."

"Where does the door lead?" Isabella asked gently.

Walker concentrated. "Comes out in the h-hot springs cave."

"Which is out at the Point," Vera said. "Well, that explains it. The only people who know about the springs are those of us who live in the Cove."

"I've been inside the hot springs cavern a few times," Fallon said. "There's a vast network of tunnels leading off of it that have never been explored. Obviously one of them leads to the shelter."

"Walker, Lasher and Rachel saw the second door when they went down into the shelter," Isabella said. "But how did they find the entrance from the hot springs cavern? They would have had to map that maze of tunnels. It would have taken weeks, at the very least. But from the looks of things, Lasher was back inside the shelter shortly after he left town with Rachel."

"Rachel," Walker said suddenly. "Rachel f-found the tunnel that leads to the shelter. She showed it to Lasher."

Fallon looked at Isabella. "Sounds like Rachel Stewart had some serious talent."

Walker chose to walk back into town. Isabella grabbed the handhold just inside the door of the big SUV and did a little hop to get up into the cab. Fallon put the remains of the Queen, together with the clock, into the cargo bay of the vehicle and got behind the wheel.

Isabella's phone rang just as Fallon drove out of the Sea Breeze parking lot. The number looked familiar.

"Norma Spaulding," Isabella said. "I've got a bad feeling about this."

"Clients are always trouble," Fallon said. "In a perfect world J&J wouldn't need any."

"That would certainly be an interesting business model." She opened the phone. "Hello, Norma," she said, going for her most professional tones.

"The buyer I had lined up for the Zander house just called," Norma said tightly. "He heard the news about the so-called Haunted House murders. He is no longer interested."

Isabella winced. "I'm sorry about that."

"Damn it, I didn't hire Jones & Jones to kill the deal."

"I assure you, it was an accident."

"Finding three bodies in the basement is an accident?" Norma's voice rose. "A serial killer dropping dead in the house is an *accident?* The property is a crime scene now. The press is having a field day with the story."

"I realize it may take some time for the media to lose interest, but I'm sure that in a few months everyone will forget about what happened at the Zander house," Isabella said soothingly.

"Not a chance. That property is never going to be marketable. The only reason I called is to tell you not to bother to send me a bill for your services. I didn't get what I paid for and I'm not about to write a check to your agency."

Outrage splashed through Isabella. "But J&J solved the case."

"There was no case," Norma said. She sounded like she was speaking through set teeth. "I hired you to help me get rid of those silly rumors about the property being haunted. I thought if a psychic detective agency declared the place ghost-free, I could sell it. But instead you killed the deal."

"It isn't J&J's fault that the property was a dumping ground for a serial killer."

"Maybe not, but I'm holding your firm responsible for killing the sale, so do not bother to send me your bill."

The connection went dead. Isabella closed the phone.

"Bad news," she said. "Norma Spaulding says she won't pay our bill. She blames J&J for making the Zander house unmarketable."

"Told you the case was a waste of time," Fallon said. "That's why we don't like to encourage that kind of work."

"It's not our fault that there were bodies in the house."

"Clients always blame the investigator when they don't get the answer they want," Fallon said. "Hell, most of the time they blame the investigator even when they do get the answer they say they want or even the one they expect. It's the nature of the business, Isabella."

She slumped in the seat and gazed morosely out the window. "It's not fair."

"Here's a little tip going forward."

"What?"

"Always get a nonrefundable retainer up front."

She drummed her fingers on the armrest. "Good idea. I'll make sure to do that next time."

Fallon turned off the main street and drove behind the J&J office. He parked under the wide overhang. They climbed out of the SUV. Fallon opened the rear of the vehicle.

"You take the clock," he said. "I'll handle the Queen."

She hoisted the blanket-wrapped clock under one arm and opened the back door of the office. They carried the curiosities upstairs to the landing. Fallon got out his key and opened the door.

Isabella walked into the office ahead of him, switched on the lights and set the clock on the floor in the corner.

"Now what?" she asked.

He closed the door and put the doll on the floor next to the clock. "Like I told Henry and Vera and Walker, an Arcane lab team will collect all of the curiosities tomorrow and take them back to the Society's main lab in L.A. I want a complete report from the experts. I'd also like to know who

175

brought the gadgets here three decades ago."

Isabella walked into the tiny kitchenette that adjoined the office and picked up the teakettle. "I sense a new conspiracy theory in the making."

There was a moment of crystalline silence behind her. She knew she had gone too far.

"Do you think that's what I do?" Fallon asked, his tone chillingly neutral. "Invent conspiracies?"

The cold, emotionless edge on the words caught her off guard. She turned quickly to face him. Fallon was watching her with a look that matched his tone. She had seen that same expression and felt the deep sense of aloneness that went with it many times since meeting him. It was as if he spent most of his life locked in some other dimension. She longed to reach out to him, but it was not as if she lived in a normal dimension, either. She was certain of one thing, though. She must not move too fast with Fallon Jones. He did not fully trust her yet, and until he crossed that boundary she had to feel her way.

Then, again, she thought, she had not entrusted him with her secrets, either. *That makes us even,* she thought.

"Of course not," she said, keeping her

176

voice light with an effort. She turned back to the sink and ran water into the kettle. "It was just a little joke, boss. I've got no problems with what you call your conspiracy thinking. After all, most of the time you're right." She shut off the faucet and looked at him. "Right?"

Some of the tension went out of him, but it was replaced by some of the soul-deep weariness that she had sensed in him the first time he walked through the door of the café.

"Most of the time," he said. "Not always. And when I do screw up, I put people in danger."

"Now you're talking about the Nightshade case, aren't you?"

"It's not just Nightshade. Yesterday at the Zander house, if you hadn't called me —" He stopped.

"But I did call you," she pointed out. "What's more I had enough sense not to go into the basement alone. Give me some credit. I told you, I can take care of myself. I've been doing it for years."

Energy heightened a little in the atmosphere. She knew that he had tapped in to his talent.

He went to the counter where the industrial-size coffeemaker sat, picked up the package of ground coffee and started to fill the machine. He did not bother with a measuring spoon.

"How, exactly, can you take care of yourself?" he asked.

She leaned back against the sink and folded her arms. "That's one of the things I admire about you, Mr. Jones. Your interrogation technique is so amazingly subtle."

He filled the machine with water. She noticed that his jaw was clenched.

"I hope you're not grinding your teeth," she said. "That sort of thing leads to crowns and root canals."

"I've tried not to push you," he said.

"I know. You've been very patient, all things considered. You weren't able to find out anything about me online, were you? Just my picture-perfect bio." She could not conceal her pride. "Even the brilliant director of Jones & Jones hit a brick wall when he went looking for me. Am I good, or what?"

He smiled wryly. "You're good. I found a nice, neat narrative of your life all the way back to your birth and it's all fake, isn't it?"

"Yep."

"I've known from the beginning that you're running from something or someone." He flipped the switch on the coffee machine. "You chose Scargill Cove as a hideout, and I'm pretty damn sure that wasn't by accident."

"Coincidence?"

"I've explained to you that we have this policy about coincidences at J&J."

"Right," she said. "Out of curiosity, how long were you prepared to wait before you pounced?"

"Pounced?" He looked baffled.

"Before you started demanding answers," she clarified.

He watched the coffee fill the pot. "I was planning to wait a little longer, but given recent events, I think maybe now would be a good time for you to start talking."

She considered that. "Okay, but I really don't see any connection between the discovery of the Bridewell curiosities and my presence here in the Cove. Aside from the fact that I have a talent for finding things, of course. I mean, it's what I do. Even when I don't want to do it, if you see what I mean."

"Talk to me, Isabella." He looked at her with his shadowed, unreadable eyes. "I need some answers."

"I understand," she said. "And now that I've worked with you for a while, I know that I can trust you. It's not like I have a choice, anyway."

"Why is that?"

"I knew the night I arrived in Scargill Cove that this was as far as I could run. I'm good at living off the grid, heck, I was born off of it. But it's only a matter of time before they find me."

They sat at their respective desks. Fallon swallowed some coffee and watched Isabella sip her green tea. He could see that she was composing herself, trying to decide where to start her narrative. He searched for a way in.

"What did you mean when you said you were born off the grid?" he asked.

She looked at him over the rim of her cup. "Ever heard of the Iceberg website?"

"That bizarre conspiracy-theory website run by some nut who calls himself the Sentinel?" Fallon grimaced. "Sure, I know it. Some folks say I've got conspiracy issues, but I'm a piker compared to the Sentinel. That guy is so far over the horizon, he'll never come back. He must have lost touch with reality long ago."

"Think so?"

"He's definitely looney tunes."

"So why do you monitor his website?"

Fallon shrugged. "Because sometimes he

hits on a nugget of solid information that I can plug in to one of my case files. Like they say, even a stopped clock is right twice a day. The problem with whatever I get from the Iceberg site is that the bits of good data are always tangled up in one of the Sentinel's crazy wheels-within-wheels, circles-within-circles fantasies. Teasing out the truth can take hours of research. There is no logical foundation to the Sentinel's theories and therefore no meaningful context. The guy is a classic paranoid conspiracy nut."

She raised her brows. "You, on the other hand, have context, is that it?"

"Makes all the difference," he assured her. "Case in point. The Sentinel will happen on a small hint of hard information about Nightshade and then embed it into a fantasy of alien abduction. It's useless in that fantasy context, so no one pays any attention. But I can sometimes fit the data into my own investigation because I do have context." He paused. "Come to think of it, I haven't seen anything new on the Iceberg site for a while. Maybe the Sentinel finally went on meds. To tell you the truth, I'll miss him."

"No," she said coolly. "The Sentinel didn't go on meds. He was murdered." She took a deep breath. "Maybe."

"Yeah, there was some chatter about that a while back online but it faded. That's the thing about the Sentinel. You can't believe anything you hear about him. I wouldn't put it past him to fake his own murder just to stir up more conspiracy theories."

"Believe me when I tell you that I am praying that she did exactly that."

Fallon stilled. "She?"

"The Sentinel is a woman. She pretends to be male online because it adds another layer of cover."

"How do you know that?"

"Because the Sentinel raised me after my parents were killed in a plane crash," Isabella said. "I'm her granddaughter."

Fallon felt as if he'd been poleaxed. He sat forward abruptly, automatically heightening his talent. "You're serious."

"The reason you never found the real me when you went looking is because I have been living under fake IDs all of my life." Isabella cradled her tea mug in both hands. "My mother did not go to a hospital to have me."

"So, no Social Security number? No birth certificate?"

"I've had a dozen Social Security numbers during my life, as well as a variety of birth certificates, credit cards and passports. My grandmother manufactured a fake ID for me before I was even born and she gives me a new one whenever I move or change jobs." Isabella glanced at the wall where her backpack hung on an iron hook. "I've got two brand-new, unused sets in my pack right now."

"Where were you born?' he demanded, fascinated. "How did you manage to stay out of the system?"

"My parents were living with my grandmother on a remote island in the South Pacific when I was born. My father wrote thrillers under an assumed name, all based on conspiracies he had uncovered. My mother was an artist. Her work hangs in some very respected museums. All the paintings are under a fake name. I was born at home, and the birth was never registered with any official government agency. I was homeschooled from the start. Every name I've ever used except Isabella Valdez has been manufactured."

He whistled softly. "I'll be damned. And people think I have a problem when it comes to the paranoia thing. Isabella Valdez is your real name?"

"Yes." She straightened her shoulders. "I decided to start using it the night I hitchhiked to Scargill Cove."

"What about the bio I found online?"

"Oh, that's a complete fake, of course. First time it's ever been used. Grandma told me to save it for this particular situation."

"Where did your grandmother get the sets of fake ID?" Fallon asked.

"From an old family firm that specializes in that kind of high-end art. They've been in business for generations. Grandma always said that if they were good enough for J&J, they were good enough for her."

"I'm going to go out on a limb here and guess that she uses the Harper family's services."

Isabella smiled into her cup. "Good guess."

Understanding whispered through him. "Why did you come to Scargill Cove, Isabella?"

"To find you, of course," she said very steadily. "Grandma always told me that if anything ever happened to her or if I got into the kind of trouble that I couldn't handle on my own, I should contact Jones & Jones."

"Why did it take you this long to tell me the truth?"

"Because I had to be sure I could trust you. We are all influenced by our upbringing. I was raised in a family of conspiracy theorists. I have certain hardwired eccentricities."

"In other words, you don't trust anyone outside the family."

"I trust you, Fallon, now that I've had a chance to know you. But I had to be sure. My grandmother's life, assuming she is still alive, depends on it."

"And if she is dead?"

Isabella's eyes darkened. "Then I will avenge her."

He steepled his fingers, thinking. "What makes you think someone would try to kill her?"

"Because they don't want her to expose the conspiracy on her website, of course. But I'm praying that she outwitted them. Grandma is really, really good when it comes to this kind of stuff. With luck, the bastards believe that she's dead."

Wheels within wheels, Fallon thought. Classic conspiracy theory logic. No context, no hard facts, no problem.

"Why would they believe she's dead?" he asked.

"There's plenty of documentation confirming her death." Isabella waved that off. "There was a notice in the local paper. A death certificate was filed. According to the records, Grandma was cremated. It's all very neat and tidy."

"But you're not buying any of it?"

"It's possible that they found her," Isabella conceded. "But I think there is also a very good chance that she is alive and has gone into hiding. I have no way to contact her. That was part of the plan, you see. She told me that if she ever had to disappear, we had to make it look solid."

"But she told you to come to J&J for help?"

"Yes." Isabella watched him with a steely determination. "They're after me, too. I got away once, but I might not be so lucky a second time."

Fallon went stone cold. "Someone tried to kill you?"

"In Phoenix about a month ago. They found me at the department store where I was working. That's when it hit me." Isabella broke off. Tears glistened in her eyes.

"When what hit you?" he prompted.

"That they might have found her, after all." Isabella opened her desk drawer, yanked a tissue out of the small box she kept there and wiped her eyes. "I had been telling myself that she was following the emergency plan. Gone into hiding. But if they found me, maybe they found her, too.

Maybe she really is dead."

Isabella was crying. He had no clue what to do in a situation like this.

"Isabella," he said.

"Sorry," she said. She sniffed into the tissue. "It's just that if she really is gone, it's as if she never even lived. She set things up that way. Her only legacy is her website, and it just sits there online like some kind of virtual tombstone. I can hardly bring myself to look at it."

"Isabella," he said again. And stopped because he could not think of anything else to say.

"If she's dead, it's my fault because I told her about the conspiracy," Isabella said into the tissue.

He was on his feet without conscious thought. He rounded his desk, yanking the clean, neatly folded white handkerchief out of his pocket. She took the handkerchief from him, looked at it for a few seconds as if she had never seen one and then she started to cry quietly into it.

He hauled her gently to her feet, wrapped his arms around her and held her tightly, as if he could somehow shield her from the dark fantasy world she had constructed.

With a small cry, she dropped the damp handkerchief onto the desk, buried her face against the front of his black pullover and sobbed in earnest.

He stood there with her while the fog off the ocean rolled in, cloaking the town and the office windows, isolating them from the rest of the world.

15

After a while, Isabella stopped crying. She raised her head and gave him a shaky smile.

"Sorry about that," she said. "Lately that's been happening to me without warning. I'm fine one minute and then I think about how she might actually be dead and that maybe I'm just fooling myself and all of a sudden I'm crying."

"It's all right," he said. He couldn't think of anything else to say. He realized that she was trying to step back. Reluctantly he opened his arms and released her.

She sat down, carefully refolded the damp handkerchief and handed it to him. She grabbed another tissue and blew her nose one last time. She tossed the tissue into the trash basket, drank some tea and composed herself.

He stood in the center of the office for a few seconds, unsure of what to do next. When nothing helpful came to mind, he went back to his desk, swallowed more coffee and forced himself to focus on the problem at hand.

"Using your line of logic," he began.

She gave him a wan smile. "That's a polite way of saying you don't believe me."

Out of nowhere anger flashed through him. "Damn it, don't put words in my mouth. I'm trying to gather facts here."

She sighed. "I know. I apologize. I've been a little emotional lately."

"Understandable," he said gruffly.

She nodded, very serious. "Yes, I think so. I've been under a lot of stress."

"That's certainly one word for it," he agreed. "All right, let's try this again. You said someone tried to kill you a few weeks ago in Phoenix?"

"Yes. Well, two men tried to kidnap me. I'm sure they planned to kill me."

"How did you escape?" he asked.

She moved one hand in a vague motion. "Turns out there's a flip side of my talent. I can find things and people, all right. But I can use my ability to conceal them, as well. I can tell someone to get lost. Literally. That's what I did with the two thugs they sent after me."

He ignored the pronoun. *They* was very popular with conspiracy buffs. There was always a mysterious *they* manipulating things from behind the scenes.

"How does it work?" he asked.

She blinked. "How does what work?"

"Your talent."

"How does any talent work?" She gave a little shrug. "I have to have physical contact to do it, that's all I know. They had me cornered on a mall roof. I sent them down an emergency stairwell and out onto the street. I don't know what happened to them after that. I assume they walked for a while until they came out of the trance."

"Or got run down?"

"I told them to only cross at the lights," she said. "When I put people into a get-lost trance, they tend to follow orders very precisely."

"Sounds like a form of hypnotic suggestion."

"I suppose so."

"Why did you tell them to only cross at the lights?"

"I assumed that if two guys from the company I used to work for got run down on a Phoenix street, it would create more problems than it would solve," she said. "Dead bodies have a way of causing trouble."

But the lack of dead bodies meant no

police records or any other kind of evidence that would lend credibility to her story, he thought. He was starting to understand how Alice had felt when she fell down the rabbit hole. He had to deal with the very real possibility that Isabella was as lost in a conspiracy fantasy as the Sentinel. But one thing was clear, Isabella believed every word she was saying.

"Tell me about the conspiracy," he said.

"I used to work for Lucan Protection Services. Do you know it?"

He paused his coffee mug in midair, all of his senses crackling. "Sure. Max Lucan is a member of the Arcane Society. He runs a high-end art-and-antiquities security agency."

"I went to work for his company about seven months ago. At the time I felt very fortunate to get the job."

"Why?"

"Let's just say that the combination of my talent plus my family history gives me employment problems. The result is that I change employers the way some folks change their socks." She paused. "I get fired a lot."

"I understand the personal history issues. It could not have been easy growing up in a family that doesn't officially exist. But what's the problem with your talent? I would think being a finder would make you a natural fit for any kind of investigation or security firm."

She took another sip of tea and lowered the mug. "The problem is that I'm picky about what I find."

"Explain."

"A lot of security and investigation work involves locating people who don't want to be found. Often those who are lost have a very good reason for disappearing. Then there are the dead bodies. Sure, once in a while those kinds of jobs are okay. I understand that sort of work needs doing."

"Like yesterday at the Zander mansion?"

"Right," she said, very earnest now. "I mean, I'm all for getting justice for murder victims and closure for families. It's important work. Honorable work. Necessary work. But it is incredibly depressing to spend your entire working life, day in and day out, searching for people who are either dead or don't want to be found."

"Hadn't thought about it," he admitted. "Is that what you did?"

"Mostly. As soon as my employers realized I could find bodies and lost people, they kept giving me those kinds of cases. But Lucan Protection Services was different. I was one of the technicians there. I enjoyed the work. No one expected me to find dead people, just lost art and antiquities."

"What went wrong?"

"I was doing a really good job. I got promoted to Department A."

"What's Department A?"

"It's an elite investigation division within Lucan," she said. "Very hush-hush."

Fallon suppressed a groan. "Right. Hush-hush."

"I was doing okay, making good money. I was even thinking about getting vested in the company retirement plan. I had a nice apartment. It almost felt as if I was starting to get a life. Finally."

"You didn't have one before going to work for Lucan?"

"Not the normal kind," she said. "Do you have any idea what it's like living under fake names and IDs your whole life?"

"No," he admitted. "But I can see where it would start to wear on a person."

"After a while, you start to wonder if you really exist. But I was beginning to feel comfortable at Lucan, probably because people like me are considered normal there, at least inside Department A."

"You mean people with some talent?"

She nodded. "Lucan hires a lot of sensitives, especially in Department A. It caters to clients who are sensitives and deal in antiquities that have a paranormal provenance. All in all, I fit right in. Then I found out what was really going on."

The rabbit hole suddenly got a whole lot darker. *I'm doomed,* Fallon thought. *I've fallen for a woman who has gone over the horizon.*

"What did you stumble into?" he asked, resigned to his fate.

"One of the lead investigators in Department A, Julian Garrett, my old boss there, is running his own private business. He's an arms dealer. But not just any arms dealer. He specializes in paranormal weapons."

Isabella waited, watching expectantly for his reaction to her bombshell.

"Huh," he said.

"That's all you have to say? I thought Arcane frowned very heavily on that kind of thing."

"It does." Fallon put his fingertips together and gave the subject some serious thought. "Hard to imagine that something like that could be going on inside Lucan Protection Services, though. I don't doubt that Max Lucan has brokered a few shady antiquities sales in his time. And I'm aware that he specializes in art and artifacts with a paranormal provenance. But Lucan is no fool. He knows that if Arcane finds out that he's dealing para-weapons to bad guys with some talent, J&J will come down on him like a very big mountain."

"I don't think Max Lucan knew what was going on. But I think he must have been getting suspicious about Department A. Julian Garrett knew that. To save his own hide, he set me up to take the fall. Now Lucan thinks I'm the one who was dealing the para-weapons. I'm sure he told Julian to find me and bring me in, but Julian wants me dead so I can't talk."

"Let's go back a step. How did you discover that you were being set up by Julian Garrett?"

"I walked into my cubicle one morning and saw a whole bunch of really ugly energy around my desk and computer. It was not there the day before when I left work. The trail led straight back to Julian Garrett's office."

"What did you do?"

"I realized Julian had been in my cubicle, but I couldn't imagine why. I started going through my drawers. I didn't find anything, so I went to work running all sorts of virus checks and searches on my computer."

"You found something?"

"A hidden file," Isabella said. "It contained a record of the sale of a number of antiquities. At first glance there didn't seem to be anything unusual about it, but I couldn't understand why Julian put the file on my computer. So I started researching the individual artifacts."

"What did you find?"

"I soon discovered that all the objects had a few things in common. In addition to having the usual paranormal provenance, every single one of them should have been classified as weapons-grade artifacts according to the company guidelines."

"Anything else?"

"All of the transactions had been handled off the books. None of the sales were recorded in the company archives. What's more, they had all been obtained from a single source, a broker named Orville Sloan. He's a major player in the black market."

"Did you confront Julian Garrett?"

"For Pete's sake, of course not," Isabella said. She looked horrified. "It was obvious he was setting me up. It would have been my word against Julian's. Julian has worked for Lucan for several years. Lucan trusts him. What's more, Lucan would have been ruthless. He would have made certain that I wound up in prison or worse."

"So you ran."

"Yes. But I also called my grandmother and told her what was going on. She's the one who said that if Julian Garrett found me, he would very likely kill me."

Isabella was not inventing any of this, Fallon thought. Her interpretation of events might be skewed, but she was giving him the facts as she knew them. What the hell was going on here?

Fallon sat forward, reached for the computer keyboard and typed in a quick series of searches. He got a ping immediately.

"What did you find?" Isabella asked.

"A report of the death of an arms dealer named Orville Sloan." Fallon studied the data on the screen. "He was shot a month ago. No suspects."

Isabella's mouth tightened. "I'll bet Julian killed him to cover up more tracks."

"Arms dealers have a lot of enemies," Fallon said mildly.

He reminded himself that Isabella was the granddaughter of the Sentinel. Conspiracy theories were second nature to her. But he couldn't restrain his instinctive response. He slid deeper into the hot zone of his talent. The vast web was starting to brighten with a cold light. A pattern was forming. There was something here, something important.

"I don't suppose you have anything resembling proof of what you think is going on inside Department A, do you?" he asked.

Isabella hesitated. "It's sort of hard to prove that kind of stuff."

"Yes, it is."

"That's why Grandma thought that I should turn the problem over to Arcane. She said that policing the psychic bad guys was part of the Society's job."

He exhaled wearily. "We do what we can, but it's not our job. It's just that when you get guys like that crazy bastard at the Zander house yesterday, there isn't a lot regular law enforcement can do."

"Exactly."

"Isabella —"

She closed her eyes for a few seconds. When she opened them, he could see nothing but stoic resignation.

"I was afraid of this," she said quietly. "You don't believe a word I've said, do you? You think I'm crazy, like the Sentinel."

"Damn it, Isabella."

"I thought maybe if I gave you time to get to know me, you would realize that I'm not a nutcase. That's why I delayed telling you the truth about myself. Maybe I should have waited a little longer before I tried to explain, but I needed to tell someone. Not knowing if my grandmother is dead or alive is just so hard to deal with. She's the only one I've got left and if she's gone —"

"Isabella." He got to his feet, rounded his desk, reached down and closed his hands over her shoulders. He hauled her to her feet for the second time. "I don't have enough information to make an informed decision on the subject of Julian Garrett's involvement in para-weapons dealing, let alone decide if your grandmother actually was murdered."

"I understand."

"But what I do know," he said, "is that you believe every word of what you're telling me. And as long as you believe it, I'll do whatever it takes to get your answers for you. If your grandmother was murdered, I'll find the killer."

"Fallon," she whispered. Her eyes glistened again. She reached up to touch his jaw. "I don't know what to say, except thank you." She stood on tiptoe and kissed him lightly.

It was a damn gratitude kiss, he thought. The last thing he wanted from Isabella was gratitude.

16

They gathered in the Scar that evening. Everyone who had lived in the Cove during the heyday of the Seekers' community showed up. Isabella made a mental note of the handful of longtime residents who had a long history in the town. Henry and Vera were there. So were her landlord, Ralph Toomey, and Marge from the Sunshine. The proprietors of the inn, Violet and Patty, were also present. The two women sat at a table with Bud Yeager, the owner of the gas station and garage. Harriet and Ben Stokes from the grocery store lounged at another table. Even Walker showed up. He hovered, jittering a little, near the door.

Oliver and Fran Hitchcock, owners of the Scar, took up positions behind the bar, solemnly pouring beers. Everyone except Walker had one.

Isabella perched on a red vinyl bar stool. Fallon occupied the stool beside her, one booted foot propped on the brass rung, his laptop in its leather case on the counter beside him.

Isabella watched the faces of the small crowd as Henry gave a brief summary of the day's events. By now the news had spread throughout the Cove. When Henry told those present that Gordon Lasher's skeleton had been discovered in the old bomb shelter, no one showed any signs of shock.

Bud Yeager snorted in disgust. "Figures he came back to steal whatever is down there. Lasher was nothing but a low-rent con man. After all this time, I still can't believe we fell for his scam."

"He was good." Marge sighed. "Real good. And we were a lot younger back in those days. We wanted to think that we were special and that there was a magic path to enlightenment that only we could experience. Lasher made it easy for us to believe."

"Only for a short period of time," Vera said grimly. "The guru magic wore off very quickly, if you will recall."

"As soon as it became obvious that the son of a bitch was going to go after every young girl who wandered into town," Patty said bitterly.

Bud Yeager drank some beer and lowered

the bottle. "Wonder who killed him?"

"Who cares?" Harriet Stokes said. "He got what he deserved. I will never forget how he used me. I let him take every dime of the money my parents left me."

Ben Stokes reached across the table to touch her arm. "He used all of us. It was never about founding a community. It was about the money right from the start."

"Good riddance." Violet shuddered. "Wanted to kill him myself, there at the end."

"Who didn't?" Ralph Toomey asked.

Henry cleared his throat and took charge again. "We always knew there was something dangerous down there in that old shelter. Turns out we were right. Fallon and Isabella say that the objects look like genuine antiques from the late Victorian era but they're actually very dangerous experimental weapons. They need to be deactivated by experts."

Bud Yeager slapped the tabletop with his palm. "Fat chance of that happening if we turn those weapons over to the Feds. We all know that."

"He's right," Marge said. "The CIA will want to find out how they work, and the military will want to figure out how to make a thousand more just like 'em."

Fallon stirred slightly. Instantly the crowd fell silent. Everyone looked at him.

"Given the unique nature of the weapons, it is highly unlikely that they could be duplicated," he said. "That's the good news. The bad news is that the clockwork gadgets that we found are not only dangerous, but they also are highly unpredictable because the technology involved is based on the principles of paranormal physics."

Isabella noticed that no one appeared shocked by that announcement, either.

"Everyone knows that the CIA and the FBI have been fooling around with the woo-woo stuff for years," Oliver Hitchcock growled from behind the bar.

A lovely warmth blossomed inside Isabella. These were her people, she thought. That was why she felt at home here in the Cove. The locals spoke her language, the language that she had been taught from the cradle, conspiracy-ese.

"That's right," she said eagerly. "Years ago, the press exposed those so-called far seeing experiments that the CIA conducted."

"And don't forget the paranormal research programs funded at Duke and Stanford decades ago," Marge offered.

"Those projects were just the ones they

let the public know about," Henry said. "No telling what they were doing in secret."

"Let's not get carried away here," Fallon said neutrally. "To date, the black-ops folks don't seem to have accomplished too much in the field of paranormal weaponry."

Vera sniffed. "Not for lack of trying. If those gadgets down there in the shelter are the real deal, we sure as hell can't turn them over to the government."

"If we do, they'll wind up in the hands of some black arts agency, sure as we're sitting here," Henry warned.

"I happen to agree with you," Fallon said patiently. "Trust me when I tell you that I don't want those artifacts falling into the wrong hands. I propose that we give them to the one organization that is capable of deactivating and storing them."

Bud frowned. "What organization is that?"

"A group called the Arcane Society," Fallon said. "Full disclosure here, the Society is my biggest client. It has been engaged in serious paranormal research for generations. What's more, it has had some experience with other gadgets just like those we found in the shelter."

Another wave of murmurs rippled through the crowd. Isabella noticed a few skeptical faces.

"The Society is for real," she assured them. "Just like Fallon is for real. You can trust him to do what's right with the weapons."

Heads nodded around the room.

"Jones, here, knows more about those weapons than any of the rest of us," Henry said. "I think we should take his advice."

"I agree," Vera declared. "Given the way the clock showed up at the old Zander place and the fact that there's a second entrance to the shelter that most of us never knew about, it's clear we can't protect those gadgets any longer."

"What about the skeleton?" Marge asked. "You're sure it's Gordon Lasher?"

"According to the ID in his wallet," Fallon said. He looked at Henry. "And a few other things."

"There was a ring with the body," Henry said. He took it out of the pocket of his coveralls and held it up for all to view. "Remember that big old flashy crystal that Lasher always wore? This is it."

"Okay, so it probably is Lasher," Marge said. "What are we going to do with it?"

"The body is a small problem," Fallon conceded.

Violet widened her eyes. "A *small* problem? It's a dead body."

"Whatever happened to Gordon Lasher happened more than twenty years ago, and judging from the comments I've heard tonight, no one seems to have missed him," Fallon said.

"That's for damn sure," Ben Stokes muttered.

"We've got a couple of options," Fallon continued. "We could tell the county cops about the skeleton but I can't see the sheriff or any of his men figuring out how to get into the shelter to retrieve the remains, let alone conduct an investigation into the death. You know what the atmosphere is like down there."

"Jones is right," Henry said. "The local authorities will realize right away that something downright weird happened down there in the shelter and they'll contact the Feds."

"That means the CIA," Fran Hitchcock said darkly. "Or some other clandestine agency. The same folks that set up that lab twenty-two years ago may still be in operation for all we know."

Oliver Hitchcock looked alarmed. "If that crowd comes back, they'll be all over the Cove this time, trying to isolate the source of the energy in that fallout shelter. I wouldn't put it past them to shut down the whole town and kick us out."

"It will be like Area 51," Isabella said, getting into the spirit of the conversation. "There will be armed guards all over the place."

"Fallon says there's some kind of cosmic energy nexus along this stretch of the coast," Vera offered. "If the CIA discovers that they can tap in to a power source like that, there won't be any stopping them. Isabella is right. The first step will be to clear out the town."

"It could be a whole lot worse," Harriet Stokes said in ominous tones. "They might decide they don't want any witnesses."

There was a vast silence while the crowd digested that possibility. Then the hubbub started up again, louder this time.

Beneath the cover of the general uproar, Fallon turned to Isabella.

"I never used the term *cosmic energy*," he said.

"Details," she said.

"*Cosmic* implies energy from beyond Earth. While some of that may be in play here, it is not, at present, measurable, and has no bearing on the nexus energy that I mentioned."

She patted his thigh. "Nobody's listening to you, boss."

"I noticed," he said.

The anxious conversations got louder and so did the level of alarm.

Fallon leaned back and extended his arms along the bar. He surveyed the crowd with a satisfied air.

"It's an amazing thing," he said to Isabella.

"What?" she asked.

"Being present at the creation of a full-blown conspiracy theory. It's like watching a galaxy being born. Lots of random, unconnected bits and pieces of matter whiz past each other, exert a little gravitational pull and bingo, they start forming an organized system. The next thing you know you have a complete, wheels-within-wheels fantasy involving the CIA, Area 51, cosmic energy and a dead guy."

She gave him a severe look. "You started this with that business about the CIA taking over the town."

"I never actually said that, either."

She blinked. "You think this is amusing, don't you?"

"I do." He gave her one of his rare smiles, the kind that heated his eyes. "You know, since I started hanging around you, I've begun to feel almost normal for the first time in my life."

"There are serious grounds for speculating about a potential conspiracy here," she told him.

"No," he said flatly. "Three people running experiments on some antique weapons twenty-two years ago and the skeleton of a dead con man do not a conspiracy make."

"Okay, what do they add up to?"

Fallon reached for his beer bottle. "A problem. One that can be easily solved."

"Really?" Isabella waved her hands to get the crowd's attention and raised her voice. "Fallon says there's a solution to the problem of the skeleton."

Silence descended again. Everyone in the room looked expectantly at Fallon.

"It appears to me," he said deliberately, "that the simplest approach is to remove the bones from the shelter and dump them into the ocean off the Point. As you know, the currents are very strong there. I calculate a ninety-eight-point-five percent chance that none of the bones will ever wash ashore, at least not near here. Even if a few do, no one will be able to trace them back to the old bomb shelter."

They all stared at him, expressions of dawning comprehension on their faces.

Henry pursed his lips. "Works for me."

Fran Hitchcock nodded slowly. "Lasher

was always talking about the forces of karma. This strikes me as a fine example of karma in action."

"I like it." Ben Stokes brightened. "I like it a lot."

"Think of it as a burial at sea," Fallon said.

"Oh, yes," Isabella said. "That's perfect."

Marge nodded quickly. "Perfect."

There were several more nods around the room.

"Let's take a vote," Henry said. "Those in favor of letting Fallon handle this problem, raise your hands."

Every hand in the room went up with one exception.

Henry looked at Walker. "How do you vote, Walker?"

Walker stopped jittering for a moment. A ferocious expression crossed his thin features. Isabella was sure that his eyes got a little hot.

"Gordon Lasher was a b-bad man," Walker said.

"I'll take that as a yes vote," Henry said. "It's settled, then. The bones go into the ocean and those weird gadgets in the shelter go to the Arcane Society."

There was a round of satisfied murmurs. Chairs scraped. People got to their feet and started pulling on their jackets and gloves in preparation for going out into the damp, misty night.

"Don't look now," Isabella said to Fallon. "But I think they just elected you sheriff of Scargill Cove."

"And here my mom always thought I should go into finance."

Outside fog enveloped the Cove, the real kind that came with the scent of the ocean. There were no streetlamps in the small community, but the handful of lights in the windows of the inn and in the rooms above the shops infused the air with an otherworldly glow.

Isabella savored the simple pleasure of walking back to her apartment with Fallon. It was good to be with him. It felt right.

Fallon took his phone out of the pocket of his jacket and punched in some numbers.

"Rafanelli? Jones here."

There was a short pause.

"What do you mean, which Jones? Fallon Jones. J&J." Fallon sounded irritated. "I need a lab team capable of dealing with weapons-grade artifacts here in Scargill Cove tomorrow. . . . Yes, I said tomorrow. Something wrong with your phone? Found a cache of Mrs. Bridewell's curiosities . . . Yes, those curiosities. The infernal devices.

Some of them are still operational."

There was another pause, much longer this time. Isabella heard an excited buzzing on the other end of the connection.

"No, I don't know yet how they got here," Fallon said impatiently. "But it looks like they've been locked up in an old bomb shelter for more than twenty years. Right. I know Dr. Tremont is the expert on glass, but I checked earlier and she's on sabbatical in London. That leaves you. Besides, you're the expert when it comes to decommissioning para-weapons, not Tremont. See you tomorrow. In the morning."

He closed the phone.

Isabella cleared her throat.

"What?" he said.

"Sometimes you have a tendency to be a tad brusque with people," she said.

He shoved his hands into the pockets of his jacket. "Brusque?"

He said it as if he had never heard the word.

"Short," she said. "Crisp. Rude."

"Huh. I like to be efficient on the phone. People tend to waste a lot of time chatting at me."

"Chatting *at* you? Chatting is generally considered an occupation that two or more people engage in together."

"I'm not a chatty type."

"Of course you are. We're chatting right now."

"No," he said, very certain. "We're having a conversation."

"Oddly enough, people sometimes resent being ordered around, especially by a person who is not even their official boss."

"You think I was brusque with Rafanelli?" Fallon sounded offended now. "I was doing him a favor. He's been fascinated by Bridewell's work for years. Taking charge of a cache of her inventions will be a huge thrill for him, not to mention a major career boost. He'll write the definitive paper for the *Journal of Paranormal and Psychical Research* and become a legend in the Society's research circles."

"I understand," Isabella said.

They walked a little farther.

"Well?" Fallon said. "What the hell should I have said to Rafanelli?"

"It's often helpful to insert a few friendly comments into a business conversation. Asking about a person's health or their children is always good."

"Are you kidding? Get people started on their health and their kids and you never get them back on track."

"Okay," Isabella said.

They walked a few more steps. Fallon muttered something under his breath and reached back into the inside pocket of his jacket. He snapped the phone open and punched in some numbers.

"Rafanelli? Jones here again. *Fallon* Jones. *Please* bring a team to Scargill Cove tomorrow to pick up the Bridewell artifacts. You're the leading expert on para-weaponry, and I wouldn't trust those gadgets to anyone else but you. How's the wife? See you tomorrow."

He snapped the phone closed.

"What did he say?" Isabella asked.

"Nothing. Not one word."

"Probably stunned."

"I outchatted him," Fallon said proudly.

"I think so, yes."

"Told you that personal nattering is a waste of time." He flipped the phone open again. "That reminds me, I'd better call Zack. He'll want to know about those curiosities."

He punched in a code.

"Zack, it's Fallon. Found a bunch of Bridewell's inventions here in Scargill Cove. Rafanelli is bringing a team here tomorrow to dismantle them and transport them back to the L.A. lab. Thought you'd like to know. Give my best to Raine. I heard she was

215

expecting. Congratulations. Bye."

He closed the phone and waited for the verdict with an air of expectation.

"Better," Isabella said. "But it strikes me that it might be a good idea if I handled more of J&J's routine business communications. That would leave you free to concentrate on your investigative work."

"Is that a polite way of saying I don't have people skills?"

"Not everyone is management material, Fallon."

"You're right," he said decisively. "In future, I'll let you do the personal chitchat."

She smiled. "Who says you can't delegate?"

They reached Toomey's Treasures and went up the outside stairs to her apartment above the shop. She was intensely aware of Fallon watching her take her key out of her pocket. He was in what she had come to think of as his brooding zone. In the dim light of the bare, low-watt bulb that lit the doorway, his hard face was cast in the light-and-shadow of film noir. The dark passions that burned deep inside him would have made it possible for him to play either the hero or the villain, but whichever role he chose, he would follow his own code.

She got the door open, moved into the

apartment and flipped the light switch. She turned to face him.

"What you did tonight," she said. "Proposing that we dump that skeleton into the ocean."

He watched her with a shuttered expression. "What about it?"

"You knew that if you gave the body to the authorities, it's possible that there would be a murder investigation."

"Unlikely. No one in this county will care about what happened here in the Cove twenty-two years ago. Nobody outside of town gives a damn about this place. Few people even know it exists."

"I'm aware of that. Nevertheless, if there ever was an inquiry into Lasher's death, everyone who attended the meeting at the tavern tonight would be a suspect."

He shrugged. "Sounds like they all had motive."

"So you didn't suggest a convenient burial at sea because you're afraid that some secret CIA black-ops agency will take over the Cove. You did it to protect the people of this community."

He did not respond.

She put her hands on his shoulders and brushed her mouth against his. "You're a good man, Fallon Jones."

217

"Just being pragmatic."

She smiled and stepped back. "Would you like to come in for a nightcap, Mr. Pragmatic?"

He loomed on the threshold, filling the doorway. His face was set in the stalwart expression of a knight preparing to go into battle.

"You probably want to talk about last night," he said.

She smiled. "Nope."

He narrowed his eyes. "Nope?"

"Last night was the most romantic night of my entire life. Why spoil it by trying to explain it?"

"I wasn't planning on explaining it. Seemed pretty straightforward to me. But I thought you might want to talk about it. Women always want to do that. Afterward, I mean."

"And you know this, how?"

He frowned. "Everyone knows that."

She almost laughed. "The one thing I know for sure about last night is that it does not involve a conspiracy."

"Definitely no conspiracy," he agreed.

"That's good enough for me."

"It is?"

She took his hand and tugged gently. "Come inside and have a drink with me,

Fallon Jones."

He moved into the room, closed the door and locked it with great care. When he turned back to her she could see the heat in his eyes.

"The most romantic night of your entire life?" he said very carefully.

"Definitely. Was it good for you, too?"

The energy in the room got a little hotter.

"Yes," he said. "The best."

"Then I don't see that further discussion is necessary."

"No," he said. "No more talking."

He swooped down upon her, scooped her up and started toward the bedroom.

Isabella put her arms around his neck.

"Guess we'll skip the nightcap," she said.

Sometime later she awoke to the knowledge that she was alone in the bed. She opened her eyes and sat up against the pillows. The clock on the night table read two-twenty.

A familiar otherworldly glow illuminated the bedroom doorway. Not psi fog, she thought. It was the light from a computer screen. Fallon had gone back to work.

She pushed the covers aside and got to her feet. She was nude and the room was chilly. She stepped into her slippers and pulled on her robe.

She tied the sash of the robe as she went down the short hallway, past the bathroom into the main room. Fallon was seated gazing into his laptop. In the glow from the screen, his face had the ruthless cast of a man obsessed. She could well believe that he was descended from a legendary alchemist.

"Fallon?"

He looked up. His hard expression relaxed at the sight of her. Energy swirled in the atmosphere. She knew that he was remembering the searing passion they had shared.

"Sorry," he said. "Didn't mean to wake you."

"What are you working on?" she asked. She moved to stand beside him. "The Nightshade case?"

"No." He leaned back in his chair. "I was just doing some background research on Julian Garrett."

"You should be in bed. You need sleep."

"I don't require a lot of sleep."

"Well, you certainly need more than you got tonight." She leaned over the desk and took his powerful hand. "It's two-twenty in the morning. Come back to bed."

"I work odd hours," he said.

"No need for them to be this odd. Come with me."

Somewhat to her surprise he got up out of the chair and let her lead him back into the bedroom. When they got there, he pulled her into his arms and down onto the bed.

This time he slept until dawn.

17

"She's the granddaughter of that wacko who operates the Iceberg conspiracy website?" Zack asked. He kept his voice pitched low, but the mix of amusement and amazement in his words was crystal clear. "Are you serious?"

Fallon stood at the window of his office and looked across the street at the Sunshine Café. Isabella and Zack's wife, Raine, had just vanished inside to pick up some of Marge's muffins for all of them to eat while they waited for Rafanelli and the lab techs.

Should have known better than to try to explain Isabella to Zack, he thought. Isabella was not easily explained. Isabella was unique, one of a kind.

"You know me," he said. "I'm always serious."

"Well, sure," Zack said. "But when it comes to your kind of serious, there are nuances."

Fallon looked at his cousin. Zack sat casually angled across the corner of Fallon's desk, arms folded. There was certainly some family resemblance between them. Like most of the men in the Jones family line, they were both dark-haired and built along the lean lines typical of the clan which had, for generations, produced a lot of hunter-talents.

That was where the physical resemblance ended, though. Zack's eyes were a glacial blue, and he was a couple of inches shorter than Fallon. But the biggest difference between them was the nature of their talents. Zack's psychic ability gave him an edge when it came to anticipating the actions of others, a major plus given his new responsibilities as Master of the Society. His talent was actually a rare form of psychometry. Zack could pick up a knife or a gun that had been used to commit murder and sense what the killer had been feeling at the time the act of violence had been committed.

He had married a woman with a similar talent. When Raine came in contact with the psychic residue of violence, her clairaudient intuition translated the energy into the form of voices. Sometimes it was the killer's voice she heard. Sometimes the victim's.

Like many in the Jones family, Zack had once worked as a J&J agent. But he was now the latest in a long line of Joneses to take the reins of the Arcane Society. In Fallon's opinion, the career change was a good move for both of them. Zack had a natural flair for giving orders, but he had never been any good at taking them.

"You want to talk about my nuances or do you want to discuss the fact that we may have located a cache of Bridewell's nasty little gadgets?" Fallon asked.

"Good to see you, too, cousin," Zack said.

Fallon winced. "Sorry. Things have been a little busy around here lately. Getting your phone call this morning informing me that you were on the way to the Cove caught me off guard, that's all. I wasn't planning on visitors."

"After we talked on the phone last night, I told Raine about what you had found. We both agreed this was a piece of Arcane history that we did not want to miss."

"You didn't come all the way from Seattle just to take a look at some old clockwork inventions."

"Okay, there is another reason," Zack said. "But I'm also interested in Bridewell's curiosities. J&J was never able to recover all of the devices after the case was closed back in the late eighteen hundreds. Couldn't even come up with an accurate estimate of how many had been made. The curiosities that were found were stored in the vault at Arcane House in England, but several vanished during the Second World War. How the hell did some of the gadgets end up here in Scargill Cove?"

"I'm still working on that problem," Fallon said. "At this point all I can tell you is that twenty-two years ago three people managed to get hold of some of the curiosities. They brought them here, tuned them up, and tried to run some experiments on them. One man evidently died in the explosion."

"They wanted to figure out how the damn things work," Zack said.

"Evidently," Fallon said. "I checked the property records. The Sea Breeze Motor Lodge was once owned by a family named Kelso. The last surviving member of the clan is a man named Jonathan Kelso. He had some kind of mental breakdown about twenty-two years ago. He's been living in an institution ever since."

"The result of the explosion?"

"That's what my talent is telling me," Fallon said. "I'm going to try to interview him when I have a chance. But right now

I've got other priorities. The first item at the top of my to-do list is to get the curiosities safely out of the shelter and into the lab."

"The secret of the weapons is in the glass Bridewell used and in her unique talent. To this day, no one understands the paraphysics involved. But why did Kelso and his companions bring the gadgets here? Obviously they knew about the old bomb shelter, but they could have found equally good shielding in a hundred other locations."

"I'm ninety-nine-point-three percent sure the deciding factor was that they knew that Scargill Cove is a natural para-nexus."

"Yeah?" Zack glanced out the window. "I didn't know that. I thought you moved the office back here because you liked the solitude."

"That was part of it, but mostly I selected it because of the energy here. The nexus currents aren't obvious at first, but they are very strong. After you've been here awhile, you can sense them. The atmosphere around here helps me to focus."

"All right, I'll buy that," Zack said. "But let's be honest: you were never what anyone would call the sociable type even before all the crap that went down three years ago. Afterward your loner tendencies got a whole lot more pronounced. Hell, you practically disappeared when you moved here."

"I like it here."

"I can see that," Zack said.

He did not say anything else for a time. Fallon waited.

"I should probably mention the other reason I decided to pay you a visit today," Zack said eventually.

"I knew it," Fallon said.

"Well, you are psychic."

"Let's have it."

"I want you to show up at the Society's Winter Conference this week," Zack said.

Fallon did not hesitate. "No."

"You've skipped it for two years in a row."

"You know why."

"Yes, but things are different this year."

"Give me one good reason I should make the trip to Sedona."

"I'll give you two. The first is that there's a move afoot to encourage the Council to replace you as the head of J&J."

Fallon felt as if he'd walked into a stone wall. It took an effort of will backed up by a little talent to pull his senses together.

"That's not possible," he said. "J&J is mine. I inherited the firm from Uncle Gresham. It's always been a privately held business within the family. It's not just another branch of Arcane like the labs or the museums. The Council can't fire me."

"There is talk to the effect that if replacing you is not an option, the Council should sever its ties with J&J and hire a new investigation firm."

Fallon gripped the window ledge. "Someone thinks I've lost it?"

"It has been suggested," Zack said neutrally. "But the politically correct argument being used is that you're spending too many resources on Nightshade."

Fallon closed his eyes. "They think Nightshade is finished because of the Hawaii case."

"Yes," Zack said.

"It's not." Fallon opened his eyes. "I can feel it, Zack. That damn organization is like a hydra. We cut off one of the snake's heads, but a new one will soon take its place. Trust me. As long as they have Humphrey Hulsey and the recipe for the formula, we can't let down our guard."

"I believe you and I'll back you all the way. But in the meantime, I need you to back me."

"You want me to do that by showing up at the Sedona conference?"

Zack watched him very steadily, his startling blue eyes cold and determined. But there was understanding in his expression as well.

"Yes," he said. "Face it, cousin, you can't stay hidden away here in Scargill Cove forever. We both know that. Those who wield power within Arcane need to see you. If you remain out of sight, the rumors will only get worse."

Fallon exhaled slowly. He had known this request was coming sooner or later, he reminded himself. His parents had dropped a few pointed hints some weeks back. Nevertheless, Zack was applying more pressure than the situation appeared to warrant. There was an underlying urgency to the demand that required a little study.

Fallon heightened his senses and watched the paranormal web light up.

"Well, hell," he said softly. "It's not just me or J&J they're after, is it?"

"I don't think so," Zack said, very serious now. "Got a feeling that severing the connection with J&J and cutting off the resources you require to fight Nightshade is part of a long-term strategy."

"You're next," Fallon said, comprehension hitting him in the gut. "With J&J out of the picture, the next logical step would be to convince the Council to remove you and put someone else in charge of the Society."

"Someone other than a Jones, to be specific," Zack said. "Someone who would be in a position to redirect not only the full resources of the Society but its goals and objectives, as well. My talent tells me we're looking at what those in the business world call a hostile takeover."

Fallon whistled softly. "More like a coup d'état."

"I want to counter it with a show of force. Within Arcane, power and talent are everything, always have been. The Jones family has a lot of both of those commodities. I want to remind the members of that. Hell, we founded the organization. We aren't going to give it up without a fight."

More sectors of the paranormal spiderweb shivered with light. "Nightshade," Fallon said softly. "Or what's left of it. Got to be."

"Maybe," Zack cautioned. "Maybe not. I haven't been able to identify the source of the recent wave of rumors, let alone whether or not the individual responsible is linked to Nightshade. This thing could be coming from an entirely different direction. There have always been those within the Society who resented everyone on our family tree."

"Because we're descended from the founder." Fallon looked around the room, mentally cataloging the antiques scattered around the space: the desk and the old inkwell, the Victorian umbrella stand and the wrought iron coatrack on the wall. All of the offices of J&J across the U.S. and in London had some mementos that reflected the history of J&J and the Society. Both of which were inextricably bound to the history of the Jones family, he thought. "They fear us because we've always controlled Arcane."

"Not just the organization," Zack reminded him. "But a lot of its deepest secrets, as well. The family has always had enemies. You know the old saying."

"Friends may come and go but enemies accumulate."

"The Joneses have had more than four hundred years to acquire our enemies."

Fallon smiled grimly. "And what's more, we're good at it."

"Comes with the territory," Zack said. "Like I told you, I don't know yet if the person who started the rumors about you and J&J is in any way connected to Nightshade, but I think it's clear that his ultimate goal is to make certain that the Joneses lose control of Arcane."

"And its secrets. It's actually a hell of a strategy, when you think about it. Why go to all the trouble and risk of resurrecting the currently broken version of Nightshade if you can take over Arcane from the inside and create a super-Nightshade? It's brilliant."

Zack cleared his throat. "Let's save the conspiracy theories until we know exactly what we're dealing with."

Fallon turned back to the window. Even those within his own family circle considered him a conspiracy nut. Zack and everyone else used the term *conspiracy theory* so loosely, he thought. They did not seem to grasp the bright, shining line that separated a valid theory of a case and a conspiracy fantasy. No wonder it had been easy for someone to fire up the new rumors at the highest levels of Arcane. *I gave the traitor all the ammunition he needed.*

"Will you come to the Winter Conference?" Zack asked quietly.

Zack was right, Fallon thought. Within Arcane, power spoke and spoke loudly.

"I'll show up for the opening-night reception," he said. "Will that satisfy you?"

"Yes." Zack came up off the desk and clapped Fallon on the shoulder. "Thanks, cousin. I knew I could count on you."

"One thing you should know. I'm working on another project at the moment."

"Sorting out the Bridewell curiosities? No problem. Once Rafanelli and his team pick up the gadgets, that old case will be closed."

"I'm not talking about the curiosities," Fallon said. "I meant Isabella."

Zack shot him a knowing smile. "Bring her to the conference. Hell, the fact that you've got a date will, uh —"

"Make me look more stable?" Fallon asked evenly. "Normal?"

"Yeah, something like that," Zack admitted.

Fallon turned back to the view of the Sunshine. "You don't understand. I'm working on Isabella's case."

"What's that supposed to mean?"

"She thinks someone killed her grandmother. She's convinced that the same person may be gunning for her."

"No offense," Zack said, "but why would anyone bother to kill the Sentinel? She's a nutcase. Everyone knows that. And why would anyone want to murder Isabella?"

"She thinks that she stumbled into a real conspiracy. She told her grandmother and now she thinks her grandmother is dead. So, yes, Isabella thinks there's a connection. I agreed to investigate."

Down below, the door of the Sunshine opened. Isabella and Raine emerged carrying paper sacks that were no doubt filled with fresh, hot muffins. Fallon could see that the two women were talking easily together, as if they were old friends. You'd never know they had met only a short time ago. Isabella's energy had that effect on people as well as dogs and plants, he thought. But, then, energy was energy. Living things always responded to it, one way or another.

Raine was tall with distinctive eyes that she tried to veil behind the severe frames of her glasses. Like Zack, she wore a lot of black.

"Let me get this straight," Zack said. "J&J is investigating the possible death of one of the nuttiest conspiracy freaks who ever fired up a website."

"More or less," Fallon said.

"You're the man who does the numbers. You never say *more or less.* What are the odds there's a real conspiracy involved here?"

"I don't know," Fallon admitted.

"You always know," Zack said.

"Not this time." He watched a big silver-gray SUV drive slowly down the narrow street. "There's the team."

The driver of the vehicle stopped and rolled down the window to speak to Raine and Isabella. Fallon watched Isabella point toward the small parking area behind the office. Then the two women entered the empty lower floor of the building.

There were footsteps on the stairs. The door opened. Isabella and Raine walked into the room preceded by the spicy aroma of the warm muffins. They brought something else into the office, as well, the subtle heat of their auras. Both women were powerful talents. Strong sensitives stirred the atmosphere in a space even when they were not running hot.

"Dr. Rafanelli and his team will be here in a few minutes," Isabella said. "We told them to get some coffee and muffins at the Sunshine first."

"Damn." Impatience flashed through Fallon. He glanced at his watch. "We don't have all day. We need to get started. It's going to take some time to make sure those gadgets are deactivated and properly stowed for safe transport."

"I'm sure the crew won't be long," Isabella said. She opened her sack and held it out to him. "Here, have a muffin. They're right out of the oven."

Distracted, he peered into the sack. "Okay, thanks."

He selected a muffin and downed half of

it before he realized that Zack and Raine were watching him with scarcely veiled amusement.

"Something funny?" he asked, munching.

"No," Zack said quickly. He took a bite of the muffin that Raine had handed to him. "You said there's a lot of old para-energy in the bomb shelter. Anything else we ought to know about?"

Isabella tossed the empty muffin sack into the trash. "We should probably tell you about the body."

Raine looked at her and then at Fallon. "There's a body?"

"Old one," Fallon explained. "Just a skeleton. Belongs to the con artist who founded an intentional community here twenty-two years ago. The members of the community kicked him out when they realized that he'd taken all their money and was trying to set up his own private harem. He returned one night to try to steal the curiosities. He got one out, the clock."

Zack dusted muffin crumbs off his hands and looked interested. "How did he get dead?"

"Workplace accident," Fallon said.

An hour later Fallon stood with Zack in the shelter. They watched Rafanelli and his

236

team painstakingly deactivate the clockwork mechanisms that animated the objects in the glass cases. Each curiosity was carefully stowed in one of the leaded-glass boxes the Society's museums used to transport artifacts infused with a hefty amount of unknown crystal or glass-based psi.

Isabella and Raine were on the other side of the room, standing over the skeleton. They talked in low voices. Zack glanced at the body with a thoughtful expression.

"That was no workplace accident," he said.

"Close enough." Fallon shrugged. "Lasher was a thief, and he appears to have been at work trying to steal stuff when he got whacked. Workplace accident, like I said."

"Who used the crowbar on his skull?"

"We think there was a woman with him. Her name was Rachel Stewart and she had some talent. From the looks of it, Rachel got really pissed off."

"You're going with a falling-out-among-thieves scenario?"

"It fits," Fallon said. "In any event, it happened more than twenty years ago. No one gives a damn now."

"And it would be a little awkward to turn the case over to the authorities," Zack agreed dryly, "given the hot psi down here."

"Uh-huh."

"See?" Zack widened his hands. "This is how the Joneses accumulate secrets."

"Another thing we're good at, like acquiring enemies."

Raine and Isabella turned away from the skeleton and walked back across the small space.

"You say you're planning to dump the remains off the Point?" Raine asked.

"That's the plan," Fallon said.

"Use your own judgment," Raine said. "But I think you should know that I can hear the echoes of the voices of the people who were here that night."

Fallon looked at her. "And?"

Shadows flickered through Raine's eyes. "There was a woman involved. But she was not the killer. There were three people down here at the time of the death. Someone else struck Lasher with that crowbar."

"Lovers' triangle?" Isabella asked.

Raine's brows tightened over the rims of her glasses. "No, I don't think so, not exactly. But there was a violent quarrel."

Fallon pondered possible revisions to the scenario for about one second, made the small adjustment necessary to his theory of the crime and was satisfied.

"Doesn't change anything," he said. "No

238

one cares."

Across the room Preston Rafanelli finished locking down the last of the curiosities. A short, sturdily built man in his early forties, he balanced his balding head with a neatly trimmed beard. He gave final instructions to one of the techs and then walked forward to join Fallon and the others. His broad face was flushed with excitement.

"This is an incredible find," he enthused. "I can hardly wait to get these artifacts into the lab. I know Dr. Tremont will want to examine them as soon as possible. I'll e-mail her tonight. Got a hunch she'll be cutting her sabbatical short when she hears that an entire cache of Bridewell's inventions has been located. I can't thank you enough for bringing me in on this project, Jones."

"No problem," Fallon said. "I live to bring joy into the lives of others."

Everyone except Isabella stared at him, mouths agape.

Isabella widened her hands. "And people say Fallon Jones has no sense of humor."

18

At four o'clock that afternoon, Zack got behind the wheel of the rental car. Raine buckled up in the passenger seat. She waved at Isabella and Fallon, who were standing on the narrow sidewalk in front of the office.

Zack put the car in gear and drove slowly along the Cove's narrow main drag, following the SUV carrying Rafanelli and his team.

"Correct me if I'm wrong," Raine said. "But I believe that the Earth may have just shifted on its axis."

Zack smiled. "Because Fallon finally hired an assistant?"

"Not just any assistant. He managed to find the one woman on the face of the planet who seems to be able to appreciate his rather unique nature. They're sleeping together."

"Yeah, I did get that impression," Zack

said. "Always knew that when Fallon finally went down, he'd fall like one of those big woolly mammoths at the end of the Ice Age."

"Hard?"

"Very. I'm surprised we didn't feel the ground shake all the way up in Seattle."

Raine drummed her fingers lightly on the seat. "I like Isabella very much, but I do sense that she's as comfortable with conspiracy theories as Fallon is. Maybe even more so."

"I think it's in the blood. Fallon says that she's the Sentinel's granddaughter."

Raine turned her head sharply, startled. "The nut who operates that weird website? Iceberg?"

"One and the same. Evidently the Sentinel died recently or faked her own death, depending on your point of view."

"Good grief."

"Isabella is convinced that someone may have murdered her grandmother because of some secret conspiracy. She thinks the killers are after her as well."

Raine rested her head against the back of the seat and groaned. "Oh, brother. Isabella really is a little out there, isn't she?"

"Looks like it."

"She seems so nice. I really like her. What

does Fallon think?"

"Fallon really likes her, too. I got the impression that he's not buying into her conspiracy theory, at least not entirely. But he's sleeping with her and he's a Jones, so he'll do just about anything for her. He's investigating the Sentinel's death."

"Wait until the rest of the Joneses hear about this." Raine's mouth twitched. "The clan is going to go into shock. Everyone has been hoping that Fallon would meet someone who could keep him anchored in reality, a woman who would serve as a counterbalance for his rather unusual nature."

"Instead he's gone right off the deep end for someone who is even further over the horizon than he is."

"What did he say when you asked him to come to the Winter Conference?" Raine asked.

"I explained the situation to him. He understood. He'll be there. He won't be staying long, though, just the night of the reception and the auction. But that's enough for my purposes."

"Get a bunch of Joneses in one room together and people pay attention," Raine said. "Any idea why Fallon hates social gatherings so much?"

"He's never been keen on them, but he

really does not want to attend this particular gig."

"Why?"

"His ex-fiancée and her family will be there."

"Whoa, slow down. I didn't know that Fallon had been engaged."

"Her name is Jennifer Austin. She's an expert in paranormal radiation. Works in the lab in L.A."

"Any relation to the Conroy Austin who sits on the Council?"

"His daughter," Zack said. "When Jennifer and Fallon got engaged, everyone thought it was a perfect match."

"What happened?"

"It didn't end well," Zack said.

"I see."

"By the way, you were wrong about the Earth shifting on its axis just because Fallon Jones got himself a new assistant."

"You're sure?"

"Absolutely certain," Zack said. "That Earth-shifting-on-its-axis thing only happens when you and I make love."

"Yes," Raine said. She smiled. "You're right about that."

19

At nine o'clock the next morning, Isabella was on the phone with Emily Crane, one of J&J's contract investigators.

"He's sitting here in my office, crying," Emily whispered on the other end of the line. "What am I supposed to do now?"

"Don't worry about the crying client," Isabella said. "Cases involving fraudulent mediums are always very emotional. Mr. Rand hoped that the fake psychic really had communicated with his dead mother. But the fact that he asked J&J to investigate makes it clear that deep down he had his doubts. Pat him on the shoulder and remind him that his own instincts were solid."

"The problem," Emily said in low tones, "is the reason why he was so anxious to contact the dear departed in the first place. Evidently his mother stashed several thousand dollars' worth of financial instruments somewhere before her death. Rand told me that his mom collapsed and died very suddenly. Heart attack. She never told anyone where she had hidden the papers."

"Oh, I see," Isabella said. "Well, that's simple enough. Tell Mr. Rand that you'll be glad to see what you can do about turning up the missing financial instruments."

"Uh, that's not such a great idea. Hang on a sec."

Isabella heard muffled voices in the background. Emily Crane was speaking to the client.

"If you'll excuse me for a moment, Mr. Rand, this is a business call. I'm going to take it in the next room."

In the background, Rand sobbed harder.

Isabella heard a door close. Rand's sobs were no longer audible.

"What's up?" Isabella asked.

"What's up," Emily said, "is that my intuition tells me that Rand is responsible for his mother's death. Not sure how he did it, maybe with her own meds. He obviously wasn't expecting the sudden cardiac arrest, though. Probably thought that if she wound up in intensive care, she would realize she was dying and tell him where the bonds were hidden."

"Oh, geez. I hate when this happens."

"Me, too," Emily said fervently. "Listen,

245

I'm one of those agents Fallon Jones likes to call his Lost Dogs and Haunted Houses people. That's why J&J referred Rand to me in the first place."

"And also because you're located in the same city."

"Right. But a murder investigation, especially one that is next to impossible to prove, is out of my league. I don't have the experience. If J&J wants to pursue this, you're going to have to bring in someone else."

"Not a problem. Let me check my file of investigators there in San Francisco." Isabella swiveled her chair around to face the computer screen and cranked up the list of Bay Area private investigators affiliated with J&J. "Here we go. Seaton-Kent Investigations. I'll give them a call."

"I know Baxter Seaton and Devlin Kent." Emily sounded vastly relieved. "Nice couple. Good investigators. I had drinks and dinner with them just last week. They can handle Rand."

"Tell Rand that you're referring him to an agency that specializes in finding lost securities. Seaton and Kent will investigate and if they actually turn up some evidence —"

"Not likely."

"You never know. If they do, they'll give everything they find to the cops. The authorities can take it from there."

"I can't tell you how glad I am that Fallon Jones finally hired someone to handle his office," Emily said. "It's so much easier dealing with you, Isabella. Jones always growled at me. I appreciated the referrals, of course, but every time he called he sounded so grouchy."

"Mr. Jones was trying to take on too much," Isabella said smoothly. "He was terribly overworked."

"I don't know about overworked, but he definitely needed an office manager and a good receptionist. Glad he found you. Call me when you get another Lost Dogs and Haunted Houses case in the Bay Area. Those are my specialty."

Isabella cleared her throat. "Actually, I'm not just the office manager and receptionist. I'm an investigator here at the agency."

"Whatever," Emily said. "Got to go deal with my crying client. Thanks for helping me unload him on Baxter and Devlin."

The phone went dead in Isabella's ear. She put it down and noticed that Fallon was watching her with his usual focused expression. He was leaning back in his chair, his booted feet stacked on the corner of the desk.

"Emily Crane wanted off the job?" he asked.

"She closed the case. Proved the medium was a fraud."

"Not what the client wanted to hear?"

"No. Emily thinks Rand killed his mom for his inheritance but his goal was a lingering death. He hoped his mother would tell him where the securities were hidden before she died. The plan didn't work. Now Rand is pursuing other courses of action."

"Emily is right," Fallon said. "Not her kind of work. Seaton or his partner can handle it. Good choice."

"I'll give their agency a call." She picked up the phone.

"Before you do that, there's something I need to tell you. I've got to make a business trip to Sedona day after tomorrow. Just an overnight."

She put the phone down. Her intuition told her that whatever was in the works, it was more than a business trip.

"You never go anywhere," she said.

"I'm not what you'd call a traveling man."

"In the whole time I've known you, you haven't gone any farther than Willow Creek."

"You've only known me for about a month."

"When was the last time you left the Cove?"

"I get out," he said, sounding defensive.

"Give me a for-instance."

His dark brows snapped together in annoyance. "There hasn't been much need to go anywhere since I arrived in the Cove."

"I see. Don't you ever get bored?"

"Somehow, what with trying to stop a bunch of bad guys who are using a dangerous drug to enhance paranormal talents, fielding an endless series of routine investigations for members of the Society, and stumbling over the occasional serial killer, I manage to keep busy."

She smiled. "Right."

"How the hell did we get off on the subject of my failure to travel?"

"Beats me," she said.

"Look," he said gruffly, "there's a regional Arcane conference scheduled in Sedona next week. The opening-night reception and auction is a very big deal as far as my family and the Council are concerned. I've managed to dodge it for the past couple of years, but Zack thinks I should attend this year to send a message."

"What message?"

"Some of the members of the Council are questioning the amount of money and resources that Zack is proposing to allocate to J&J this year to pursue the Nightshade investigation. They think that William Craigmore's death was a knockout blow to the organization. They don't see why we have to keep up the pressure."

"Ah, yes, corporate politics in action."

"They've got a point." Fallon exhaled wearily. "Pursuing Nightshade is damned expensive and the Society does have other priorities. Also, several people on the Council have pet research projects that they want to see better funded."

"I understand," she said.

"It's not as if Arcane can draw on unlimited resources. The Society is like any other organization. It runs on money. Mostly it relies on membership dues and fund-raisers like the auction at the Sedona conference. All of the high-ranking members from the western district of the Society will be in Sedona. The idea is to pull as much money out of them as possible."

"What gets auctioned off?"

"Periodically the curators of the Society's museums go through their basements and weed out some of the less important artifacts. Paranormal antiquities always hold great interest for collectors. Lot of money involved."

"Sort of a Sotheby's or Christie's for the Arcane crowd, hmm?"

"That's the idea," Fallon said.

"Do you want me to schedule one of the Arcane corporate jets or do you want to fly commercial to save money?"

"Book one of the Arcane jets and put it down as a Nightshade expense."

She cleared her throat. "Uh, doesn't that send the message that J&J is not particularly budget-conscious?"

"I like to think of it as being efficient. Time is money. I don't want to waste any more than necessary on the Sedona conference."

"Okay." She reached for the phone again.

"Have them pick us up at the regional airport outside of Willow Creek. It's the closest."

She paused, phone in hand. "Us?"

"You're coming with me."

Her fingers clenched around the phone. "I am?"

"You're my assistant, aren't you?" He pushed himself to his feet and started toward the door. "No self-respecting executive goes anywhere without an assistant."

He took his jacket down off the hook and wrapped his hand around the doorknob.

"Wait a second," she yelped. "I don't have

251

the right clothes for a business conference."

"Order up what you need online. Overnight delivery." He paused, frowning. "You'll probably need a dress or something for the reception and the auction."

For a second she could not breathe.

"I'm attending the reception with you?" she finally whispered.

"Like I said, no exec goes anywhere without an assistant."

He opened the door and went out onto the landing.

She leaped to her feet. "Where are you going?"

"To pick up the mail," he said. "I feel like getting some exercise."

He closed the door.

She dropped into her chair and listened to his footsteps on the stairs. After a few seconds she rose again and went to the window. Down below, Fallon appeared on the street. She watched him turn right and disappear around the corner, heading toward Stokes's Grocery, which also housed the Cove's small post office.

Fallon had insisted on picking up the mail for the past three days. Prior to that he had been content to let her handle the small, daily chore. Fallon was not exactly a creature of habit, but he had a number of established routines. Any break in the pattern was of great interest.

She gave it a few minutes and then went to the window on the other side of the room. She was just in time to see Fallon walking back from the grocery store. But he did not turn toward J&J. Instead, he disappeared again through a stand of trees, heading toward the bluffs and the path that led down to the Cove.

Another break in the pattern.

She turned, grabbed her coat off the wall hook and went out the door.

A bank of fog hovered just offshore, waiting to swallow the town whole. When she reached the top of the bluffs, she saw Fallon. He was already down on the rocky beach, walking toward the Point at the far end of the Cove. His hands were thrust deep into the pockets of his jacket. Even from this distance she could sense the dark, moody tension that shivered in the air around him.

She went down the steep path with some care. Loose pebbles skittered beneath her shoes. By the time she reached the bottom of the path, Fallon was nearing the Point. She paused briefly to open her senses. Fallon was illuminated in icy para-fog. But, then, he was always enveloped in the stuff.

She went after him, picking her way between tide pools and rocky outcroppings. Small crabs and sharp-billed shore birds scuttled out of her way.

She knew that Fallon could not have heard her approaching over the background roar of the surf, but he must have sensed her presence, because he stopped and turned to wait for her.

When she got closer, she could see the solemn set of his face and the dark shadows in his eyes.

"What are you doing down here?" he asked.

She ignored the brusque tone.

"You got something important in the mail, didn't you?" she asked. "Something you've been expecting for the past couple of days."

For a few seconds she thought he might not answer. Then he looked out toward the horizon.

"Yes," he said finally.

"Can you tell me what it is? Or is it too personal?"

He took the box out of his pocket and looked at it. "I received a ring."

The stoic resignation in his voice sent a frisson of alarm through her. The ring was connected to something very painful.

"Whose ring is it?" she asked gently.

"It belonged to a man who died three years ago. Last year I got his watch. The year before that I received a photo of his casket."

She studied his hard face. "What's going on, Fallon?"

"Someone wants to make certain that I never forget."

"That you never forget what?"

"That I killed my friend and partner."

20

They sat down on a large rock facing the wild surf. Holding it in his gloved hand, Fallon studied the black metal ring that was set with a green stone.

"His name was Tucker Austin," he said. "We were both J&J agents at the time. My uncle was running the agency back then. He was preparing to retire and turn the business over to me."

"But you worked as an agent, first?"

Fallon shrugged. "Family tradition. Tucker and I handled a number of cases together that year. We made a solid team, at least for a while. He was a high-end light-talent."

"I've never heard of that kind of ability."

"Probably because it's rare. A medium-range light-talent can manipulate the light that comes from the normal end of the spectrum. A dreamlight-talent can read the radiation from the dark ultralight sectors. But people like Tucker can bend both visible and paranormal wavelengths in such a way that they can make themselves invisible."

"The government is working on a super-stealth fighter plane that uses that principle," Isabella said. "Top secret black arts stuff. My grandmother broke the story on her website a few months back."

"The news was in all the popular-science magazines and several newspapers long before it appeared on the Iceberg site," Fallon said dryly.

"Really?"

In spite of his dour mood, Fallon's mouth kicked up a little at the corner. "You do realize that if it's in the *New York Times,* it isn't exactly a big secret."

She sniffed. "Not because the black-arts people didn't try to keep it secret."

"Okay, I'll give you that point. Back to my story. Tucker was especially useful to J&J because he could make himself invisible not only to those with normal vision but also to those who can see or sense energy in the paranormal ranges. He could conceal his own aura."

"Wow. He could hide from aura-readers and hunter-talents?"

"Tucker could move through a crowd of high-end auras and hunters like a ghost."

"I can see why he was so useful to J&J. He would have been the perfect psychic spy to send out against bad-guy talents."

"Tucker loved the work. The more dangerous, the better as far as he was concerned. He was a real adrenaline junkie. Like I said, we made a good team."

"You're an adrenaline junkie?"

"No. I was the plodding research guy. I handled the investigative and planning phase of the cases. I identified and drew up the list of suspects. Tucker went inside to get the evidence. Then we put it all together and gave the package to my uncle at J&J. He decided whether the case could be turned over to regular law enforcement or if it was a situation that J&J had to take care of on its own."

She nodded. "The way we handled the killer at the Zander house yesterday."

"You know, in some quarters that kind of activity is called taking the law in our own hands," Fallon said. There was a deep weariness in the words. "And it is frowned upon."

"Arcane polices its own because no one else can do the job."

"That has certainly been the rationale for J&J's existence since it was founded," Fallon agreed. "I've never told any of my agents or even anyone in my family, but sometimes in the darkest hours of the night I wonder if that makes it right."

She turned toward him. "We both know we can't leave para-psychopaths free to prey on the public. Not if it's in our power to stop them. Regular law enforcement doesn't even acknowledge the existence of criminals with paranormal abilities. How could the cops possibly track down the bad guys, let alone keep them in prison?"

"Don't think I haven't asked myself that question a million times." Fallon leaned forward, rested his forearms on his thighs and cradled in his gloved fingers the box that held the ring. He watched the surf pound on the rocks. "But sometimes I wonder, Isabella."

She put her hand on his arm. "The fact that you even ask the question is what makes you the right man to head J&J, Fallon Jones."

They sat together for a time, watching the relentless waves.

"What happened to Tucker?" she asked after a while.

"I killed him."

There was no trace of emotion in his voice. That told her everything she needed to know. Fallon was haunted by the death of Tucker Austin.

At first she thought he was not going to tell her the rest of the tale. But eventually he started to talk again.

"Tucker and I were assigned to the biggest case of our careers. A nightclub not so coincidentally named Arcane had popped up on the J&J psi-dar. It catered to sensitives, many of whom were not members of the Society. Some didn't even realize they had a little talent. But they were drawn to the club consciously or unconsciously by the energy of the place."

"All nightclubs have to give off a lot of intense energy or they go bankrupt," she said.

"Yes, but most clubs get their energy from the music and the crowd and a good marketing image."

"And the alcohol and the recreational drugs that are frequently available," she added.

"The Arcane Club attracted its patrons with all those things, but it offered one additional lure, an elite club within a club."

"Wait, don't tell me, let me guess. The insiders' club was called the Governing Council?"

He looked at her. "You're good."

"Thanks," she said. Pride tingled through her. Fallon Jones did not give praise lightly.

"So whoever operated the Arcane Club got a kick out of creating a shadow version of the real Arcane Society, including the Council. Creepy."

"It was," Fallon agreed. "Also smart marketing."

"Did the club offer a parallel version of Jones & Jones?"

"Within the world of the club, J&J provided security."

"For crying out loud," she said, incensed. "They made the J&J staff the bouncers? That's just wrong. We are an elite investigative firm."

He smiled a little at that and went on with the story. "Unlike most insider clubs, the big draw wasn't a drug; it was the lighting fixtures in the rooms that were reserved for the exclusive patrons."

"The lights?"

"They were called magic lanterns," Fallon said. "They were based on crystal technology. The paranormal radiation they emitted acted like an intense hallucinogen on people with talent. The higher the talent level, the bigger the hit."

"Lot of energy in light," Isabella mused. "All across the spectrum."

"My uncle was aware of the club, but he was not too concerned at first. Even when it became obvious that there was some kind of drug dealing going on, he figured it was a problem for regular law enforcement. J&J didn't get concerned until people who were deeply involved in the scene in the Arcane Club started dying."

"How did they die?"

"Two thought they could fly. They jumped out windows. A couple of others were so disoriented by the state of altered consciousness that they engaged in high-risk behavior that got them killed. The authorities investigated the deaths but never made the connection to the club because no evidence of drugs showed up in the autopsies. My uncle decided it was time for J&J to take a look at the situation."

"What happened?"

Fallon focused on the crashing waves. "He assigned Tucker and me to the case. We both realized immediately that there was no way we were going to get the kind of evidence that would stand up in court. Tucker suggested that we recommend to my uncle that he put pressure on the club owners to shut down. I agreed."

"Did that work?"

"The club closed, but my uncle wanted to know who had designed and built the magic lanterns. He asked me to look a little deeper."

"Wait," Isabella said. "Let me get this straight. Your uncle assigned you but not your partner to conduct the more detailed investigation?"

Fallon looked down at the ring. "I think my uncle had his suspicions about Tucker by then. Once I started looking, though, I could see the connections myself. Just a few things at first, but it didn't take long before they formed a pattern. Should have seen it much sooner."

"The pattern pointed to your friend, Tucker?"

"I couldn't believe it. Didn't want to believe it. I had trusted Tucker with my life in the course of some of our investigations. But in the end I had to face the truth. He was the secret owner of the club. He was responsible for the magic-lantern deaths."

"Something tells me you did not go straight to your uncle with the results of your investigation."

Fallon frowned. "Why do you assume that?"

She waved off the question. "Because he was your friend and partner. You had to be absolutely certain."

"I should have turned things over to my uncle at that point. But you're right — I needed to be sure. I confronted Tucker. I hoped that I was missing some piece of the puzzle that would exonerate him. Like everyone else I know, he had been warning me that my talent gave me a skewed vision of reality, that it made me inclined to see conspiracy fantasies where there was nothing but random chance. He told me more than once that some day I'd go too deep into the darkness and never return."

"So you gave him a chance to convince you that you were wrong. I'll bet he had a really good explanation."

"He laughed at me," Fallon said, sounding resigned. "He told me that I really had lost it. He said he could prove that he was innocent. He asked me to give him twenty-four hours. I said okay."

"What happened?"

"He tried to kill me."

"With his talent?"

"With an overdose of magic-lantern psi."

"Oh, crap."

"I had dinner with my fiancée that night."

An odd little chill fluttered through Isabella. "I didn't know that you were engaged."

"I was at the time," Fallon said. "Obviously I'm not now."

"Right." She did not know how to take

that. The thought of Fallon Jones having had his heart broken by another woman left her feeling slightly unnerved for some inexplicable reason. She did not want to think that someone else had ever had the power to hurt him in that way. "Go on."

"We had dinner at Jenny's condo. Tucker must have used his talent to slip into her place and conceal a magic-lantern lightbulb in one of the floor lamps. The visible light waves given off by the crystals look normal. You don't notice the paranormal effects of the lanterns until it's too late. The radiation hit both Jenny and me, of course, but I'm a more powerful talent than she is."

"So it hit you harder."

"It slammed my senses straight into overdrive." Fallon's jaw tightened. "Never felt anything like it in my life. I went into what I thought was an enlightened state. Suddenly I could see all the mysteries of the cosmos. I was sure I could comprehend them if only I looked a little deeper."

"What happened?"

"I was in a state of altered reality, completely disoriented. It was as if I was moving through a dream. I went out onto the balcony of Jenny's condo, convinced that I would be able to see the heart of the universe. While I was in that condition, Tucker entered the apartment. He tried to force me over the railing. Actually, he tried to talk me into going over under my own willpower."

"What?"

"I was hallucinating," Fallon said. "Out of my head. He tried to convince me that there was a crystal bridge that connected the balcony of Jenny's condo with the roof of the building across the street."

"I think I saw that movie."

"So did I. According to Tucker, all I had to do was step out onto the bridge. When that didn't work, he resorted to force. There was a struggle. In the end, I . . . killed him. He went off the balcony, instead of me."

"Dear heaven. How on earth did you manage to save yourself when you were in such a disoriented state?"

"This is going to sound weird," Fallon said. "Even though the magic lantern affected my talent, I think it was my talent that somehow saved me."

"Nah, it was your willpower and self-control that saved you, not your talent."

He looked at her. "You think so?"

"Sure. You've got more self-control than any talent I've ever met. When push came to shove, it was that ability that saved you, not talent." She paused. "Then again, the two are sort of linked, I suppose. The fact that you can handle such a powerful talent means that you've got a lot of built-in control. Chicken-and-egg thing, I guess. If you didn't have a lot of control, you'd have gone crazy by now."

"Thanks for that visual," Fallon said.

"Just trying to clarify here."

"You have a way of doing that."

"Doing what?" she asked.

"Clarifying."

"Oh. Okay."

"The bottom line is that I survived and Tucker died."

"You did what you had to do," Isabella assured him.

"Maybe. Maybe not."

"What do you mean?"

"I was out of my head," Fallon said. "Who knows how I might have handled the situation if I'd been in a normal state of mind? Jenny started screaming and crying. She was hysterical with grief and rage."

"Why was she so upset? Because of the hallucinogenic light of the lantern? Surely when she came back to her senses, she understood that you had been forced to fight for your life."

"Tucker Austin was her brother."

Isabella sighed. "I see. Well, that certainly explains her distraught reaction."

"Tucker was her older brother. She idolized him. Hell, he was the golden boy of the Austin family. Jenny and her parents have never believed that Tucker was running the club or selling the magic-lantern light. They have what you might call another theory of the crime."

Understanding hit her hard.

"They think you were the one running the Arcane Club and dealing the magic-lantern light."

"Their version of events is that after J&J fired up the investigation, I decided to cut my losses, shut down the club and set Tucker up to take the fall. Literally, in this case."

"To cover your tracks?"

"Yes," Fallon said evenly. "They also believe that my family protected me."

"Of course they can't prove that because there is no proof, so they comfort themselves with their own version of history. It's actually a pretty solid conspiracy theory, because within Arcane the Joneses wield a lot of power. It would be easy to believe they would circle the wagons around one of their own."

Fallon's eyes were bleak. He said nothing.

"That's one of the hallmarks of conspiracy theories, isn't it?" She shook her head. "As someone once said, they are the losers' version of history."

"Never thought about it like that."

"Probably because you weren't raised in a family of dedicated conspiracy freaks." She glanced down at the ring. "So every year on the anniversary of Tucker's death someone sends you a nasty little memento mori. Who is it? Jenny?"

"Probably, although I suppose it could be Tucker's mother or father."

"You've never tracked down the sender?"

"Didn't seem to be much point. I got the message."

"Will the Austin family be at the Sedona conference?"

"The Austins are power brokers within Arcane. Yes, they will be in Sedona."

"No wonder you're not keen on attending."

"At least this year I'll have a date."

21

The following morning Isabella took a break at the Sunshine with Marge. As was the custom, Violet and Patty walked over from the inn to join them. Isabella sat at the counter and sipped tea from a heavy mug. The other three drank Marge's high-test coffee and told tales about the brief heyday of the Seekers' community.

The arrival of an overnight delivery van interrupted yet another denunciation of Gordon Lasher. They all watched the vehicle roll down the street and stop in front of Jones & Jones.

"They found me," Isabella yelped. She set down her mug and jumped to her feet. "I was so afraid that there would be a screwup and they wouldn't be able to find Scargill Cove."

"I'm assuming that's the dress and the shoes?" Marge asked.

"I sure hope so," Isabella said. She headed

for the door. "Otherwise, I'm in bad shape for that business conference in Sedona."

"Bring the clothes back here," Violet called after her. "We want to see them."

"Especially the shoes," Patty said.

Isabella paused, her hand on the doorknob. "Why the shoes?"

Patty grinned. "I want to see if they really are glass slippers."

Isabella frowned. "I keep telling you, this visit to Sedona is a company business trip."

"Sure," Marge said. She chuckled. "A business trip that involves a corporate jet, a dressy reception and high-end fund-raiser auction. Woo-hoo! Go get the dress and the shoes and bring them back here so we can see them."

Isabella hurried outside. The driver of the delivery van had the rear door of the vehicle open. He removed two boxes.

Isabella rushed across the street. "Are those for me?"

He glanced at the labels. "Address says Jones & Jones."

"That's me. I mean, I work for Jones & Jones. I'll take the packages."

"Sign here."

She scrawled her signature, took the boxes and went back inside the Sunshine. Marge was waiting with scissors. She got the first box open in a flash.

Isabella parted the packing tissue and removed a long sweep of midnight blue. There were gasps all around.

"Oh, my," Violet said in prayerful tones. "What a beautiful dress. You're going to look gorgeous in it."

Isabella touched the liquid fabric. "It is nice, isn't it? Cost a fortune, but Fallon told me to bill it to the agency."

"Of course," Marge said. "He's the one who told you this was a business trip."

"The shoes," Patty said impatiently.

Marge used the scissors to open the second package. There was a shoe box inside. Isabella opened it and took out the pair of black evening sandals. Jet crystals gleamed discreetly on the gleaming patent leather straps.

"Oooh, they're so sexy," Patty said.

"Very nice," Marge agreed. "Not exactly glass slippers, though."

Violet smiled and touched one of the delicate black crystals. "Close enough. You can always count on Zappos."

Marge looked at Isabella. "Just think — you're going to the ball, Cinderella."

22

The glittering hotel ballroom was awash in power, both the kind that came with money and status and the psychic sort.

"Feels like the whole room is ever so slightly electrified," Isabella said.

Raine smiled. "When you gather this many people of talent together in one space, the atmosphere does tend to get a little hot."

"Yes, it does."

Isabella looked across the room at Fallon, who stood with Zack and two other men. As she watched, a distinguished-looking woman with silver-gray hair joined the men.

"The man on Zack's right is Hector Guerrero," Raine said in low tones. "The other one is Paul Akashida. The woman is Marilyn Houston. All three are on the Council. Zack considers them to be allies. They understand the true danger of Nightshade and they will support measures to make sure J&J remains vigilant."

"Fallon tells me some of the other Council members are wobbling because of some vicious rumors about him."

"Which is why Zack insisted that Fallon come tonight." Raine smiled. "I've got to tell you, though, I wasn't sure he would show up."

"Why not?"

"Fallon isn't the kind of man who responds to social pressure. But I suppose a threat to cut off funding for his precious anti-Nightshade project did the trick." Raine wrinkled her nose. "I'm afraid Zack is very good at figuring out exactly what it will take to get someone to do what he wants that person to do. It's part of his talent. One of the two reasons they put him in charge of Arcane."

"What's the other reason?"

Raine raised one shoulder in an elegant little shrug. "He's a Jones. There has always been a Jones in the Master's Chair. Technically speaking, since the changes made by Gabriel Jones back in the Victorian era, the Council has the power to elect anyone it pleases to the Chair."

"But somehow the result of every election has been a Jones?"

Raine raised her brows. "Yes. Coincidence?"

"I think not." Isabella smiled. "Sounds like the Society operates more like a hereditary monarchy than a democracy."

"Power rules in this organization, just as it does in any group," Raine said simply. "Within Arcane that means, among other things, a lot of raw talent. There happens to be a great deal of that in the Jones bloodline. In addition, the Joneses have been running Arcane a long time. They know where all the bodies are buried. In fact, they buried a few of them."

"Hmm."

Raine's brows went up. "What?"

"I'm not so sure that Fallon is here just because he's worried about the J&J budget. At least I don't think that's the only reason he agreed to show up tonight."

"Really? What other reason might there be?"

"I don't know," Isabella admitted. "Fallon is not always entirely forthcoming."

"You mean he's devious."

"No, he's just a very private person, and he's not accustomed to sharing his thoughts with others because most people don't understand how he thinks."

"That's certainly one way of putting it," Raine said. She gave Isabella a searching look. "I think you may understand him better than anyone ever has."

Isabella took a sip of champagne and lowered the glass. "I expect that somewhere along the line he got tired of trying to explain himself and his talent."

Raine switched her attention back to Fallon. "You may be right. I hadn't thought about it quite like that."

An attractive, expensively dressed woman in her late fifties approached the alcove.

"Good evening, Raine," she said warmly. "You look lovely tonight, as always."

Raine smiled. "So do you. Nice to see you, Maryann. Have you met Isabella Valdez, Fallon's new assistant?"

"No, I haven't had the pleasure." Maryann turned quickly to Isabella. "I'm Maryann Jones, one of Fallon's many aunts. Ours is a somewhat extended family, to say the least."

Raine grinned. "That tends to happen when one of your ancestors sires offspring by three different women."

"Old Sylvester was a bit of a rogue," Maryann sighed. "Then, again, he considered fathering a lot of children part of his research program. He was anxious to test his theories of the laws of psychic inheritance."

"How do you do, Maryann," Isabella said politely.

"It really is nice to meet you," Maryann said. "All of us in the family are so relieved that Fallon finally hired an assistant. He has been trying to handle far too much alone for far too long."

Isabella cleared her throat. "Actually, I'm an investigator at the agency now."

Maryann looked intrigued. "Is that so?"

"In addition to being the office manager," Isabella added hastily.

"Well, regardless of the title, I'm just grateful that Fallon found someone who could work with him day in and day out," Maryann said. "I'm afraid most people find him rather difficult."

"He needs his space," Isabella said. "Given the nature of his talent, he has to spend a lot of time in his own head."

Maryann's expression sharpened. "Yes, he's always been somewhat of a loner. Not everyone understands that. Oh, there goes Linda McDonald. I must speak to her. If you'll both excuse me?"

"Of course," Raine said.

Isabella waited until Maryann had been swept up in the crowd.

"A woman of strong talent," she said.

"Oh, yeah," Raine said. "Like everyone

else in the family."

"Uh, mind if I ask what kind?"

Raine smiled. "Didn't you know? Maryann Jones is one of the top matchmakers at arcanematch.com. In fact, she is considered to be the best. Runs the agency."

"I see," Isabella said. She couldn't think of anything else to say.

"No," Raine said.

"I beg your pardon?"

"You're wondering if Maryann matched Fallon with his former fiancée, aren't you?"

"The question did cross my mind."

"I don't know the whole story, mind you, but Zack told me that Fallon is convinced that with his talent he's not a good candidate for arcanematch. He became even more convinced of that when Zack got a disastrous match through the agency."

"Not you, I take it?"

"No."

"What happened?"

"Zack's fiancée tried to kill him."

"I'd say that qualifies as a poor match."

"Fallon's case was a little different. Since he didn't have any faith in arcanematch, he decided to find his own partner. Legend has it he went about it very methodically, using a computerized matrix, a detailed personality inventory and his own personal theory of para-compatibility. It didn't go well."

"I gathered that."

"And, yes, she's here tonight. That's Jenny Austin over there near the terrace doors. The redhead. She's talking to William Hughes."

Isabella looked toward the doors and saw a strikingly attractive woman chatting to an older man. Jenny was dressed in a sleek black gown that, although elegantly cut, managed to convey a funereal air. Something in the atmosphere around her, Isabella thought, a faint, telltale disturbance.

She opened her talent very cautiously and immediately regretted it. Glacial mist filled the entire room. Everyone in Arcane had secrets, and a lot of them were the deep, dark kind. Hastily she shut down her other sight. From this distance she could not see the precise sort of energy that swirled around Jenny Austin, anyway.

"What kind of talent is she?" Isabella asked.

"Jenny's a spectrum energy-talent. Quite brilliant. She's a very respected researcher in the L.A. lab. Actually, I think that was part of her appeal for Fallon."

Isabella could feel a small cloud of gloom gathering over her head. Of course Fallon would be intrigued by a woman who was not only beautiful but also a gifted researcher.

"I can see where he would have been attracted to her because she has a scientific mind," Isabella said, trying not to let her glum mood show.

"That was no doubt part of it," Raine said. "But according to Zack, there was an additional feature as far as Fallon was concerned."

"Well, she is lovely."

"It wasn't just her looks," Raine said. "It was the fact that one of Fallon's several times great-grandmothers was also a scientist — a botanist, as a matter of fact. Lucinda Bromley Jones lived in the Victorian era and was married to Caleb Jones."

"The other half of the original Jones & Jones?"

"Right. I'm afraid that Fallon went with the assumption that if the founder of J&J had good luck marrying a scientist, it made sense for his descendant to find himself a wife with scientific inclinations."

"In other words, Fallon tried to apply logic to the problem of finding a wife."

"Typical Fallon."

Isabella stifled a small sigh and switched her attention to the other side of the room where Maryann Jones was chatting with a group of distinguished-looking people that included Fallon's mother, Alexia Jones. Fallon had introduced his parents at the start of the reception. Alexia and Warner Jones had been very gracious but that was only to be expected, Isabella reminded herself. There was no way to be sure what they really thought of her. Fallon had made a point of presenting her as *my new assistant.*

"Fallon's aunt was checking me out, wasn't she?" Isabella asked.

Raine smiled. "She certainly was."

"Think she knows that Fallon and I have a personal relationship as well as a business relationship?"

"I think everyone in the room is aware of that."

"Good grief." Isabella tried to squelch a tiny surge of panic. "How on earth could they possibly know? And don't you dare tell me it's because everyone in the room is psychic."

"You don't have to be clairvoyant to sense the energy in the atmosphere when the two of you are close together. The fact that you and Fallon are involved in a personal way was obvious the minute you walked into the room tonight."

"Ack. I think I need another canapé and a

second glass of champagne."

"I'll come with you to the buffet table. I need to fortify myself for another round of socializing."

They made their way around the fringes of the crowd, pausing occasionally so that Raine could greet someone or introduce Isabella.

"I imagine being the wife of the Master of the Society can be somewhat demanding at times," Isabella said as they neared the buffet table.

"You have no idea."

Isabella fixed her attention on a platter of tasty-looking puff pastry canapés. "Those look good."

"Go for it," Raine said. "I'm off to check out the cheese tray."

Isabella picked up a small dish and circled around the small group blocking the path to the puff pastries.

"From what I hear, Fallon Jones is getting worse," a man said in low tones. "He's become obsessed with that conspiracy he calls Nightshade."

"Now, Hal, that's just gossip," a woman observed. "You have to agree that Nightshade represented a genuine threat."

"Past tense," Hal insisted. "That's the point, Liz. Look, I give J&J credit for breaking the back of that organization, but with Craigmore gone, there's no way Nightshade will ever recover. With its leader dead and five of the drug labs destroyed, the organization is finished. We should be directing our resources elsewhere."

"Jones is convinced that Nightshade will reconstitute itself," a younger man volunteered. "According to what I've heard, he believes that the scientist who re-created the formula is still out there somewhere, probably concocting another version of the drug for a new boss."

"Doubtful," Hal said. "But here's the real issue, Adrian. There's no way to know if Jones is right or if he's simply sunk so deep into his own fantasies that he can't find his way back to reality. We need someone in charge of J&J who can put things into perspective. The agency should refocus on handling routine investigations for members of the Society. That's why it was founded in the first place."

Adrian looked thoughtful. "I talked to Fallon earlier this evening. He's not real great with the social chitchat thing but he didn't strike me as a wacko."

"It's in the blood," Liz said. "Everyone knows that the men in that line who inherit a high-level version of chaos theory-talent eventually become paranoid and get lost in their conspiracy fantasies."

"Is that right?" Adrian asked.

"Well, there was that old story about one of Fallon's multiple-great-grandfathers, Erasmus Jones," Hal said. "A mad-scientist type who eventually committed suicide. And there were tales of Caleb Jones, as well."

Liz's expression tightened. "The speculation is that Fallon's version of the talent came directly from his ancestor, Sylvester Jones."

Adrian's brows shot up. "He's got the same talent that the founder had?"

"No two talents are ever exactly alike," Hal said. "But it's no secret that Sylvester was half mad and completely paranoid at the end. Liz is right, that kind of thing can come down through the bloodline."

Adrian drank some wine and looked thoughtful. "What do you suggest?"

"A lot of people are saying that the Council should appoint a new director of Jones & Jones, someone known to be stable and level-headed," Hal said. "A strong strat-talent, perhaps."

"There has always been a Jones at the head of J&J," Liz pointed out.

"Just as there has always been a Jones in the Master's Chair," Hal said grimly.

"Doesn't mean it has to be that way. Maybe it's time for a change. Arcane should start by severing its connection with the agency."

Isabella popped a stuffed pastry puff into her mouth. "Now that," she said to Hal, "would be a real dumbass thing to do."

Hal, Liz, Adrian and everyone else within earshot turned to look at her. There was a great hush around the buffet table.

"And you would be?" Adrian asked. Curiosity and a tinge of masculine interest lit his eyes.

"Isabella Valdez," she said. "I'm an investigator with J&J. I work at headquarters. Also, I manage the office for Mr. Jones."

"Ah, so you're the new assistant. I'm Adrian Spangler." Adrian stuck out his hand. "Nice to meet you."

"You, too." Isabella brushed crumbs off her palms and shook his hand.

No one else moved. No one else said a word. It was as if everyone in the vicinity except Adrian and Isabella had been flash-frozen.

"So, why would firing Fallon Jones and dumping J&J be a dumbass thing to do?" Adrian asked. There was no challenge in his tone, just curiosity.

"Because with J&J and Fallon Jones, the Society has the best psychic investigation agency on the planet," Isabella said briskly, "at least for the kind of investigative work that Arcane needs. The agency is uniquely qualified to handle Arcane business because it has a grasp of the history of the organization as well as access to all of the private files pertaining to the old cases."

"Good point," Adrian said. "It would be hard for another agency to step in and take over."

Hal frowned. "It might take some time for a new agency to get up to speed, but the trade-off would be a higher level of professional stability at the top."

"Oh, for pity's sake," Isabella said. "Stop trying to imply that Fallon Jones is unstable and crazy. I doubt that you would know a real conspiracy nutcase if you tripped over one."

Adrian grinned. "And you would?"

He was enjoying himself, Isabella realized. She noticed that Raine had quietly joined the small crowd at the buffet table. Raine, too, looked amused. But everyone else appeared to be teetering on the fine line between shock and fascination.

"Absolutely," Isabella said. "I happen to be an expert on the subject of conspiracy theorists. I can spot 'em a mile away. That's one of the assets I bring to the firm, by the way. Trust me, Fallon Jones is no conspiracy freak. Polar opposite, in fact."

Hal scowled, but Liz and Adrian and several others were starting to look intrigued.

"All right," Adrian said. "I give up. What is the polar opposite of a conspiracy freak?"

Isabella smiled. "A real detective, of course."

This time a few whispers rippled across the gathering crowd.

Isabella reached for another canapé. "Don't you get it? Fallon Jones thinks like a detective, not a conspiracy kook. He uses his talent to link facts and make connections, but he doesn't invent those facts and connections and he doesn't manipulate them the way true conspiracy nuts do. He's a psychic Sherlock Holmes. Holmes and Jones would be the last people on earth to be sucked into a conspiracy fantasy."

It dawned on her that the crowd was no longer staring at her. Everyone's attention was focused on a point behind her.

She turned around and saw Fallon watching her with an inscrutable expression. There was a little heat in his eyes.

"What do you say we go outside and get some fresh air, Watson?" he said.

"Watson got to carry a gun."

"Forget the gun."

"You never let me have any fun on the job."

"Not true. I let you find a serial killer and some dead bodies, didn't I?"

"Well, there is that." She plucked two more hors d'oeuvres off the tray. "You've got to try one of these little puff pastry thingies. They're yummy."

"Thanks," Fallon said.

He took a canapé in one hand, nodded briefly at the small crowd watching the scene and wrapped his other hand around Isabella's arm. He ate the puff pastry as he steered her toward the glass doors that opened onto the terrace.

"Good, aren't they?" Isabella said.

"Not as good as Marge's muffins."

"No," she agreed. "Nothing else is that good."

"Except your grandmother's ginger soup."

"Except for that."

23

They stood at the terrace railing and looked out at the night. The towering red rocks that gave Sedona so much character were transformed into dark, looming monoliths beneath the crystal-sharp moon. Isabella shivered a little with a bone-deep awareness.

"It's true what they say about this place," she said. "You really can feel the energy."

"It's not a nexus because it lacks ocean currents, but it definitely has its own kind of power," Fallon agreed. "There are several vortexes in the region."

"I can see why the Society likes to hold some of its meetings here."

"Trust me, Zack and the Council didn't choose this location just because it sits on a vortex site."

"No?" She glanced at him. "Why, then?"

"Because it's got a certain reputation. Notice all those brochures in the lobby advertising vortex tours, crystal healing and spiritual guides?"

"I see what you mean. You can hold a convention of psychics here and no one will think it's weird."

"It's called hiding in plain sight," Fallon said.

She shivered again, this time because of the chill in the air. "It's a lot colder than I thought it would be. This is supposed to be a desert."

"It's January and the altitude here is forty-five hundred feet," Fallon said. "We're lucky it's not snowing."

"Leave it to you to know exactly why I'm freezing my rear off out here." She folded her arms around herself. "I should have thought to check the weather report when I packed for this trip. Guess I was a little too focused on the dress and shoes. I was so worried they wouldn't arrive in time."

Fallon looked at the dress. "The dress is nice."

"Glad you approve, but don't thank me until you get the bill."

"No problem. It's a business expense."

"Right."

Nothing personal, she thought. It wasn't as if he had bought the dress for her as a gift. Just a business expense.

"The dress was pretty pricey," she warned.

He shrugged.

"But not as expensive as using one of the Arcane corporate jets to get here," she added.

"Doesn't matter."

"I had to spend some bucks on the dress because it's hard to fake quality in a fancy evening gown, you see. But the shoes are a knockoff."

"Don't worry about it, Isabella. Like you said, the jet cost a hell of a lot more."

"Okay."

He took off his jacket and draped it around her shoulders. It carried the warmth and scent of his body. She suddenly felt much warmer.

"Thanks," she said.

He nodded once, dismissing the small act of gallantry and propped one foot on the low rock barrier that rimmed the terrace. He leaned forward, one arm braced on his thigh.

She edged a little closer to him. He looked so sexy and so devastatingly masculine out here in the shadows, she thought. There was the distilled essence of the relentless avenger, the protector and the warrior in the energy that enveloped him. He was the kind of man you could always depend on, she thought. His word was his bond. Honor mattered to Fallon Jones.

He moved one hand, slightly revealing the face of his black watch and one of the old-fashioned gold-and-onyx cuff links that secured the cuff of his crisp white shirt.

"Did someone give you those cuff links?" she asked.

He glanced down at his left wrist. "Family heirlooms. Once upon a time they belonged to Caleb Jones. They've been passed down the line to me."

"That's nice," she said. "Things like that help keep you in touch with the past. They remind you of who you are and where you came from and what you need to be."

"Yes," he said.

"Someday you can pass them down to your own son. Or daughter. No reason a woman couldn't wear cuff links."

Fallon frowned, as though the prospect of having offspring was a new concept.

"Hadn't thought about that," he said.

"Must be nice to have a big family like yours," she said wistfully.

"It's a pain in the ass most of the time."

"But you know they're there for you if you need them to be there."

"Yes," he said.

"Did you hear what those people were

saying at the buffet table?" she asked after a while.

"About severing the connection between Arcane and J&J? Zack warned me there was talk."

"If whoever is behind the talk succeeded in getting Arcane to dump the agency, it wouldn't stop there, would it?"

"No," he said. "If the coup is successful, it would result in the Joneses' losing control of Arcane. In one sense it wouldn't matter."

She smiled. "Because the Joneses would take their secrets and fire up another version of Arcane?"

"We wouldn't have any choice. Someone has to do what Arcane has been doing since the Victorian era."

"Keep a lid on the damage done by the bad guys who happen to be psychic and hunt down the folks who try to re-create the formula."

"The problem," Fallon said, "is that it would take time to rebuild a new Arcane, and time is the one thing we don't have a lot of right now. Meanwhile Nightshade would almost certainly use the lull to reposition itself within the heart of Arcane."

"So that's what we're dealing with. A conspiracy to oust the Joneses from Arcane and take over the Society."

"It depends on your definition of conspiracy," Fallon said. "Zack thinks of it as hostile a takeover."

"Nope, I know conspiracies when I see them, and this is the real deal."

His mouth twitched. "What did I ever do without you to help me see things clearly, Isabella Valdez?"

She wrinkled her nose. "You're laughing at me, aren't you?"

"No," he said. "I'm laughing at myself." He wrapped one arm around her and pulled her close. "I didn't do that a whole lot before I met you, at least not in a very long time."

"I'm not sure how to take that."

"I was slipping into the darkness before you came along, Isabella."

"No," she said quickly. "I think you were just physically and psychically exhausted and maybe a little depressed because the job was overwhelming you."

"All I know is that with you I feel centered again."

It wasn't exactly a declaration of love, she thought, but at least Fallon was aware of the bond between them. That would do for now.

She reached up and touched his hard jaw. "When I'm with you, I feel as if I've found something I've been looking for a very long time."

His eyes burned. He lowered his head and kissed her, slowly at first, letting the hunger grow between them. The heady psi of the Sedona night closed around them, enhancing sensation across the spectrum. Isabella opened her senses to savor the invisible fire.

"Excuse me if I'm interrupting anything."

The voice, iced with rage and pain, came out of the darkness behind Isabella. Jolted, she gasped, took a step back out of Fallon's arms and turned quickly, nearly toppling in her stiletto-heeled shoes. Fallon caught her easily, steadying her.

They both looked at Jenny Austin, who stood in the shadows. Searing fog flared around her.

"Hello, Jenny," Fallon said quietly.

Jenny walked closer. Her hands were clenched in small fists at her sides. Dressed in black and bathed in moonlight she looked like the doomed heroine of an opera that was destined to end in tragedy. She seemed oblivious to Isabella's presence.

"I can't believe you had the gall to show up here tonight, Fallon," Jenny said. Her voice was tight as though she was struggling to breathe or to restrain tears. "How could you do this to my family?"

"I'm sorry," Fallon said. "But we both know it was inevitable that sooner or later we would come face-to-face at some Arcane event. The Society is a small world at the top."

"And your family controls that world," Jenny said bitterly.

Fallon did not react.

Jenny abruptly turned to Isabella.

"You must be the new office manager everyone is talking about. The one who thinks Fallon is some kind of modern Sherlock Holmes."

"Well, as a matter of fact, in addition to managing the office, I'm an investigator in the firm," Isabella said.

"The way I hear it, you're providing some additional services on the side," Jenny said coldly.

At that, Fallon stirred. Ominous energy shivered in the atmosphere. "That's enough, Jenny. Isabella has nothing to do with you and me."

"Does she know why we broke up?" Jenny whispered. "Does she know that you killed my brother?"

Isabella studied the fog that threatened to consume Jenny. "I know what really happened the night your brother died," she said gently. "I can also see that the secrets you

296

are keeping are slowly but surely destroying you. You know the old saying, the truth will set you free."

"You don't know what you're talking about," Jenny said. "Fallon Jones killed my brother."

"You were the one who exposed Fallon to the magic-lantern lights that night, weren't you?" Isabella said gently. "Tucker didn't use his talent to slip into your condo to set up the lantern. You did it so that Fallon would be disoriented when your brother came to murder him."

Fallon was suddenly very still. But his reaction was nothing compared with Jenny's. She looked stricken.

"You're crazy," Jenny whispered.

"I'm sure Fallon knows the truth. He has probably known it all along."

"That's not true." Jenny's voice rose. She turned to Fallon. "Make her stop talking."

"That's not so easy to do," Fallon said.

Isabella took a step toward Jenny and stopped. "Don't mean to scare you, but I really don't think you're going to be able to keep the secret much longer. I've seen this kind of hot fog before. If you were a sociopath, it wouldn't be a problem. They feed on the flames. But you are a decent person and you once cared about Fallon so you feel the heat, don't you? You know what it's doing to you."

"Shut up," Jenny pleaded. "Just shut up. Please."

Isabella said nothing. Fallon did not move.

Jenny started to cry. Everything about her seemed to crumple beneath the crushing weight of the secrets she had been holding.

Isabella went to her and put her arms around her. Jenny resisted for a few seconds and then the last of the dam gave way. Jenny sobbed against Isabella's shoulder.

After a while Fallon offered a pristine square of white linen. Isabella smiled a little. How many modern men carried a crisp white handkerchief on the off chance that they might need to produce it for a distraught woman, she wondered. Then, again, the small gesture suited Fallon. In many ways he was a man from another era, some mythical time and place where honor and chivalry were important concepts.

"I believed him." Jenny took the handkerchief and blotted her eyes and took a deep breath. "I'm so sorry, Fallon. But he was my brother. I had to believe him."

"I know," Fallon said. "He was my friend and my partner. I wanted to believe him, too."

Jenny sighed. "You probably know everything. You're Fallon Jones. You always have the answers."

"Not always," Fallon said.

"In this case I'm sure you do." Jenny looked at him. "You're right, I did expose you to the magic-lantern lights that night. I hid the device in a floor lamp. I was subjected to the radiation as well, but it didn't hit me as hard as it hit you because your talent is so powerful. I . . . I knew it would be like that."

"Tucker told you that I was the one who was running the club and selling the light in the insider rooms," Fallon said. It was a statement of fact, not a question.

"Yes." Jenny sniffed. "It's all my fault. I'm responsible for everything that happened because I'm the one who created those damn lanterns in the first place."

"Why?" Fallon asked.

"It was an experiment," Jenny said. She sounded dull and lifeless now. "So many psychoactive pharmaceuticals don't work well on those who possess a high level of talent. I was trying to come up with a naturopathic approach to treating problems like depression and anxiety and PTSD in strong para-sensitives. There is a lot of work being done with light to elevate moods in normal people. I thought there might be a way to use light from the paranormal end of the spectrum on those with talent to achieve similar positive effects."

"I understand," Fallon said.

"I was working from the records of one of my ancestors, a spectrum energy-talent who lived back in the nineteen thirties. I came up with a device that combined various kinds of amber and quartz that are naturally para-luminescent and para-phosphorescent."

"Oh, boy," Isabella muttered. "Geek talk. I think my eyes are starting to glaze over."

Jenny ignored her. She continued talking earnestly to Fallon. "On their own, the rocks don't have much effect, but when arranged in certain ways and activated by the right kind of mirrors, well, you know what happened. The effects ranged from euphoria to hallucinations and disorientation. All short-term but highly unpredictable."

"I admit this isn't my field," Isabella said. "But the theory behind your research sounds very intriguing."

"It is," Jenny said. "And I still think there is a lot of potential in it. But as soon as I ran some tests on my own version of what Tucker called my magic lantern, I realized that although it was a mood enhancer in very small doses, the side effects could be devastating. I could not come up with a safe way to use it in a naturopathic manner."

"But by then Tucker had learned about your experiments and concluded that it might make an attraction at his club," Fallon said.

"I swear, I didn't know that he was the secret owner of the Arcane Club," Jenny whispered.

"I didn't know it, either, until the end," Fallon said.

Jenny sniffed into the handkerchief. "It doesn't matter now, but I want you to know that I didn't construct the magic lanterns for him. He used my notes and made them himself. They aren't that hard to build if you have the right quartz and amber and an obsidian mirror."

"I never believed that you were involved in the club lanterns," Fallon said.

Jenny gave him a wan smile. "The thing is, I believed him when he told me that you were the real owner of the club and that you were dealing some kind of terrible psychic drug. After he . . . died I had to go on believing that what he had told me was the truth. The alternative was just too awful."

Isabella touched Jenny's shoulder. "You've accepted your brother's guilt, haven't you?

That's no longer the source of your pain. It's your sense of responsibility that is driving you into despair."

"It was all my fault." Jenny sighed. "If I hadn't run the experiments with those damn rocks and if I hadn't demonstrated the results to Tucker —"

"If it hadn't been the magic-lantern technology, it would have been something else that got Tucker into trouble," Fallon said. "He liked living on the edge. As time went by, the adrenaline rush of proving that he was smarter and faster than everyone else became his personal drug of choice."

"Yes," Jenny said. "I think you're right. His need to take risks was an addiction. Everyone in the family knew that. My poor mother worried constantly that he would get himself killed on one of his J&J assignments."

"Proving that he could outmaneuver Jones & Jones was the ultimate challenge," Fallon said.

Jenny dabbed at her eyes with the handkerchief. "Even knowing Tucker as well as I did, I still let him convince me that you were the bad guy. Can you ever forgive me?"

"I never blamed you," Fallon said. "You had to make a choice between believing your brother or a man you did not know very well. Hell, if I'd been in your shoes, I would have made the same choice."

Jenny looked at him with unconcealed desperation. "Do you really think so?"

"Family is something we Joneses understand," Fallon said.

Jenny crushed the handkerchief in her hand and closed her eyes. "I don't know what to say. Thank you, Fallon."

Isabella hugged her again. "Now you need to forgive yourself, Jenny. That's the only way to make the fog go away."

Jenny opened her eyes, bewildered. "Fog? What are you talking about?"

Isabella smiled and released her. "Never mind. Just a figure of speech."

Jenny turned back to Fallon. "You were right."

"About what?" he asked.

"A moment ago you said that I'd been forced to choose between believing my brother or a man I did not know very well. That's the truth. I didn't know you very well, Fallon."

"No," he agreed.

"Even if things had been different, I don't think that would have changed," Jenny said.

"Probably not."

"There's something else I need to tell you about that night. Even if there had been no

Arcane Club and no magic lanterns and things had not ended the way they did, I was going to give you back your ring."

"I know," Fallon said.

She shook her head, rueful now. "Of course you do. You're Fallon Jones, the brilliant chaos theory-talent. You can see the pattern before anyone else."

"Not always," he said. "But you were right, Jenny. It would never have worked between us."

She gave him another misty smile. "We both made the same mistake when we got engaged. We thought we could rely on logic and reason when it came to choosing a mate."

"Obviously a false assumption," Fallon said.

Jenny turned back to Isabella. "Fallon may not have done a very good job when he tried to find a wife, but I think he did very well, indeed, when he hired an assistant."

She turned and walked back toward the lights of the ballroom. Isabella jacked up her other vision. The terrible fog was already diminishing. With luck, Jenny would allow herself to heal.

Fallon came to stand beside Isabella. They waited until Jenny had disappeared into the crowd.

"You knew she was going to give you back your ring that night?" Isabella asked.

"Doesn't take a lot of talent to know when you're about to get dumped. Even I could see it coming."

"And if she hadn't ended things first?"

"I would have had to do it," he said. "You heard her. Jenny felt as if she never really knew me. That problem went both ways."

"Everyone has secrets. Everyone has a private place. I don't think it's ever possible to know anyone completely. I don't think we would want to know someone that well even if it were possible. Part of what makes other people interesting is that there is always some mystery beneath the surface."

"The kind of knowing I'm talking about goes deeper than secrets," Fallon said.

She thought about that. "I see what you mean."

"Do you?" He shook his head. "Then you're way ahead of me because I sure as hell couldn't define it."

"But you'll recognize that kind of knowing if you ever find it?"

"Yes," he said. "So? What does it mean?"

"To want to know someone in a way that goes deeper than just learning a person's secrets? It means you're a hopeless romantic, Fallon Jones."

There was a heartbeat of stunned silence. And then Fallon began to laugh. The sound started out as a hoarse, harsh, little-used chuckle. But it quickly gathered depth and volume. In a moment, Fallon was roaring with laughter. The sound reverberated across the terrace, spilling out into the night.

Isabella sensed a presence behind her. When she turned around she saw Zack and Raine silhouetted in the entrance of the ballroom. As she watched, a number of other Joneses, including Fallon's parents, gathered to watch the spectacle on the terrace. The expressions on their faces ran a short gamut from stunned to fascinated.

She poked Fallon in the ribs. "We've got an audience," she whispered.

His laughter faded. He turned to look at the crowd in the doorway.

"Good joke?" Zack asked.

"Best one I've heard in a long time," Fallon said.

24

The auction started at ten. Fallon stood with Isabella at the back of the room. A hush fell over the crowd. The auctioneer picked up his gavel.

Fallon took Isabella's arm.

"We can leave now," he said, keeping his voice low.

She glanced at him, surprised. "Don't you want to see who bids on those weird artifacts in the display cases?"

"No. I've had about as much socializing as I can handle for one evening. I've done what Zack asked, helped him provide a show of force. He can handle the Society's politics from here on in. That's what he gets paid to do."

Her eyes narrowed a little in suspicion, but she allowed him to steer her out of the ballroom and into the hallway.

"You're up to something," she whispered. "I can tell."

"You know us small-town folks. Early to bed and early to rise."

"Ha. What's going on, Jones?"

"We're leaving first thing in the morning."

"Define first thing," she shot back.

"After breakfast."

"Okay, that's not so bad. You're anxious to get back to Scargill Cove?"

"We have a lot of work waiting for us." The *we* surprised him, coming out of his mouth as it did. For so long he had thought of the agency as his sole responsibility. But lately he had begun to think of Isabella as something more than an assistant or even an investigator. He was starting to treat her like a partner. That was probably not wise.

"Yes," she said, looking satisfied at the prospect. "J&J never sleeps."

"There's another reason for getting an early start."

She gave him an expectant look.

He drew her through the lobby toward the elevators. "We're going to make a stop on the way back to the Cove."

"Where?"

"Cactus Springs."

She halted abruptly, forcing him to halt, too. Her eyes widened. "That's where my grandmother lives. Lived."

"I've done all the investigation I can do

308

online. Now I need to take a look at the scene of the crime. Isn't that the kind of thing Sherlock Holmes would do?"

"But you don't believe that there was a crime."

"I told you, I'm reserving my opinion until I have all the facts."

She gave that some thought. "Grandma warned me not to go to her place if something happened to her because she was afraid they might be watching, waiting for me to show up. But I suppose there's no reason you and I can't go there together. As long as you're with me, it should be safe. Grandma is the one who told me to find you if I couldn't hide from them. She said they would not want to involve Arcane."

"*They* being Julian Garrett's people?"

"Right." She wrinkled her nose. "I know you don't believe my theory of the case."

"Your *conspiracy* theory of the case," he corrected. "Thus far I haven't found anything to indicate that Garrett or anyone else was involved in any way with your grandmother's death, assuming she is dead."

"It's okay." She gave him a glowing smile. "You don't have to explain. You're still investigating. That's all that matters. Sooner or later you'll find the proof."

They started up the stairs to the second floor.

"You do understand that we may be trying to prove a negative here," he cautioned. "There is no way to do that. Which is, of course, how conspiracy theories work in the first place and why they manage to stay alive."

"You never know, we might find a solid clue in Cactus Springs."

"Don't get your hopes up," he said.

"I'm pretty sure that Sherlock Holmes never said that to a client."

"You're my assistant, not a client."

They reached the landing and went down the hall to Isabella's room. He took out the card key and opened the door for her. She stepped into the room on the impossibly high heels and turned to face him.

"We didn't really need to go to the expense of booking two rooms," she said. "Evidently everyone back there in the ballroom knows that we're personally involved."

"How the hell did they find out?" Outrage crackled through him. "Zack or Raine must have said something, although how they knew is an interesting question. I'll have a talk with Zack in the morning."

"No, no, no," she said hastily. "Zack and Raine didn't gossip about us. It's just something about our energy. Even nonsensitives can often tell when two people are involved in a physical relationship. The energy of that sort of attraction is very strong."

Annoyed, he gripped the door frame and checked the hallway to see if anyone was watching. Then he turned back to her. "Damn it, I won't let anyone embarrass you."

"Trust me, I'm not in the least embarrassed."

"You're sure?"

"Absolutely," she said. "What about you? Do you mind people knowing that we're sleeping together?"

He gave the question a couple of beats, trying to sort out his reactions. Deep down he liked the fact that everyone knew that Isabella was his, at least for now. He wanted other men to know that she was not available. And since when had he developed a possessive streak?

He finally got to the bottom line.

"Only if it makes you feel awkward," he said.

She put her arms around his neck. "Poor Fallon. How did an old-fashioned gentleman endowed with such quaint Victorian virtues ever survive in the modern world?"

He groaned. "You think I'm some kind of throwback?"

"Only in the nicest sense of the word."

"Calling me old-fashioned and Victorian makes me feel ancient. I know I'm a little older than you, but not that much. I just look old."

"No." She stood on tiptoe and brushed her mouth against his. "You don't look old. You look perfect."

The touch of her mouth acted like an electrical switch. Everything inside him went to flashpoint in a heartbeat.

"You're the one who is perfect," he rasped.

He moved into the room and shut the door. The action plunged the small space into a shadowed realm, a world lit by the silver light of the canyon-country moon.

He took off his tux jacket for the second time that evening and tossed it across the back of the nearest chair. When he started to loosen the black bow tie, Isabella stopped him.

"Let me," she said.

He opened his senses and saw the heat in her eyes.

When she reached up to unknot his tie, her fingers trembled a little. He caught her hand and kissed her palm. She let the ends of the tie dangle around his neck and went to work unfastening the onyx cuff links. There were two faint clinks when she put the cuff links carefully on the table. The small, intimate sound jacked his senses even higher. He was certain he had never been so hard in his life.

She went to work on the black studs that secured the front of his shirt.

He kissed her and began to strip her with quick, focused motions. The evening gown collapsed into a dark pool at her feet. He got the lacy bra off next. The panties followed, leaving her in the sexy high heels.

Energy ignited the atmosphere of the shadowed room. Isabella's effect on him could only be described in terms of alchemy, he thought. She was the fire that transmuted the cold iron inside him into gold. With her he could look into the heart of chaos and glimpse the ultimate goal of the ancient art, the Philosopher's Stone. With her he was, for a time, complete.

Desperate now, he picked her up and braced her against the nearest surface, the wall. She put one bare leg around his waist and then the other. Her scent was more intoxicating than any drug. He cradled her with one hand and stroked her with the other until she was wet and frantic.

"For me," he said. He caught her earlobe

between his teeth and bit down a little, needing to reinforce the words. "I want you like this only for me. No one else."

"It has never been like this with anyone else. It couldn't be. Only you." She clutched at his shoulders and looked at him with her mysterious eyes. "This had better work both ways or it's over now."

"Only you," he said. He was shatteringly aware that his voice was hoarse with passion. He could barely speak at all. "Never like this with anyone else."

She smiled her devastating smile.

"Good," she said.

Her fiercely wonderful energy filled the room, enveloping him.

He managed to unzip his trousers and then he was pushing into her. She closed tightly around him.

He thrust again and again, fast and hard. She clung to him, wrapping herself around him. He could hear her breathing: quick, shallow gasps that betrayed her rising excitement.

"Fallon."

He forced himself to stop pounding into her long enough to lift her away from the wall and put her down onto the bed. He got rid of his trousers and briefs, kicked off his shoes and lowered himself onto the bed beside her.

"My turn," she said.

She flattened one hand on his chest and pushed him onto his back. He went willingly. And then she was on top, sliding slowly downward, fitting her tight core to him.

She rode him slowly, tormenting him until he thought he could not endure it. But he forced himself to let her set the pace. He gripped her soft thighs and opened his senses fully. He did not try to focus his talent. Rather, he gave himself up to the glittering exhilaration of the moment. It was only at times like this, when he was so intimately connected to Isabella, that he could safely slip the bonds of his self-control and fly free.

Sensation and the heat of desire carried him on a relentless tide. The knowledge that Isabella was riding the same wave thrilled him beyond measure.

When she came undone in a storm of energy, he followed her over the edge into the endless night.

25

She came back to her senses a long time later, aware of a faint rustling sound. Fallon was no longer in the bed.

She opened her eyes and saw him dressing by the light of the moon. She pushed herself up on her elbows and watched him tuck the white shirt into the waistband of his trousers. She was not sure whether to be amused or annoyed or hurt.

"You're leaving?" she asked, trying not to show any emotions at all.

"If I stay here until morning, there's a good chance that someone will see me leaving your room."

She relaxed, smiling a little. "I told you, everyone at the conference already knows we're sleeping together."

"I don't have a problem with that."

He walked to the bed, bent down and braced a hand on either side of her. He kissed her, his mouth deliciously rough on hers. It was a branding kiss, she decided. He was letting her know that on this level she belonged to him. He straightened reluctantly.

"But there's something called discretion," he said.

"Gosh. Haven't heard that word used in a long time. You are aware that's another old-fashioned concept?"

"Is it?"

"Yeah, but it's very sweet." She yawned and waved a hand toward the door. "Go on back to your room. I'll see you in the morning."

"Breakfast at six-twenty. I want to talk to Zack before we leave and then I've got to say good-bye to my parents. Plane leaves at eight. I haven't told the pilot that we're making a detour. I'll inform him just before we take off."

"Why not let him know earlier so he can revise the flight plan?"

"Just a precaution." He went to the table and collected his cuff links. "No sense advertising our schedule in advance."

A tiny chill shivered through her. "You don't want anyone to know that you're investigating my grandmother's death, do you?"

"Zack and Raine know."

"Sure, but they won't say anything because they've got the same concern that you do. My point is that the three of you don't want folks on the Council to suspect that you're wasting valuable time and money checking out a conspiracy theory about the murder of a known crackpot."

His hand closed tightly around the cuff links. He watched her steadily. "I didn't say that."

"But it's what you're thinking."

"What I'm thinking," he said evenly, "is that the fewer people who know that I'm looking into your grandmother's death, the better. Nothing more, nothing less."

"Ha. With you there's always something more. But never mind. I understand. Heck, I even agree with you. The fewer people who know about this, the better. See you in the morning, Fallon."

For a moment he did not move. She held her breath, wondering if he was reconsidering his decision to leave. But after a couple of seconds he went to the door, opened it and checked the hall.

"Lock the door after I leave," he ordered.

"Yeah, sure."

She waited until he moved out into the hall and shut the door before she got out of bed. She padded barefoot across the room and put on the safety lock. There was no sound out in the corridor for at least three full seconds. Then the light shifted under the door. She knew that Fallon had finally walked back to his room at the end of the hall.

She crawled into bed, pulled up the covers and pondered the ceiling for a very long time.

After a while she drifted off and tumbled into a troubled dream in which her grandmother appeared in the heart of a storm of icy fog. Grandma was speaking, trying to send a warning, but as was so often the case in dreams, the words made no sense.

She came awake on a current of fear, pulse racing, heart pounding. The primal instincts of childhood took over. *Do not move. Maybe the monster under the bed won't see you.*

She forced the crushing wave of panic aside, but she remained very still. Her other sight, aroused by the surge of adrenaline, was already at full throttle and sending her a confusing flood of stimulation. The psychic senses operated both independently and in conjunction with the normal senses. Engaging one's talent without also getting feedback from the regular senses could be wildly disorienting unless a person was accustomed to dealing with only the psychic sense.

Cautiously she opened her eyes partway. She was curled on her side, facing the sliding glass doors that opened onto the little patio.

The curtains were still parted, allowing moonlight to slant into the room. But something was different. The atmosphere was much chillier than it had been earlier. She realized that she was inhaling the fresh, clean scents of the desert night, not air-conditioning. As she watched, the edge of one of the curtains fluttered.

The sliding glass door was partially open. Paranormal fog boiled through the entrance. Someone had entered the room. She remained frozen for another instant, trying to adjust to the shock.

And then she tried frantically to leap from the bed. She discovered she could not move.

"I know you're awake." The voice came out of the shadows behind her, the voice of an irritatingly unctuous salesman. "I've used my talent to trap you in the twilight zone between sleep and wakefulness. Don't bother trying to move. You can't even twiddle your thumbs."

The hot acid of adrenaline splashed through her. She struggled desperately to get to her feet and managed to twitch, if not actually twiddle her thumbs. Her left foot jerked an inch. That was more than the intruder expected but not nearly enough to get her out of bed and through the sliding glass door to safety.

Damn it, Fallon, why didn't you stay? This wouldn't have happened if you'd been here with me where you belong. You see where those old-fashioned notions of discretion get you?

She stared fixedly at the open window, fighting the terrible panic so that she could concentrate on her psychic senses. They seemed to be fully functional. She had no problem perceiving the river of hot fog that seethed and roiled across the floor and past the foot of the bed.

"You can talk," the intruder said, "but if you try to scream, I'll have to use more energy to silence you. You won't like it, trust me."

"What do you want?" She tried to speak as loudly as possible, testing her voice. But the words emerged as a thin whisper.

"I won't hurt you. I don't do that kind of work. I'm staying out of your range of vision because that's one of my policies. Clients and those who receive the message never see my face."

"What are you talking about?" she hissed in the same reedy whisper.

"They call me the Messenger. I consider myself a go-between. I'm here to make you a very handsome offer."

"And if I refuse it?"

"Let's not go there. It will be more profitable for both of us if we start on a positive note."

Beneath the bedding she succeeded in getting one hand clenched into a fist. The gesture of rage was useless. Her only hope was to somehow find the strength to roll off the edge of the bed onto the floor. If she got out of the intruder's line of sight for even an instant, he would likely lose focus for a couple of seconds. That might give her enough time to scramble out the door into the night. At the very least she would be able to scream for help.

"I'll keep this short," the Messenger said. "I represent an individual who is extremely interested in acquiring inside information about Jones & Jones. You are uniquely placed to provide that sort of data."

"Forget it," she mumbled.

The fact that the intruder could hold her virtually paralyzed was extraordinary on its own. That he could do so without making physical contact meant that his talent was truly off the charts. Nevertheless, he had to be using a great deal of energy to control her movements. He could not go on for long generating power at such a rate.

She had to find a way to make him touch her. If he put a hand on her, she was sure she had enough power to disorient him.

"Listen to the rest of the pitch before you make your decision," the Messenger said smoothly. "First, the money will be excellent. A hundred thousand dollars has already been wired into an offshore account just to show my client's good faith. There will be more as soon as you start to forward information to a certain e-mail address."

She poured everything she had into moving one leg an inch closer to the edge of the bed. She succeeded but the effort cost her. She was drenched in sweat.

"No," she said hoarsely.

"I put a slip of paper with the number of the account and details for accessing it on the console."

"No."

"You really do want to think about the offer before you make up your mind."

"There's nothing to think about. The answer is no."

"Your decision, of course, but I have been instructed to inform you that turning down the offer would not be a wise move in terms of your future health and well-being."

The old dream started out in the usual manner.

He was lost. He had traveled too far out on the multidimensional grid. He had gone too deep into the dark zone. This time he would not be able to find his way back.

The endless night was illuminated here and there by small galaxies composed of points of light. Each tiny sun was important; each was connected to another but he could not quite grasp the patterns.

The clusters of stars were like swarms of fireflies in an endless garden of night. He was well and truly lost.

But someone was calling to him across the vast reaches of time and space.

Isabella.

He looked for her but he could not see her in the shadows. He had to find her. She was infinitely more important than whatever fabulous discoveries awaited him in the heart of chaos. And she was in danger. . . .

Fallon awoke on a rush of energy, all of his senses at full throttle. He had to find Isabella *now*.

He was out of bed and reaching for his pants before he could assess and analyze the decision. The part of him that was always engaged in probabilities and possibilities did a fast assessment of the situation. If Isabella was in danger, that danger would have arrived via the patio.

Given the hotel's desert landscaping, that meant he would be covering some rough ground. He paused long enough to pull on the low boots that he had worn on the plane. He was going to look like a lust-crazed idiot if he showed up on her patio half-naked with no good reason.

He jerked open the sliding glass door and went out into the night.

"Are you threatening to murder me?" Isabella asked. The new tide of energy slamming through her was enough to propel her to the very edge of the bed. Another inch and she would fall onto the floor. She was battling the invisible psychic thrall the whole time, but she was making some progress.

"No, no, no, Miss Valdez. I assure you I am not a hit man. I told you, I'm the Messenger."

"You know what happens to messengers."

There was no sound out on the patio, just a sudden shifting of the shadows. But suddenly Fallon was there, sweeping into the unlit room on a pressure wave of energy. He went straight toward the intruder like a hawk zeroing in on prey.

"Shit." The Messenger no longer sounded like a silver-tongued salesman. He sounded panicked. He leaped for the only available exit, the door that opened onto the hallway.

Isabella felt the paralysis lift instantly as the intruder lost his focus. She rolled out of bed and got to her feet in time to see Fallon grab the fleeing Messenger and spin him around. For the first time, she saw the ski mask that covered the man's face. He had relied on more than his unnerving talent to conceal his identity.

"No, wait," the Messenger gasped. He flung up his hands to ward off a blow.

Energy flashed in the atmosphere.

"Don't kill him," Isabella said quickly. "Not yet. He knows stuff. We need to talk to him first."

"Yes," Fallon said. "We'll definitely have a chat first."

He slammed the Messenger onto the floor. The man groaned. Fallon leaned down and ripped off the ski mask.

"Always knew you'd come to a bad end, Lockett," Fallon said. "Didn't know I'd be the one to take you out, though. I assumed it would be some other disgruntled client."

Lockett stiffened. He stared up at Fallon. "You know my name?"

"I never do business with people I don't know."

Lockett sat up slowly, clearly dazed by more than just the body slam. "I don't understand. No one knows my identity. I never let clients see me. How the hell did you find out?"

"I don't think that's important at the moment. What are you doing in this room?"

"He said that someone wants me to spy on J&J," Isabella said indignantly. "There was a huge bribe involved. And a threat."

Fallon looked at her. "Robe."

"What?"

"You're in your nightgown. Put on a robe."

She looked down. "Oh, right."

Her nightgown was made of soft cotton. It was ankle length and long-sleeved. All in all it was far more modest than the evening dress she had worn earlier, but she suspected that it was the principle of the thing that worried Fallon. She grabbed her robe and slipped into it.

Fallon turned back to Lockett. "What's this about a bribe and a threat?"

"I never threatened her," Lockett said

forcefully. "I wasn't the one trying to bribe her, either. I simply relayed the message. That's what I do. You should know that, Jones."

"What was the message?" Fallon asked.

Lockett heaved a world-weary sigh. "My client wanted me to offer Miss Valdez a sum of money in exchange for transmitting certain details concerning the operation of Jones & Jones. That's all there was to it."

"I told him no," Isabella said, still incensed. "Then he informed me that a hundred thousand dollars had already been wired into an offshore account. The number is on the table."

"What about the threat?" Fallon asked.

Lockett cleared his throat and managed to regain his salesman's voice. "Uh, that would seem to be moot at this point."

"No," Fallon said. The word was etched in steel. "It's not moot."

Isabella moved to stand at the foot of the bed. "He said that turning down the offer from his client would not be good for my future health and well-being."

"That's all there was to it," Lockett said earnestly. "I swear it. I don't know what the client had in mind. You know my policy, Jones. I always deliver the exact message, word for word, that I was commissioned to carry and I never deliver any threat that could get me arrested."

"In that case, I will just have to use my imagination." Fallon said. "Which is not a good thing for your client. Go deliver that message."

"Of course, of course," Lockett said.

"I want it delivered exactly twenty-four hours from now," Fallon added.

"Always happy to oblige a long-standing client such as yourself, sir."

"Get out of here before I change my mind."

Lockett scrambled upright, grabbed the ski mask and headed for the patio door.

"My apologies, Miss Valdez," he said, skittering past Isabella. "Just business, nothing personal."

He vanished into the night.

Isabella turned on Fallon, outraged all over again. *"You let him go?"*

"He's a rat, but rodents have their place in the feeding chain." Fallon crossed the room to close the sliding glass door. "Occasionally he's my rat. Besides, I know how to find him."

"You've actually used that dreadful little man to deliver messages to people?"

"Lockett is a professional, and he has connections at all levels of our world."

"You mean the world of private investigators?"

"No, the community of people with talent. Sensitives inhabit the entire ecosphere of society. We've got our thieves, scam artists and drug runners, just like we've got our CEOs, academics and politicians. There are good guys and bad guys in our world just as there are in the rest of society. Lockett is one of the few people I know who can move from the streets to the boardroom to government circles and back again. In his own way, he's trustworthy. I've used him before and I'll probably use him again."

"I see." She sniffed. "Well, I suppose professional investigators like us have to be practical about this sort of thing."

"I'm afraid so. Talent is talent and in my experience, really good, reliable talent is hard to come by."

"He's a little weasel of a man, though."

"I'll give you that," Fallon said. "But if it's any comfort, he won't ever bother you again."

She thought about the panic in the Messenger's voice when, for a brief moment, he thought he was facing death at Fallon's hands. "I think you're right about that. What about the money?"

"Hang on a second." He took his phone

out of his pocket and punched in a code. "Dargan, it's Jones." There was a short pause. "What do you mean which Jones? Fallon Jones . . . You're right, I'm the only Jones who would be calling you at three o'clock in the morning. Unfortunately for both of us, you happen to be the best tracking hunter on my list in the Sedona area. I want you to keep tabs on a man named Kit Lockett. He'll be using some other name, but I'm going to e-mail you a photo and profile, which includes his home address, make and model of his car, credit card info and favorite bars. He just left the Cloud Resort here in Sedona. He'll be staying somewhere nearby. Find him and keep an eye on him."

Isabella folded her arms and listened while Fallon issued instructions with surgical precision.

"No, I don't want you to grab him," Fallon said. "I gave him a message to deliver to one of his clients twenty-four hours from now. He always does that part of his job in person so that there is no electronic trail; otherwise I'd have one of the cryptos handle this. He'll be making contact with someone soon. I want the name."

And suddenly Isabella understood.

Fallon closed the phone and dropped it

into his pocket. He paused, brows slightly elevated, when he saw Isabella looking at him.

"Of course," she said, satisfied. "You want to find out who tried to bribe me."

"That's the idea," Fallon said.

"Ha. I should have thought of that right away. Can't wait to see which dumbass in the Society thinks I can be bribed for a lousy hundred thou."

Fallon grinned briefly. "A *lousy* hundred thou?"

"Okay, so I've never seen that much money in one place at one time in my life. That's hardly the point."

"What is the point?"

"I am deeply offended. Pissed off, actually. My honor has been impugned or something."

"I'm a little irritated myself." He picked up the slip of paper that was on the console.

"Wonder what the client will do when he realizes I'm not going to take the money," Isabella said.

"I don't think the client cares whether or not you accept the bribe."

"What makes you say that?"

"The idea is to make sure that there's a trail from this account that leads straight back to you," Fallon explained. "Trust me, whoever goes looking will soon find out that it is in the name of Isabella Valdez. Word of the bribe will be all over Arcane within hours after the discovery is made."

"In other words, it's all about making me look guilty."

"Yes." Fallon opened the slider again and made a move onto the patio.

"Wait." She hurried to the door. "Where are you going?"

"Back to my room. I need to go online."

"What are you going to do?"

"Close that bank account and make sure there is no link to you."

"But what about the money?"

He kissed her lightly. "I've got a plan for that."

"What plan?"

"No reason it shouldn't go to a good cause. I'm going to transfer it into the Society's Foundation Trust."

She smiled. "Someone just made a generous donation to further paranormal research?"

"At the moment it's an anonymous donor," Fallon said. "But I hope to be in a position to personally thank the individual very soon."

26

The aging trailer sat on the last concrete slab in the last row of the Desert Palms Trailer Court. Fallon brought the rental car to a halt.

"This is it?" he asked.

"Yes." Isabella contemplated the trailer, afraid to open her other vision. There was a forlorn air of neglect about the place. The inside shades were pulled shut. "What if I'm wrong, Fallon? What if she really is dead?"

"We'll deal with that when we have more data."

She half smiled at his bracing, no-nonsense statement. "I love it when you do that, you know."

"When I do what?"

"Insist on collecting the facts before leaping to a conclusion."

He opened the door. "I've been told that it drives most people nuts."

"That's because they don't understand. I

really can't imagine why so many people think you're prone to finding conspiracies around every corner."

She got out and waited while he came around the car to join her.

"See anything?" he asked.

She knew what he meant.

"I'm afraid to look," she admitted.

"But you'll do it because you're an intrepid J&J investigator."

"There is that." She braced herself and raised her talent.

Energy enveloped the trailer. She drew a sharp breath.

Fallon watched her. "Something needs finding?"

"Yes." Jolted, she started forward. "Whatever it is, it's very hot. That means it's important. Oh, Fallon, I should have come here sooner."

"Take it easy." He caught up with her. "You handled things the way your grandmother wanted them handled. If there's something in that trailer to be found, we'll find it. In fact, she probably meant for you to find it with me, not on your own."

"Maybe." She dug the key out of her purse and went up the three steps.

The door of the neighboring trailer swung open. A woman with tightly permed blue hair peered out. "About time you showed up, Elly."

Isabella exchanged a quick glance with Fallon. She could tell that he understood that when she came here to visit her grandmother she used yet another ID.

"Hello, Mrs. Ragsdale," Isabella said politely. "Nice to see you again."

Mrs. Ragsdale glowered. "I suppose you didn't bother to come here until now because you didn't think that your grandmother left you anything of value, eh?"

"I've been busy dealing with her business affairs," Isabella said weakly. "Lawyers, wills, that sort of thing. You know how it goes with estates, even small ones."

"Bernice always said that if anything ever happened to her, you'd be along eventually to take charge of her things." Mrs. Ragsdale peered at Fallon. "Said when you did show up, you'd most likely be with a man."

Fallon looked at her. "Were you and Bernice good friends?"

"Played bridge every Wednesday and Friday night," Mrs. Ragsdale declared. "Bernice was a fine player."

Isabella tightened her grip on the key. "Were you here when my grandmother died, Mrs. Ragsdale?"

"Yep. Watching the late-night talk show.

She must have called the ambulance, herself." Mrs. Ragsdale sighed. "We all saw it pull up. They took her away. She never came out of the hospital. Heard later it was a heart attack. Everyone here at the Court is going to miss her, that's for sure."

"So will I," Isabella said. "If you'll excuse me, Mrs. Ragsdale, I need to get started on organizing her things."

"She said you'd probably give everything to charity except for the pictures, of course."

"Probably."

Mrs. Ragsdale cleared her throat. "I could take that old microwave of hers off your hands, if you like."

"I won't be able to make any final decisions today," Isabella said. "I just came to pick up her personal papers."

"And the pictures," Mrs. Ragsdale said. "She said that's all she had that would be important to you. She really wanted you to have the pictures. Told me to remind you when you turned up."

"I'll be sure to take them," Isabella said.

"I cleaned out her refrigerator and emptied her garbage," Mrs. Ragsdale said. "Didn't want things to spoil and stink up the place."

"That was very thoughtful of you," Isabella said.

Fallon looked at her with veiled interest. "You have a key?"

"Oh, yes, Bernice gave it to me a couple of weeks before she passed. She said she was having some chest pains and was getting concerned. I told her to go to the doctor, but she refused. Said it was just a bad stomach."

"Did anyone else stop by after she died?" Fallon asked.

"Nope." Mrs. Ragsdale paused. "Well, except the manager, of course. He comes by occasionally to check on things. Told me the only reason he hadn't sold Bernice's trailer and her things was because she had promised him that if anything happened to her, Elly, here, would pay him whatever was owed."

"Was the manager the only person who went inside the trailer besides you?" Fallon asked.

Mrs. Ragsdale snorted disapprovingly. "Nosy, aren't you, young man?"

To Isabella's amusement, Fallon gave the elderly woman his rare, wickedly charming smile, the one that should have been registered as a dangerous weapon.

"Been a while since anyone called me a young man," he said.

Mrs. Ragsdale responded right on cue.

Her faded eyes sparkled, and she suddenly glowed.

"It's all a matter of perspective," she said gruffly. "Trust me, at my age, you look young. In your prime, as they say." She gave Fallon a head-to-toe perusal. "Yep, in your prime and a mighty fine prime it is, too."

Isabella coughed discreetly.

Mrs. Ragsdale seemed to realize that she had gone off topic. She smiled warmly at Fallon. "To answer your question, the only other person I've seen go inside was the new man on the maintenance crew. He checked Bernice's trailer after it rained. Said he wanted to make sure there wasn't any water damage. Old trailers leak like sieves, you know."

"So, to the best of your knowledge, no one except you, the manager and the guy from maintenance has entered the trailer," Fallon concluded.

"Nope." Mrs. Ragsdale snorted. "Trust me, someone would have noticed straight off if an outsider got within fifty yards of that trailer. Everyone in the Court pays attention to everyone else's business. It's about all the entertainment we get. Some days it's more interesting around here than one of those reality TV shows."

"Thank you for looking after things," Isabella said.

"No trouble at all, dear. And I'm real sorry your grandmother is gone. She was a live wire. Kept up with all the latest news on her computer. Always seemed to know what was going on behind the scenes. Bridge won't be nearly as interesting without her. Let me know if you need anything. And don't forget about that microwave."

"I won't," Isabella promised.

She got the door of the trailer open. Stale, musty air spilled out. She took a breath and stepped inside. Fallon moved in behind her and shut the door.

Isabella looked around. The interior of the trailer lay in shadow, but it looked very much as it had the last time she had visited three months earlier. The small space was neat and carefully organized.

"Grandma always says that living in a trailer is like living on a boat," she said. "A place for everything and everything in its place."

"She was the methodical, organized type?"

"Oh, yes. To a fault."

"That makes it easy then. We just look for whatever seems wrong or out of place."

"Easy for you to say. Grandma may have been organized but she had a lot of stuff."

Fallon took in the tiny kitchen, the dining

340

nook, the bed and the miniature bathroom in a single sweeping glance.

"Where's her computer?" he said.

Startled, Isabella turned toward the dining nook. It took her a second or two to register what was wrong.

"It's gone," she said. "Grandma had a new laptop. I gave it to her. She kept it on the dining table. If she was going underground, that is the one thing she would have taken with her. But if someone did murder her, that is the one thing the killer would have grabbed."

"It is also the one thing that a thief looking for electronics to sell in order to support a drug habit would have stolen," Fallon said patiently.

"True." Isabella pulled herself together. "But you heard Mrs. Ragsdale. No one has been inside the trailer since the night Grandma was taken away."

"Except Mrs. Ragsdale," Fallon said. "And the manager. And some guy from the maintenance crew. I'm sure Mrs. Ragsdale does her best to keep on top of things, but she's a seriously senior citizen. Probably hard of hearing. And this trailer sits at the far end of the Court. Late at night a thief could have gotten inside without being seen."

"Not in this trailer park," Isabella said. "Everyone here is elderly."

"Your point?"

"Older people don't sleep well. Grandma said that this place was like a Vegas hotel. Someone is always watching because someone is always awake."

"I'm not trying to argue with you," Fallon said. "But the fact is that the computer is gone and there are a number of possible explanations. The one that has the highest probability is the theft scenario. It may have been ripped off by one of the maintenance crew or the manager or a burglar."

"Okay," Isabella said. "But there are other possibilities, right?"

"Yes, Isabella, there are other possibilities. They just aren't very likely."

"Unless my grandmother is alive."

Fallon started to methodically open and close the myriad built-in drawers and storage cabinets that lined the interior of the trailer. "If your grandmother is alive, that changes everything."

She watched him glance into another drawer. "What are you looking for?"

"Something else that looks wrong or out of place. Get busy. You're the one who knew her best. Take a good look around. Do it first without your talent. You don't want to miss what your normal senses can tell you. Too many agents rely on their psychic abilities and wind up missing obvious clues."

"Got it." Isabella opened the cabinet beneath the sink and peered inside at the half-empty bottle of dishwashing liquid. "You know, what Mrs. Ragsdale said about the pictures was sort of strange."

Fallon closed a drawer and looked at a calendar that hung on the wall. "Why was it strange?"

"Because in my family we never took photographs." Isabella felt sudden hot tears in her eyes. "I don't have a single picture of my parents or of my grandmother."

Fallon offered no sympathy. He was still studying the calendar. "I can understand that a dyed-in-the-wool conspiracy theorist like the Sentinel would not go in for family photo albums, especially in this day and age when the pictures might wind up online."

Isabella dashed away the tears with the back of her hand. "That's what Grandma said."

"So what pictures was she talking about?"

"I don't know. If she had any here in the trailer, she never told me about them." She closed another drawer. "Nothing looks strange or out of place, Fallon. Except for the missing computer, of course."

"All right, use your finder-vision. Your grandmother was aware of your talent. If she hid something that she wanted you to locate, it should be obvious to your para-senses."

Isabella opened her other sight carefully. She knew what to expect. Her grandmother's secretive nature had generated layer upon layer of fog in the trailer. But most of it was in the cool, gray zone.

The exception was the searing mist that swirled around the wall calendar. She took a closer look at it.

"That calendar is locked in hot fog," she said.

"Wrong month," Fallon said. "It should be showing the month that your grandmother was taken away in an ambulance."

Isabella felt her pulse kick up. "Maybe she wrote something important on one of the dates."

Fallon moved to stand directly in front of the calendar. Isabella joined him. Together they studied the colorful, glossy picture of a stretch of beach complete with crashing waves. The focal point of the shot was a large, oddly shaped rock. Eons of wind and tides had formed the stone into the shape of a roughly hewn arch.

"I don't understand," Isabella said. "It's

just a generic calendar landscape. The rock is a little unusual, though."

"Yes," Fallon said. "The rock is very unusual."

"I've seen rocks similar to that on the beach in Santa Cruz."

"That's not Santa Cruz," Fallon said.

He reached up to remove the thumbtack that secured the calendar to the wall.

Voices sounded outside. Mrs. Ragsdale was talking to someone.

"She just got here," Mrs. Ragsdale said. "About time, if you ask me. It's been a month since Bernice passed."

"Everyone handles this kind of loss in a different way, ma'am," was the response.

Isabella went cold.

"Fallon," she whispered.

He folded the small calendar, stuffed it inside his jacket and took out his gun.

There was a sharp rap on the door followed by a low, chillingly familiar male voice.

"I know you're in there, Angela, and I know that Jones is with you. I'm unarmed and I'm alone. Open the door. We need to talk."

"You know that guy?" Fallon asked, keeping his own voice equally low.

"It's my old boss at Lucan Protection Services, Julian Garrett. When I worked

345

there I used the name Angela Desmond. Julian's the one who set me up and then sent those two men to kidnap me in Phoenix."

"About time the guy from the maintenance crew showed up," Fallon said.

27

Fallon opened the trailer door, making sure to keep the gun out of Mrs. Ragsdale's line of sight. He made certain the man on the front steps got a clear look at it.

"Ah, shit," Julian Garrett said, weary and resigned. "Take it easy. I just want to talk to Angela. I swear, she's got it all wrong. No one is trying to hurt her."

"That's good," Fallon said. "Because anyone who lays a finger on her will wake up dead."

Julian was dressed in a green work shirt, pants and low boots. The logo for a company named Desert Sun Maintenance was stitched on the pocket of the shirt. Garrett looked to be in his midthirties. His gray eyes, high cheekbones and sharply etched features gave him the air of a lone wolf. There was energy in the atmosphere around him, a lot of it.

"Trust me, the last thing my boss wants

me to do is bring Arcane down on his neck," Julian said.

Isabella moved up behind Fallon and looked at Garrett. "My name is Isabella Valdez now, and if you don't want to hurt me, why did you send those two thugs to grab me in Phoenix?"

Julian glanced meaningfully over his shoulder and then lowered his voice another notch. "I admit that was badly handled. My men had instructions to pick you up, that's all. Look, I can explain everything. Mind if I come inside? I don't want to get too dramatic here, but there's a small matter of national security at stake."

"Oh, bullshit," Isabella said.

Julian's mouth tightened. He switched his attention back to Fallon. "Department A has done some jobs for some very black-arts agencies. Just like J&J."

Isabella rounded on Fallon. "You never told me that we do work for the Feds."

"We try to avoid those jobs," he said patiently. "But we have been known to do some consulting for certain agencies."

"Consulting." Julian's mouth twisted in a humorless smile. "Nice turn of phrase. It's the same kind of consulting work that Department A does at Lucan. And that's what this is all about." He looked at Isabella. "Give me five minutes. That's all I ask."

Fallon did not take his eyes off Julian. "What do you think, Isabella?"

"Well," she said. "I guess we can't just shoot him here in front of Mrs. Ragsdale. The gossip would be all over the Court in about twenty seconds. And then there's the problem of the body."

Julian winced.

"You're right," Fallon said. He realized he was starting to enjoy himself in a perverse way. "Probably be better to do the actual shooting somewhere else where there aren't any witnesses."

"Lot of desert out here," Isabella observed.

Julian's jaw tightened. "Very funny. Five minutes. That's all I'm asking."

Isabella stepped back. "Okay, there's not much he can do here in the Court. He's got the same problem that we've got, too many witnesses."

"True," Fallon said. He moved back but he kept the gun visible. "Five minutes."

"Thanks." Julian stepped into the trailer and pulled the door closed behind him. He gave Isabella a wry smile. "Isabella Valdez?"

"That's my name."

"Glad to meet you," Julian said dryly.

"You don't know how glad I am to see you."

"Can't say the same." She narrowed her eyes. "Did you kill my grandmother?"

"No, I swear it," Julian said. "I only discovered a few days ago that she even existed. When I finally tracked her down to this trailer park, hoping to find you, she was already dead. Heart attack, according to what I could determine." His expression softened. "I'm sorry for your loss."

"Yeah, right. Explain those two men in Phoenix if you can."

"As I said, Phoenix was a bungled operation. I apologize."

"For sending two men to kidnap me?" Isabella said, her voice rising. "You *apologize?*"

"You were never in any danger from that team," Julian said.

"They chased me up to the roof of a department store. They had guns. They were trying to grab me."

"Like I said, it was clumsy work and that was my fault." Julian shoved his fingers through his hair. "All I can say is that we were desperate to find you and bring you in before some really bad guys got to you first. I knew that you were running scared. I was afraid that if you got wind that anyone associated with Lucan was in the vicinity, you'd disappear again."

"Good guess," she said.

"I told the team to do whatever they had to do to bring you in. Figured I could explain everything once I met with you face-to-face. I made it clear you were not to be hurt. But you ditched my men and we lost you again."

"You set me up, damn it. You were dealing para-weapons out of Department A. You knew Max Lucan was getting suspicious, so you put that incriminating file on my office computer. As if I'd be dumb enough to actually use an office computer to keep a file that could get me fired or sent to prison. You don't think very highly of me, do you, Julian?"

"You were set up, all right," Julian said. "But not by me. Caitlin Phillips was the one dealing the para-weapons. She's the person who installed that file on your computer."

Isabella felt blindsided. "Caitlin?"

"My administrative assistant, remember?"

"Of course," Isabella said, struggling to process the new information.

"She resigned and then she disappeared. We think one of her connections in the black market killed her."

"I don't understand."

"After we found the file of para-weapons sales on your computer, Max and I tracked it back to Caitlin. But by then she was gone."

Isabella frowned. "If you know I'm innocent, why are you looking for me?"

"Because you're in danger. Listen to me, Isabella. Caitlin did one last deal before she was murdered. She arranged an acquisition for one of her clients, a South American drug lord. But the transaction was never completed because the broker got himself shot."

"That would be Orville Sloan?" Fallon asked, as if he were only remotely interested in the answer.

Julian frowned. "You know about Sloan?"

"J&J is a detective agency, if you will recall," Fallon said.

Julian sighed. "Right. Sloan was the broker Caitlin used. It looks like he was killed by a disgruntled client. It was bound to happen, sooner or later, given the nature of the profession. But the problem for us is the timing."

"I'm assuming that means that the broker was shot after he had arranged for the delivery of the artifact but before he told Caitlin Phillips where the package could be found," Fallon said.

"Yeah, that's about it." Julian turned back to Isabella. "Word of the missing artifact

352

has hit the underworld. A lot of people are looking for it, including the drug lord and a certain black-ops agency. The agency wants that para-weapon found before the drug lord gets it."

Isabella shrugged. "So?"

Julian cleared his throat. "Due to the rumors that circulated after you took off, a lot of people, including, we believe, the drug lord, think that you might be able to find the weapon."

"Crap," Isabella said. "Now I've got a drug lord looking for me?"

"Luckily I found you first. We have to recover that para-weapon and get it out of circulation. Once the drug lord realizes the Feds have it, he'll stop looking for you because you won't be of any use to him."

"Nice theory," Fallon said.

"For Pete's sake, Julian, I can't just pull missing stuff out of thin air," Isabella said. "That's not how my talent works. I need some kind of trail or a connection. Something."

"Take it easy," Julian said. "We know the general whereabouts of the weapon because we had a team following Sloan. But they lost him for a short time. When they picked him up again, they realized he no longer had the artifact. And then he got shot."

"Where did he leave the weapon?" Isabella asked.

"Turns out the broker had a thing about old movies," Julian said. "He went on a tour of the Vantara Estate. He had the artifact when he went into the mansion, but it wasn't on him when he came out. We think he left the weapon inside."

"You're talking about the old film star's house?" Isabella asked. "The mansion near Santa Barbara that's open to the public for tours?"

"That's it," Julian said, grim-faced. "Ever been there?"

"No," Isabella said.

"The house is an architectural monstrosity on the outside, but it's even more over-the-top inside," Julian said. "Dozens and dozens of rooms filled with an incredible amount of art and antiques. Sloan's intention was to get safely away from the estate before letting Caitlin know exactly where he had hidden the weapon."

Fallon thought about that. "Not a bad hiding place for a paranormal gun that in all likelihood won't look anything like a real gun."

"Tell me about it," Julian grumbled. "I've sent people inside the mansion posing as tourists. I even got one of my hunters hired

354

on as a night guard and had him take a look around. I went in myself twice. The mansion is crammed with antiques. It's like the basement of a very large museum in there. Talk about a needle in a haystack."

"Now you need Isabella to help you find the weapon," Fallon said.

Julian looked at him. "We're on the same side here, Jones. Arcane doesn't want a potentially dangerous para-weapon falling into the hands of some drug lord who happens to have a little talent any more than the black-ops people do."

"Agreed," Fallon said.

"One way or another, we have to recover that artifact," Julian said. "It's the only way to guarantee Isabella's safety. As long as the drug lord thinks she can find it, she's in danger."

Fallon looked at Isabella. "Your call."

She folded her arms and looked at Fallon. "Do you believe him?"

Fallon opened his senses again. Points of light appeared on the multidimensional grid. Connections sparked and flashed, and the sector in which Julian Garrett moved was starkly illuminated in both light and shadow.

"I think he's telling you part of the truth,"

he said. "And I can call Max Lucan to verify."

Julian looked at him. "You do that. Max will back me up."

Fallon took out his phone, ran through a list of contacts and punched in a number.

"Lucan? This is Fallon Jones. Yeah, that Jones. I'm with a woman who used to work with you. Called herself Angela Desmond. Her name is Isabella Valdez now. One of your people is here with us. Julian Garrett."

Fallon went silent, listening.

"Tell me about Caitlin Phillips," he said after a while.

More silence.

"All right," Fallon said eventually. "That's it for now. No, I don't know yet if Isabella will agree to look for the weapon. It's up to her. Hang on, I'll ask her." Fallon looked at Isabella. "Lucan confirms the facts that Garrett gave us. He says the black-ops people do want the artifact and so does the drug lord."

Julian looked at Isabella. "Satisfied? Do we have a deal?"

"I'll look for the para-weapon at the Vant-ara Estate," she said. "But no guarantees."

"Understood," Julian said. "Thanks."

She narrowed her eyes. "But I'm with J&J now. If you want to hire me, you have to pay our fees. We charge for this sort of work, you know. We're running a business here, not a philanthropic society."

Julian did not argue. "Name your price."

"Oh, we will," Isabella said.

Fallon spoke into the phone. "We'll take the case, Lucan."

He closed the phone.

Julian cleared his throat and smiled at Isabella. "So, uh, I've never actually watched you work. Do you need to examine something that belonged to the broker to pick up the scent or whatever it is you do?"

"I'm not a dog, Julian," she said.

Fallon did not say a word. He simply looked at Julian with a cold, unwavering stare. Energy crackled in the atmosphere.

Julian reddened. He closed his eyes briefly and then gave Isabella an apologetic smile. "Sorry. I didn't mean it that way. It's just that I never really understood how you do what you do. None of us did. All we knew was that you were the best tech we'd ever had in Department A. But I was under the impression that when you searched for something that was connected to an individual, you liked to get a psychic reading on the person."

"I'm a little touchy when it comes to how I work," Isabella said. "You're right. It would be helpful to have some physical contact with an object that the broker, Orville Sloan, also would have handled. The stronger his emotional connection to the item, the better."

"How about his computer?" Julian said. "He had it with him when he was shot. One of the hunters I had tracking him managed to grab it."

"That'll do nicely," Isabella said.

Fallon looked at Julian. "You can leave now. We'll meet you at the Vantara Estate tonight. I'll call you later with a time."

Julian's jaw tightened. "I don't like the idea of leaving Isabella unprotected."

"Don't worry about me," Isabella said. "I've been doing fine without any protection from Lucan for the past month."

"The drug lord is serious," Julian said.

Fallon looked at him. "So is J&J. Get out of here, Garrett."

Julian hesitated, clearly unhappy. But he seemed to realize he could not win the argument. He left.

Isabella waited until the door closed behind him. She uncrossed her arms and leaned back against the kitchen counter, hands braced on either side.

"So Caitlin Phillips was the one running the arms-dealing operation," she said. "I never would have guessed. But I suppose it makes sense. As Julian's administrative assistant, she had access to all the data and records and connections that Julian had."

"Maybe." Fallon pulled out his computer and set it on the dining table.

"When I look at Julian, I see lots of fog, but then I see that when I look at you as well," she mused. "Everyone has secrets."

"What are you getting at?"

"I'm a walking lost-and-found department, Fallon, not a human lie detector," Isabella said. "You're the one who can assess the subtle details and spot tiny inconsistencies. Do you really think Julian is telling the truth?"

"He definitely wants to recover that device and he needs you to do it. No question about that."

"But?"

"But I think he knows more about the nature of the weapon than he's letting on."

"Well, that's no surprise." She hesitated. "So Lucan really is working for a government client. And here I thought Julian was the one doing the illegal deals."

"It can get complicated in the black market."

Isabella was quiet for a moment.

"The beagle," she said, perfectly neutral.

He frowned. "What's that supposed to mean?"

"That's what Julian and the others used to call me behind my back when I worked for Lucan. Whenever one of the agents came up against a brick wall in an investigation, someone would say, get the beagle. She can find anything."

"Beagles are born to hunt."

She brightened. "Never thought of it like that."

"Doesn't matter now. You don't work for Lucan anymore."

"That's true." She looked around the trailer. Tears glistened in her eyes. "I guess I'm going to have to accept the fact that Grandma really did die of a heart attack."

"I'm ninety-seven percent sure that your grandmother is alive."

"What?"

He took the calendar out from under his jacket. "I think she left this picture behind because she knew that I'd be with you when you finally came here to the trailer park. She knew I'd recognize it. Your grandmother has gone to ground like the former intelligence agent that she probably is."

"Are you telling me that Grandma once worked for some secret agency?"

He studied the picture. "Got a hunch

she's hiding out with an old colleague."

"But that beach scene means nothing to me."

"It does to me." He held out the calendar so that she could read the caption beneath the photo.

"Eclipse Arch, Eclipse Bay, Oregon," Isabella read. She looked up. "Never heard of the place."

"I have. Your grandmother is safe, but we can't risk contacting her until this thing is over. She was right about one thing. Communication between the two of you at this juncture might put both of you in danger."

"You said if my grandmother was alive, it would change everything."

"Yes," Fallon said. "It does."

28

Shortly before midnight, Isabella stood with Fallon in the night-darkened gardens of the Vantara Estate. They were not alone. Julian and the Lucan agent who was posing as a security guard were with them. They all contemplated the theatrically illuminated mansion. With its pastiche of Baroque, Renaissance and Iberian architectural elements, the ornate structure looked like a fairy-tale castle.

"Got to admit, those old 1930s film stars knew how to do over-the-top," Fallon said.

Isabella smiled. "I like it."

"Let's go," Julian said. Urgency and impatience crackled in the atmosphere around him.

"I've got the code," the hunter said. "I'll let you into the house through one of the side doors. I turned off the alarm system just before you got here. You'll have the mansion to yourselves. You should be okay

362

if you stick to pencil flashlights, but don't turn on any lights in the main rooms. There's not a lot of traffic out here at night, but the county cops run regular patrols every couple of hours."

"I don't need visible spectrum light to do my job," Isabella said.

The hunter led them through a section of gardens steeped in shadows. He wielded a flashlight, but Isabella knew that he did not need it for himself. His preternatural night vision allowed him to move through the darkness as confidently as if the path were lit with floodlights.

He stopped at a discreetly concealed side door and punched in a code. The door opened. He ushered Isabella, Fallon and Julian into a hallway.

"Got the floor plan?" he asked.

"Yes," Julian said.

"I'll leave you to it, then," the hunter said. "I need to check in with company headquarters. Don't want to break routine or they might send someone to check."

He closed the door, plunging the hall into darkness.

Fallon switched on a pencil flashlight. Julian did the same. Isabella raised her talent.

There were always secrets aplenty in old houses and the Vantara mansion was no exception. Traces of psi fog swirled in the hallway. Layer upon layer of wispy mists indicated decades of small, private secrets that were nobody's business but that of the individuals who harbored them. Isabella suppressed her awareness of the old radiation and concentrated on the newer mysteries. As usual in a space that had been well traveled, there was a great deal of fog, including some very hot stuff that she recognized as having been left by the hunter.

"Nothing here that looks like it ever had any connection to your broker," she said.

Fallon consulted the map. "According to the team, he entered the mansion on a regularly scheduled tour. All the tours start in the Grand Hall."

"To the left," Julian said.

He led the way around the corner and down a long, high-ceilinged corridor paneled in rich, dark hardwood.

Isabella lowered her senses, not wanting to waste energy that she might need later for more nuanced detective work. Still, even when perceived with only a fraction of her talent, there was an abundance of fog to wade through. There were no such things as ghosts, but sometimes she wondered if down through the centuries, others endowed with her kind of talent had started the rumors of spirits from the Other Side. It was easy enough to imagine phantoms in the eerie light.

She followed Fallon and Julian through another doorway and into a heavy sea of fog.

"Whoa." She stopped abruptly, adjusting her senses down another notch. "This, I take it, is the Grand Hall?"

Even in darkness lit only by moonlight slanting through high, Gothic-style windows and the two thin beams of the flashlights, the vast space glowed with gilded splendor. The walls were hung with huge ancient tapestries depicting medieval hunting scenes. Marble tiles covered the floor. Heavy, ornate furniture adorned the room. Couches and chairs covered in velvet and embroidered brocades were arranged in groupings around tables inset with lapis and malachite. Massive chandeliers hung from the ceiling.

"We know for certain that the broker was in this room," Julian said. "He was seen entering. He exited the house with the rest of the tour group through the kitchens."

"There's a high probability that your broker had some serious talent in order to survive as long as he did in his line of work," Fallon said. He studied the cavernous space, keeping his flashlight aimed at the marble-tiled floor and the richly woven rugs. "Probably a strategy-talent or an intuitive."

"He definitely had some juice," Julian agreed, "although he seemed unaware of it."

"Strats and intuitives often take their psychic side for granted," Fallon said absently. He crossed the room to examine a wall of glass-fronted bookcases. "Their abilities don't strike them or those around them as unusual unless they are extremely powerful."

"If he did have some talent, he would have been jacked when he entered this hall," Isabella said.

"Right." Fallon aimed the beam of the flashlight at a gilded red lacquer console table. "He knew that what he was about to do was dangerous. There would have been a lot of adrenaline, and that means his senses would have bounced sky-high."

"Which would heat up the fog," Isabella said.

Julian frowned. "What fog?"

"Never mind," Isabella said. "Just give me a minute to take a closer look." She opened her senses slowly. "Sheesh. There's a ton of energy in here."

"What the hell are you talking about?" Julian demanded.

"This place gets half a million visitors a year, according to the brochure," Fallon said.

"Well, no wonder the mist is so thick," she said. "There's so much stuff in this house that anything smaller than a refrigerator would be hard to find unless you knew where to look."

"Damn it, Isabella," Julian said. "Can you handle this or not?"

"Oh, shut up, Julian," she said. "I don't work for you anymore, remember? I'm a J&J investigator now."

Fallon's shadowed smile bordered on the macabre.

Julian shut up.

Isabella ignored them both and concentrated on calibrating her senses. She tuned out the older fog, concentrating on the brighter, more recent traces. Then she refined the search further, looking for only the very hot, icy light that she had detected on the broker's computer.

And suddenly, there it was, the unique trail of searing fog that could only have been laid down by the broker.

"Got it," she said softly. "You're right, Fallon, he was running very hot. He was definitely nervous but mostly he was excited, thrilled."

"No surprise there," Julian said. "It was probably the biggest deal of his career."

Fallon watched Isabella. "You're in charge here. We'll follow you."

"This way," she said, confident now that she had the trail.

She went quickly up the wide, curving staircase at the far end of the Grand Hall to the second floor. The river of fog flowed along another paneled passageway, past rooms and chambers and alcoves that gleamed and glowed and glittered in the shadows.

"Wouldn't want to have to pay the utilities bill for this place," she said.

"It would be the salaries for the staff required to maintain the mansion that would ruin you financially," Fallon observed.

"Could you two try to stay focused here?" Julian muttered.

Isabella ignored him. So did Fallon.

She followed the searing mist down another hallway, past a large ballroom. She hated to admit it, but at times like this she did feel a little like a dog that had picked up the scent. Fallon's words floated through her head. *Born to hunt.* Somehow that made her talent sound a lot more impressive.

She rounded another corner and came to a halt. Fallon and Julian stopped behind her.

"What do you see?" Julian asked urgently.

She studied the energy on the carpet. "He went into this room," she said. "But the others on the tour did not."

Fallon aimed his flashlight at the doorway of the room. A velvet rope blocked the entrance. "He hung back, waited until the tour group had moved on and then he ducked under the rope."

"Looks like it," Isabella said.

Julian moved to stand beside Fallon. Together they speared the shadows with their penlights.

Isabella stood on tiptoe behind the men, trying to peer past the barricade created by their broad shoulders.

"How sweet," she said. "It's a little girl's bedroom."

"Vantara had a daughter," Julian said. "She inherited this place. Couldn't afford to maintain it so she sold it to the historical foundation that runs the tours."

The bedroom was a frilly fairyland of pink and white. The small bed was adorned with ruffles and flounces and covered with a herd of stuffed animals. Lacy curtains bracketed the windows. A child-sized dressing table and stool stood in one corner. Dolls, rocking horses and stuffed pandas littered the floor.

"I don't see anything that even remotely resembles a weapon," Julian said.

"No," Fallon agreed. "But there's something of a paranormal nature in here. I can feel the energy."

Isabella tapped the shoulders of both men. "Excuse me. Mind if I take a look?"

Fallon stepped back. So did Julian.

She ducked under the velvet rope and stepped into the bedroom, concentrating on the trail of fog.

The mists led straight to the top of a pink-and-gilt chest of drawers. For the first time, Isabella took out her own flashlight and switched it on. She started opening and closing the drawers. Most were crammed with dainty petticoats, nightgowns and other items that had been made for a little girl.

The bottom drawer was filled with small pink and white socks and a cauldron of boiling fog.

"Got it," Isabella said.

"What is it?" Julian asked urgently.

"Hang on." Isabella dug beneath the neatly arranged socks and saw an elaborately wrought hand mirror. She aimed the beam of the flashlight at the object and caught her breath. The mirror was spectacular. The gold-and-silver frame was intricately worked in an elaborate Baroque design that subtly incorporated ancient alchemical symbols. Strange crystals glittered in the light. Although the object looked as if it had been crafted during the seventeenth century, the glass was not dark with age.

Captivated, she reached down to grasp the curved handle.

Electricity sparked through her. She flinched but she did not let go.

"This thing is definitely hot," she said softly.

"Are you okay?" Fallon asked.

"I think so."

She looked into the mirror, aware that Fallon and Julian had come up behind her and were doing the same thing. They were all fascinated, she realized.

It was like looking into a pool of liquid mercury. She could almost see her image but not quite. The seemingly solid glass of the mirror appeared molten. Silver energy swirled just beneath the surface, compelling her to look deeper.

"It's incredible," she whispered.

"Lower your senses," Fallon ordered.

The razor-sharp words snapped her out of the mini-trance. Startled, she hastily cut her talent. The surface of the mirror took on a more normal appearance. She could still sense the power in the artifact, but it no longer exerted the strong pull that it had a few seconds earlier.

Julian plucked the mirror from her hand. Energy whipped the air around him. His triumphant excitement was palpable.

"Damn, you did it, Isabella," he breathed. "This has to be the para-weapon that the broker left here."

"But what does it do?" Isabella asked.

She half expected Fallon to respond. He was always the one with the answers. But for once he had nothing to offer.

"I told you, I don't know exactly how it works." Julian examined the back of the mirror. "All I can tell you is that the black-ops folks who hired Lucan to make the buy are willing to pay a hell of a lot to get it off the market."

"Time to go," Fallon said. "We got what we came for. Let's move."

The chillingly neutral quality of his voice sent a shiver of awareness through Isabella. Something was wrong. In that moment she knew that he had recognized the mirror and had some knowledge of its power.

She looked at him, but in the deep shadows it was impossible to read his face. She heightened her talent a little and saw the heat in Fallon's eyes. It was not the kind she associated with their lovemaking. Fallon was jacked and dangerous.

"Jones is right," Julian said. "Let's get the hell out of Dodge."

He went swiftly toward the doorway. Fallon grabbed Isabella's arm, his grip uncharacteristically rough. She turned to look at him in surprise. But he was already shoving her across the room toward the bed.

She landed with a jolt and a shocked gasp. When she opened her eyes, she saw that Julian had spun around in the doorway. The mirror in his hand flashed white-hot.

The room was suddenly ablaze with a blinding paranormal fire. Isabella realized that although she could still see and hear and feel, she felt terrifyingly numb. It took her a heartbeat to understand that was because her para-senses were frozen.

She was vaguely aware that Fallon was in motion, launching himself through the raging storm of psi. He slammed into Julian. His momentum took both of them to the floor in the hallway. They landed with a sickening thud.

The energy storm cut off abruptly when Julian lost his grip on the mirror. But when Isabella tried to raise her talent, she discovered that her senses were still numb.

The sickening sounds of hand-to-hand combat brought her up off the bed. She found the flashlight she had dropped and staggered across the room to the doorway. She had to grip the frame to stay on her feet.

Fallon and Julian were locked in a cage fight because of the narrow confines of the hallway. The primal nature of the battle sent a nauseating wave of panic through Isabella. Fists rose and fell, smashing again and again into muscular flesh. Boots and shoulders struck the wall. She caught glimpses of blood as the two men heaved and rolled and collided again and again.

A lethally thin blade flashed evilly in the shadows. She could not tell which man gripped the knife. But in the next moment she heard a terrible crack. Fallon had slammed Julian's hand against the floor.

The knife dropped on the carpet. Julian howled, rolled onto his side and clutched his broken wrist.

"Bastard," he snarled. "You son of a bitch. You should be dead."

"You're not the first person to tell me that." Fallon got to his feet. There was blood on his face. He took his gun out from under his black leather jacket. "The Quicksilver

Mirror can kill," Fallon said. "But only in the hands of a talent who is powerful enough to control the maximum amount of energy latent in it. You just weren't strong enough, Garrett."

"Shit." Julian groaned. He sat up, cradling his injured wrist. "The last thing I need is a lecture on para-physics from Fallon Jones. Just shoot me now."

"Good idea," Isabella said.

Fallon looked at her. "Are you okay?"

"Yes — no." Another flicker of panic shivered through her. "Fallon, my senses are frozen."

"So are mine." Keeping the gun trained on Julian, he picked up the mirror. "But they'll recover in time. If the mirror doesn't kill you, the effects are temporary."

"Oh, good. For a moment there I was a little worried."

Fallon prodded the groaning Julian. "On your feet. We're leaving before the maintenance people show up and start asking a lot of questions about the damage to the hall-way."

Julian got to his knees. "How the hell do you plan to get me out of here? That's my hunter who's standing guard down there."

"Not anymore," Fallon said. "After he got us inside, he was replaced by a J&J agent. I called in some talent from L.A."

Julian's face twisted in disgust. "How did you figure it out?"

"I didn't know you were after the Quicksilver Mirror until I saw the damn thing," Fallon said. "But there were a few details that didn't sit right. You gave off the vibes of a guy who was working his own agenda. What pissed me off and made me decide that you were one of the bad guys was how you used Isabella and then sent that hunter team to grab her in Phoenix when you discovered that you needed her after all. That's no way to treat a lady, Garrett."

Julian shot Isabella a fulminating look. She gave him her most dazzling smile.

"I was following Lucan's orders," Julian said, turning sullen.

"I called Lucan again after you left the trailer today. Gave him a different theory of the crime. He agreed to play it out and see what happened."

"Whose theory of the crime?" Julian demanded.

"Isabella's. I've learned the hard way not to ignore the gut reaction of a trained investigator. She was sure you were behind the arms dealing in Department A."

"She's not an investigator — she's just a

finder-talent," Julian muttered. "A technician."

"Who is now a full-fledged investigator at J&J," Fallon concluded.

Isabella picked up a flashlight and aimed the beam at Julian's battered face. "What's this all about Julian? What kind of operation were you running? And what really happened to Caitlin Phillips?"

Julian said nothing.

Fallon turned thoughtful. "I think you were right, Isabella. There was something going on inside Department A. Garrett and Caitlin Phillips were running a small, private arms-dealing operation. They had a buyer for the mirror, but I doubt that it was one of Lucan's black-ops clients. They set up the deal with the broker, Sloan, who chose the mansion as the drop point. But things fell apart when Sloan got shot before he could tell Garrett and Phillips where he had hidden the mirror. So they went looking for you."

"At that point you knew that you would need the resources of Lucan's company to find me, didn't you, Julian? And once you did grab me, you knew you would need my full cooperation. That wasn't likely as long as Lucan and everyone else thought I was guilty of arms dealing. So you changed your story to point the finger of blame at poor Caitlin Phillips. You killed her, didn't you? You planted evidence in her house to make Lucan believe that she was the guilty party."

"Have fun weaving your little conspiracy fantasy," Julian said. "You can't prove a damn thing. The worst you can do is get me fired."

"No," Fallon said. "That's not actually the worst thing I can do."

"We both know you're not going to murder me in cold blood and dump my body." Julian managed a hoarse chuckle. "Give me a break — J&J doesn't work that way."

"Don't be so sure of that," Isabella warned.

Fallon raised his brows. "We're supposed to be the good guys, remember?"

"Well, yes," she grumbled. "But we decided that there are exceptions to every rule, remember? And Julian constitutes a really big exception if you ask me."

"He is, but as it happens, Garrett isn't our problem. Max Lucan hired him. He can terminate his own employees. No reason we should do his job for him."

Julian went very still. "It will be your word against mine."

Fallon's smile widened. "Then you have nothing to worry about, do you? Go on, get out of here."

Julian looked flummoxed. "What the hell are you trying to pull, Jones?"

"You're right. I can't prove a thing, so get lost while I'm still in a good mood."

Julian scrambled to his feet. "What happens to the mirror?"

"It goes back to its rightful owner."

Julian grimaced. "Guess I should have seen that coming."

He half loped, half limped down the hall and disappeared around a corner. Isabella drummed her fingers on the side of the door frame.

"I really hate to see him go free like that," she said. "It's not right."

"Maybe not," Fallon said. With one hand he pulled a pristine handkerchief out of his pocket and wiped his cheek. He used his other hand to take out his phone. "But letting him run might give us the answer to one lingering question."

Isabella speared the flashlight at Fallon. Blood glistened on his jaw and dripped down the front of his jacket.

"You're *bleeding*," she wailed.

He looked down at the handkerchief. "Yeah."

She rushed to him, took the handkerchief from his hand and gently blotted up more of the blood.

"You need to sit down," she ordered. "You could go into shock."

"I don't think so," he said. "Let's get out of here."

He started to bend down to pick up the mirror but stopped midway, groaning a little, and gingerly reached inside his jacket.

"I'll get it," Isabella said quickly.

"Thanks." Fallon spoke into the phone. "He's running. Don't lose him. He's injured and will probably seek medical help. Don't interfere. Just keep an eye on him until one of Lucan's people takes over."

He ended the call and punched in another number. "Max? Jones here. Isabella was right about everything. Looks like Caitlin Phillips is most likely dead. She was Garrett's partner, but he needed another fall guy after he realized he required Isabella's help to locate the artifact. What is it? The Quicksilver Mirror. Yeah. Worth a fortune in some quarters. We've got it and Garrett is running. I've got a hunter following him until you can get someone on it. I'll give you the whole story tomorrow. What? Of course we'll send you our bill."

He closed the phone.

Isabella picked up the mirror and took Fallon's arm to steady him, although he did not seem to be wobbly. She drew him carefully down the staircase.

"What's the one lingering question?" she asked.

"The name of the person who commissioned the Quicksilver Mirror."

"You let Julian run because you want to know the identity of his buyer."

"Well, that plus the fact that there wasn't anything else I could do with him except try to convince the local cops that he's guilty of breaking and entering and something tells me that wouldn't fly."

"But Garrett doesn't have the mirror to sell now. Why would he contact the buyer?"

"He might not," Fallon said. "But I'm thinking there's a high probability that the buyer will contact him."

"Why?"

"Because we are not going to let it be known that Arcane recovered the mirror," Fallon said patiently. "That will be our little secret."

A cold thrill of comprehension swept through Isabella. "You think that the buyer will believe he's been double-crossed. That Julian has sold the mirror to someone else."

"It's been my experience that not only is there no honor among thieves, but there's also not a hell of a lot of trust or mutual affection, either. What's more, that type tends to be vindictive."

"One more thing. You said the mirror is going back to the rightful owner."

"Yes."

"Who is that?"

"The Arcane Society. The Quicksilver Mirror was stolen from one of the museums."

"Oh, geez. That raises some troubling questions doesn't it?"

"Sure does," Fallon said.

29

"Caitlin Phillips's body was found buried in her own backyard," Max Lucan said. "Looks like she was drugged and then strangled. Garrett has gone to ground in a third-rate motel outside of Sacramento. I've got a team on him. I'll let you know if he contacts anyone or if someone attempts to contact him."

"Don't let the disgruntled customer get to them first," Fallon warned.

"In spite of recent evidence to the contrary," Max said, "my people do know what they're doing."

"Too bad *you* didn't know what they were doing," Isabella said.

Fallon looked at her. "Play nice, Isabella. We need Max's help at the moment."

She wrinkled her nose. "Oh, all right."

Max raised his brows at Fallon. "Vindictive, isn't she?"

"Not usually," Fallon said. "But this

particular situation is a little different."

It was the day after the events at the mansion. The three of them were sitting in the executive suite of Lucan Protection Services. It occurred to Isabella that although she had worked for Lucan for nearly six months, she had never been in Max Lucan's office. Her career path was clearly trending upward. When you worked for J&J, you got some respect.

She had not been keen on the idea of coming face-to-face with her former boss on his own turf, but Fallon had said that it was important for her to be seen in the company of the president and CEO. It was, he claimed, the quickest and most efficient way of dispelling any lingering gossip about her. She knew he was right, but it made her uneasy. A lot of people were now aware of her real name, she thought. Her life was getting complicated. Then, again, maybe that was what happened when you finally got a life of your very own.

"Garrett and Phillips were running their little side business out of Department A," Max said. "Looks like it was going on for damn near a year. They were obtaining weapons-grade paranormal artifacts and selling them to buyers on the black market. Orville Sloan was the broker who handled the arrangements."

"They had to be very careful because they knew that your company has an agreement with Arcane," Fallon said.

"Any devices or antiquities that appear to be potentially dangerous must first be evaluated by one of the Society's labs," Isabella stated. "If they are found to be weapons-grade, they must be dismantled or rendered inoperable. If that is not possible, the artifacts go into cold storage in a secure vault until such time as the techs can figure out how to de-energize them."

Both men looked at her. She gave them her most charming smile.

"Sorry if I'm lecturing," she said sweetly. "But you deserve it, Mr. Lucan. You actually thought I was the one behind the illegal arms sales. How could you believe such a thing?"

Max fixed her with a considering expression. "Maybe because you ran?"

"I ran because I found those files on my computer and I knew I'd been set up."

"You should have come directly to me."

"Oh, yeah, like you would have believed me instead of Julian."

"And maybe I liked you for the dealer, because of all the people I've got working in Department A, you're the one with the talent to pull it off," Max said.

"So my talent made me look good for the part of the bad guy, is that it?"

"It was certainly a major factor."

She thought about that. "Okay, that's a much better reason."

Fallon's eyes gleamed with amusement but he said nothing.

"There was also the fact that you were a relatively new hire," Max continued. "You'd been here less than six months. And when I pulled your personnel file, I got a real queasy feeling."

She was incensed. "What was wrong with my file? It was perfect."

"A little too perfect," Max said. "Trying to track down your previous employers or close relatives turned out to be impossible. It was as if you were a ghost."

"Good description," Fallon said. "I ran into the same problem when I hired her."

Isabella gave him her most repressive glare.

"On the other hand, Garrett and Phillips had been working for me for a few years and had an impressive track record," Max continued. "In addition, they were very convincing. When Caitlin vanished under suspicious circumstances and Garrett made a production out of finding the record of the last deal with Sloan, I gave Garrett everything he needed to track you down."

"All he cared about was recovering the mirror," Isabella said. "After that he probably planned to pull the plug on his career at Lucan and disappear with the artifact."

"I may have to rethink my employee benefits program," Max said. "Clearly I'm not offering a competitive salary package. I've lost three high-level talents this month. You, Phillips and Garrett."

Isabella glared. "That is not amusing, Mr. Lucan."

"You have my most sincere apologies," Max said.

"Fat lot of good that would have done me if I hadn't had J&J watching my back."

Fallon stirred ever so slightly. "I think it would be a good idea if we all stay focused here. Is there a drug lord involved in this thing?"

"No," Max said. "Looks like Julian embellished that story a bit. But a certain black-ops agency did pick up the rumors of the artifact and asked Lucan to try to get it off the market."

"Well, Julian certainly had a client," Isabella said. "And I doubt very much that it was a spy agency."

"We're still waiting for him to come out

of the woodwork," Max assured her. "Don't worry, if and when he shows up, we'll grab him."

"Surely you have a list of possible suspects," she said.

"We do," Max said. "We're checking it, trust me."

"For heaven's sake, how many collectors would be interested in old weapons infused with paranormal properties?"

Max and Fallon looked at each other. Fallon shrugged. So did Max.

Isabella sighed. "Okay, more than a handful, I take it."

"You'd be surprised," Max said.

"We've got two problems," Fallon said. "We need to find both the client and whoever was supplying Phillips and Garrett with the para-weapons." He looked at Max. "I take it that you didn't come up with anything helpful on Sloan's computer?"

"My people are still digging but so far nothing," Max said. "Sloan was a very careful man. Which makes me wonder who got to him."

"Given the timing of his death, I'm thinking whoever was supplying him with the para-guns was the one who shot him," Fallon said.

"Really?" Isabella asked, fascinated.

Max frowned. "Hadn't thought about that possibility."

"But why would the person who was obtaining the weapons want to ice the broker?" Isabella asked. "And why kill him before the mirror sale was completed. Seems to me the supplier needed Sloan just as much as Caitlin and Julian did."

"That may have changed," Fallon said. "Arms dealing is a dangerous line of work. Lot of tough competition. We can assume that the supplier concluded that he no longer needed Sloan and that the broker had become a liability."

"Sloan was the one person with a direct connection to the supplier," Max said. "With the broker out of the picture, there is no one who can identify the person who provided the weapons to him. I agree with you, Fallon. Sloan's death was no coincidence. The supplier was severing all connections in preparation for firing up a new business arrangement."

"But what about the mirror?" Isabella said. "It was worth a lot of money and it was good as lost in the Vantara mansion."

"Looks like in the grand scheme of things, the mirror was no longer important," Fallon said. "The loss of the artifact was minor collateral damage."

Max leaned back in his chair. "Which makes you wonder what the supplier's new business arrangements look like."

"Yes," Fallon said. "It does. It also makes you wonder what he plans to sell next."

Isabella shivered. "Whoever it is must think he can make a lot more money with his new partners than he could with Caitlin and Julian."

Fallon contemplated Max. "Keeping an eye on Garrett and identifying the client who commissioned him to acquire the mirror is your problem. You know the paranormal black market better than anyone, including me. The supplier, however, is a J&J problem."

"I agree," Max said. "The Quicksilver Mirror came out of an Arcane museum. It probably wasn't the first artifact that Phillips and Garrett got from that source."

"Got a hunch someone has been cleaning out the museum basements for a while," Fallon said. "Easy to see how it could happen. The Society has been collecting for more than four hundred years. Like most museums, most of the collection is in storage. Who would notice if occasionally a couple of items went missing?"

"I'll leave the problem of identifying the supplier to you, Jones." Max sat forward.

"Been meaning to ask you, where did you get the black eye? You look like you fell off a cliff."

Fallon touched his ribs and winced. "Feels like it, too."

Max opened the bottom drawer of his desk and took out a bottle of whiskey. "Try some of this stuff. Good for what ails you."

"Thanks." Fallon eyed the bottle. "I believe I will."

"Hold it right there." Isabella held up a hand. "Is this some kind of male bonding ritual?"

"It's what colleagues in the investigation business do occasionally when they are working a case together," Max said.

"Got it." Isabella smiled. "Pour me a glass as long as you're at it. I'm in the investigation business, too, remember?"

Fallon smiled his rare smile. "Not likely to forget."

Fallon's phone rang just as they walked out the front door of the office tower. Isabella waited while he took the call.

"Dargan. What have you got for me? Right. No surprise. I thought that might be it. You're done. Send us the bill. What do you mean, who is us? I've got a new full-time assistant and investigator. I'm not the only one in the office anymore."

He closed the phone.

"Dargan ID'd the Messenger's client?" Isabella asked.

"Carolyn Austin. Jenny's mother."

30

Walker finished a circuit around the gas station and garage. All was well. He walked past Stokes's Grocery, turned right and started to work his way back through town, following the usual pattern of his rounds.

It was three in the morning. Every window was dark, even the one on the second floor of Jones & Jones.

Fallon Jones and Isabella Valdez were still out of town. Walker was worried about them. The pressure in his head told him that they were in danger but there was nothing he could do except guard the office and Isabella's apartment. Jones would take good care of Isabella, he told himself. Jones was strong.

He walked past the inn and then went around behind Seaweed Harvest. Methodically he checked out the backyards, parking areas and garbage cans behind the shops. You never knew what you were going to find in the trash.

The pressure in his head rose suddenly when he went past the back of the Sunshine. He walked faster, letting the pressure guide him. He was on the road that led to the highway now. He rarely walked this far beyond the town limits. He searched the shadows on either side of the pavement with his special vision.

He spotted the dark, hulking outline of the SUV parked in the trees alongside the road. The headlights were off. As he watched, a man and a woman opened the doors and got out. They started walking through the trees, heading toward town. The man led the way, moving with an easy confidence that indicated he, too, possessed a special kind of vision. The woman, however, stumbled and came to a halt.

"Not so fast," she said. "I know you can see where you're going, but I can't."

"I'll guide you." The man moved back to take her hand.

Outsiders, Walker thought. They did not belong in the Cove.

He started toward the vehicle, walking very fast now.

"Shit," the man whispered. "Some guy is coming this way. Doesn't move like a hunter, but I think he's got night vision."

"Must be the one they call Walker. Everyone says he's a nut."

"Crazy or not, he's seen us. Want me to take him out?"

"Yes," the woman said. "Hurry. But make it clean. No blood. No evidence. We'll dump the body in the ocean off the Point. He's a known crazy. Everyone will think he jumped."

"A broken neck will fit that scenario."

The man plunged toward Walker, tearing through the trees like a big hunting cat intent on bringing down a deer.

Walker did not move. He knew his special vision would protect him.

The attacker pulled up sharply a couple of yards away. He turned on his heel, searching the trees.

"Lost him," he snarled. "The bastard is good. Never even saw him move."

Because I didn't move, Walker thought.

"Find him," the woman ordered. "He's seen both of us."

"He's not here, I'm telling you. He got away."

"A talent of some kind," the woman said. "All right, let's get out of here. I need to think."

They scrambled into the front seat of the SUV. The engine roared to life. The headlights came up. The heavy vehicle wheeled back onto the road and sped off, heading toward the highway.

Walker stood guard until dawn but the intruders did not return. When the sun rose, he walked back into town. The muffins were sitting on a plastic plate on top of the trash can lid behind the Sunshine, as usual. He could hear Marge rattling pots and pans in the kitchen.

He thought about talking to Marge. But it wouldn't do any good to tell her what had happened. She would not know what to do. No one else in town would know what to do, either. The only one who could handle the problem of the intruders was Fallon Jones.

There was no way around it, Walker concluded. He would have to wait until Jones returned to the Cove. He had overheard Marge tell one of the regulars that Fallon and Isabella were due back this morning. In the meantime, he would take his bath in the hot springs out at the Point and do his daily meditation. The waters of the hot springs always calmed him and his head always felt more clear after a couple of hours of meditation.

He could usually sleep after the bath and meditation ritual. By the time he woke up

Fallon Jones would be back in town. Jones would know what to do.

At nine o'clock, his inner agitation temporarily soothed by the waters of the spring and the meditation ritual, he walked back to his cabin to sleep for an hour or two.

The music of the waltz invaded his fevered dreams. He awoke, the anxiety slamming back as it always did. The pressure in his head was excruciating this time. He managed to get out of bed and stagger down the hall to the small living room.

The music grew louder and more relentless. He thought his skull might explode.

He collapsed on the rug. The violent energy of the waltz carried him off into the night.

31

Marge folded her elbows on the counter and gave Isabella an expectant look.

"Well?" she said. "Did you have a good time at the ball, Cinderella?"

Isabella sipped her tea and swiveled slowly from side to side on the stool while she considered her answer.

"It was very exciting," she said, choosing her words with care.

"Any pictures?" Marge asked.

"No, to be honest, I didn't even think about taking pictures."

"Darn."

The bell over the door chimed. Violet and Patty walked into the café, raincoats dripping.

"We came for a full report," Violet announced. "Are there pictures?"

Isabella set down her mug. "I was just explaining to Marge that there are no photos. To tell you the truth, things got a little complicated down in Sedona. This guy broke into my room and tried to bribe me to make it look as if I was on the take and Fallon had to beat him up. Then we went to Cactus Springs to check out my grandmother's trailer and another guy showed up who convinced us to help him find an old artifact. When I located the artifact, he tried to kill Fallon, and Fallon had to beat him up, too, and then we came home."

Marge, Violet and Patty exchanged looks.

Marge frowned at Isabella. "That's it?"

"Pretty much," Isabella said.

"Gee," Violet said. "Guess that's the last time we let you and Fallon go off on a romantic getaway trip."

Marge shook her head. "I can't believe it. We send the two of you off to a glamorous ball with a beautiful gown and glass slippers, and you and Fallon end up getting attacked?"

"The best part is that I found out my grandmother is alive, but I can't contact her yet because it might put her in jeopardy."

Violet looked blank. "I thought you said your grandmother was dead?"

"Fallon is sure she is okay. She's gone underground until we wrap up the case."

Marge's brows rose. "Your grandmother sounds like a very interesting woman."

"She is," Isabella assured her. "All in all, it was a very busy trip, but it's good to be home."

"You can take the girl out of Scargill Cove but you can't take the Cove out of the girl," Patty said. "Welcome home, Cinderella."

"Thanks," Isabella said. "If it's any consolation, I can tell you that Fallon looked great in a tux."

Marge smiled. "I'd have paid good money to see Jones in a tux."

"Worth every penny, trust me," Isabella said.

Violet laughed.

Marge snorted and straightened. She looked at Patty and Violet. "You two want coffee?"

"Of course," Patty said.

She plunked herself down on one of the stools. Violet hopped up onto another one.

Marge went to the coffee machine.

"Anyone seen Walker today?" Isabella asked.

"The muffins are gone," Marge said. "So he must have come by on his morning rounds."

"He's probably at the hot springs," Violet said. "He spends a lot of time there during the daylight hours. Why?"

"I don't know," Isabella said. "For some

reason, I've been thinking about him a lot this morning."

Marge poured coffee into two mugs. "Don't worry, he'll show up sooner or later."

Isabella slipped off the stool. "I'm going to the grocery store to collect the mail. But first, I'll drop by Walker's place and see if he's there. Maybe he's ill."

"Just be sure you don't do anything to startle him," Marge warned.

"I'll be careful," Isabella promised.

She slipped into her yellow raincoat, collected her umbrella and went outside onto the street. She paused briefly and looked up at the window of Jones & Jones. Fallon was not visible. She knew that he was probably at the computer, phone to his ear, multitasking as he searched for a trace of the person who had supplied the Quicksilver Mirror to Sloan.

She walked to the end of the street and followed the bluff path to the weathered cabin that Walker called home. The cabin looked much the same as it always did, lonely and forlorn. But it always seemed to her that there was a certain stalwart air about the place, as if the cabin would persevere, regardless of the ravages of time and the elements. Walker had infused the place with his own energy and aura, she thought.

She went up the tumbledown steps, careful to avoid the broken middle tread, and then stopped. The shades were pulled down but that was par for the course with Walker. There was no smoke from the chimney but that, too, was normal. Still, something in the atmosphere was raising goose bumps on her arms. She opened her senses.

A terrible cold fog enveloped the cabin. Walker's home was always awash in a haze of secrets, but until now, the mists had been tinted with the chill of old mysteries. Not today.

Today the fog seethed and burned with the ominous dark radiance that warned of impending death.

Heedless of Marge's advice, she pounded on the door.

"Walker, it's me, Isabella. Are you in there?"

For the first time she became aware of the faint notes of a delicate melody. The light, tinkling strains of the waltz were barely discernible above the crashing of the waves below the bluffs. There was an eerie undercurrent in the music that rattled her senses. Her intuition was screaming at her.

Run.

She was suddenly certain beyond a

shadow of a doubt that Walker was in mortal danger.

Pushing past the panic, she twisted the old knob, expecting to find the door locked. But to her surprise, it opened. The music was louder now. Searing fog swirled in the small, rustic front room. Walker lay unmoving on the floor in the center of the energy storm.

"Walker."

She moved into the room and crouched beside him, searching for a pulse. Relief swept through her when she found one. Walker was alive but unconscious. There was no blood. She ran her hands through his unkempt hair but found no signs of a wound.

The music seemed to be getting louder now. For some reason the icy strains of the waltz made it hard to think.

She glanced around, looking for the source of the disturbing music. An elegant gilt-and-enamel music box sat on a small table. The glass lid was raised. Two tiny dancers, a man and a woman, dressed in late-nineteenth-century ballroom attire, twirled slowly, their movements jerky.

The box looked Victorian.

It was getting harder to see now. The room was spinning slowly around her. She had to get outside.

She heard footsteps in the short hallway. A figure wearing a set of high-tech head-phones appeared.

"Oh, crap," Isabella said.

Frantically she called on her talent, and for a few seconds, she was able to push back the dark waves of the waltz that threatened to drown her.

She jammed a hand into the pocket of her raincoat. The business card was still there. Clutching it in her fingers, she crumpled to the floor.

Fallon would come looking for her. He would notice every detail that seemed wrong or out of place. A business card did not fit into Walker's decorating scheme.

The steady beat of the waltz was in control now. She could not fight it any longer.

The music pulled her into an endless night.

32

"Wyman Austin came to see me this morning," Zack said. "Told me that he's resigning from his seat on the Council. The official reason will be the usual."

Fallon cradled the phone against his ear and propped his heels on the corner of his desk. "He wants to retire and spend more time with family and friends?"

The call from Zack was important but Fallon was having a hard time focusing on the conversation. An unpleasant restlessness had set his senses on edge.

"Right," Zack said. "The steam has already gone out of the rumors. Word is spreading fast that Carolyn Austin started them. This morning I had a conversation with Hector Guerrero and Marilyn Houston. They are both convinced now that the Council will vote to continue funding J&J and the Nightshade project."

"Good, because it isn't finished yet."

Fallon rubbed the back of his neck, trying to get rid of the tension that had been building within him for the past few minutes.

"I agree," Zack said. "Wyman Austin explained that Jenny finally told him the full story of what really happened the night Tucker died, including her role in it. She had been trying to protect her parents from finding out what kind of man her brother really was and dealing with her own guilt. I'm sure you're aware that Carolyn Austin went into a very deep depression after the loss of her son."

"Yes."

"Took more than a year for her to recover. When she did, she became obsessed with revenge. She blamed you and the rest of the Joneses. She set out to try to destroy the family's grip on Arcane."

"Sure," Fallon said. "I understand vengeance. It's a solid motive, but there's something wrong with the timing here."

"What do you mean?"

"It's been almost three years since Tucker died. Why go after the Jones family now?"

There was a long pause on the other end of the connection.

"Must have taken Carolyn that long to concoct a plan."

"I don't think it was her plan."

"Got any ideas?" Zack asked.

"I've got a feeling that someone played on Carolyn Austin's obsession with revenge. That person suggested a way to destroy the Jones family's grip on Arcane, and Carolyn ran with it."

"You're thinking Nightshade, aren't you?"

"Yes."

"I'll let you work that angle. I've got a budget to get through my Council while everyone is feeling more charitable towards J&J."

"Congratulations," Fallon said. "The Jones show of force seems to have worked."

Zack laughed. "I don't think that filling the room with a lot of Joneses was what turned the tide."

"Maybe it was my new status as a psychic Sherlock Holmes."

"Don't knock it. Isabella's defense of your investigational talents is definitely proving to be an asset. Several key members of the Council are now referring to you as Sherlock."

Fallon groaned. "Just what I need."

"Goes to show that language is everything," Zack said. "You can thank your new assistant for giving you a new image within Arcane."

"You can thank her for Wyman Austin's

resignation, too."

"Yeah?" Zack sounded interested.

"Jenny and I had a long talk out on the hotel terrace. Isabella was there. She helped Jenny deal with what happened on the night of Tucker's death. There was a lot of crying, and afterward Jenny seemed relieved or something."

"Thanks to Isabella?"

"Yes."

"Lot of good energy around your new assistant," Zack said.

"She's a full investigator here at the firm now."

"Right. So when are you going to marry her and make her a partner?"

Fallon felt something snap inside him. *"It's not that easy, damn it."*

"Hey, hey, calm down, cousin. Didn't mean to shock you. I just assumed —"

"When it comes to Isabella, don't ever assume anything." Fallon surged to his feet, phone clenched in his hand. "You think it's easy to marry her?"

"Well, Aunt Maryann approves of her. She told your folks that it was a perfect match. Naturally your parents told mine."

"And now everyone in the family thinks I'm going to marry Isabella?"

"It would seem to be the logical next

step," Zack said, speaking carefully now.

"This hasn't got a damn thing to do with logic."

"With you, everything comes down to logic. Am I missing something in this equation?"

"People in Isabella's family don't get married," Fallon said through his teeth.

"Some kind of religious thing?"

"Some kind of conspiracy theory thing. Marriages mean licenses. Isabella was raised not to leave a paper trail. She doesn't even have a birth certificate."

"So we're just talking about a piece of paper?"

Fallon exhaled slowly, forcing himself to regain control. "I'm overreacting here, aren't I?"

"You do sound uncharacteristically emotional," Zack agreed. "But you're a Jones and you're in love. We get emotional about this kind of stuff in our family."

"It's not just the license," Fallon admitted after a while. "I don't want her to stay with me out of gratitude or pity."

"Gratitude? Pity? Trust me, Fallon, a lot of people feel a lot of things when it comes to you, but gratitude and pity are rarely on the list. Why would Isabella feel either?"

"Can't talk about it right now. Got work to do."

"Wait, don't hang up."

"Serves you right after all the times you hung up on me when you were working as a contract agent for J&J."

Fallon cut the connection and went to the window. From that angle he could see most of the counter inside the Sunshine. Isabella was no longer inside the café. She must have finished her morning break and must have now been on her way around the corner to the grocery store. She would spend a few minutes chatting with Harriet Stokes while she collected the mail.

She's okay.

But his Jones intuition was riding him hard now, lifting the hair on the nape of his neck. He needed to find Isabella. There was no logical reason to take the gun, but he pulled out the lowest drawer of the desk and picked up the weapon and the holster.

He buckled the gun in place, took his leather jacket off the wall hook and went to the door. He would just amble down the street to the grocery store and intercept Isabella when she emerged with the mail. They could have another cup of coffee and tea together at the Sunshine.

The computer pinged. Something important had just come in. He went back across the room to see the new data that had arrived.

I'm like one of Pavlov's dogs, he thought morosely. *I respond to that damn ping the way the animals did to a bell. I start salivating. My reward is another dot of light on the paranormal grid instead of some kibble, but that's the only difference. I'm a creature of habit and a lousy conversationalist. Even the bad guys get bored listening to me. What was it Garrett said? Not a lecture on para-physics. Just shoot me now.*

Why would Isabella want to marry him even if she didn't have a phobia about licenses and paper trails? Great. Now he was feeling sorry for himself.

The encrypted message was from Max Lucan.

The buyer who commissioned the delivery of the mirror showed up at the motel where Garrett was staying. Sander Clay. The name should ring a few bells. He's the CEO of Clay Tech Industries. Turns out the Feds have been watching him for months because they think he's involved in illegal arms dealing (the normal kind). My people grabbed him when he tried to terminate Garrett. Got it all on video

411

complete with sound. Turned everything over to the FBI. Garrett is talking as fast as he can. He even admitted to killing Caitlin Phillips.

My work here is done. Any luck on your end?

Fallon straightened. He did not have time to respond to the query. The need to find Isabella was escalating.

He was heading back to the door when another ping sounded. He wanted to ignore it, but his intuition told him something important had come in.

The new e-mail was from the head of security at the L.A. Arcane museum.

. . . Can confirm that the entire staff submitted to a Q&A with Clare Lancaster Jones, the lie detector-talent you recommended. Everyone passed with flying colors. The list of names is attached. I'm at a loss to explain the theft of the mirror. A full inventory is currently being conducted to determine what other artifacts, if any, were stolen. . . .

The sense of urgency was pushing adrenaline through his veins, but he desperately needed answers. He pulled up the list of museum employees who had passed the psychic version of a lie detector test and compared it with the list he had ordered from the museum's personnel department.

There was one name on the list of employees that was missing from the list of people who had submitted to Clare's Q&A.

Lights lit up all over the grid as the connections slammed into place. He now knew who had sold the Quicksilver Mirror and, most likely, a number of other artifacts on the black market. But first he had to get to Isabella.

He went down the stairs to the empty first floor. When he reached the street, he headed for the grocery store.

Harriet Stokes was at the counter. She looked up from a gardening magazine when Fallon entered.

"Morning, Fallon. How's it going?"

"Fine." Fallon looked around, taking in the shelves of canned goods, the small freezer section and the bins of bulk nuts and grains. "Where's Isabella?"

"Haven't seen her yet this morning." Harriet put down the magazine. "Expect she's over at the café having coffee with Marge and Violet and Patty. Everyone in town wants to know how Cinderella got on at the ball."

"What ball?"

"That would be the one which required a fancy dress and glass slippers."

"What are you talking about?" Fallon headed for the door. "Never mind. I don't have time now."

He went outside and cut back across town to the Sunshine. When he yanked open the door, Marge, Violet and Patty stared at him.

"Where's Isabella?" he asked.

Marge frowned. "She left a while ago. Said she was going to pick up the mail."

Fallon went cold. "She never made it to the grocery store."

Violet smiled. "Take it easy. She said she was going to check up on Walker first. She was a little worried about him for some reason."

"Son of a bitch."

He broke into a run, heading toward Walker's cabin on the bluffs. He was dimly aware of Marge, Violet and Patty following him. Other people peered curiously out of doorways and shop windows.

When he went past the Scar, Oliver Hitchcock came out of the front door.

"Hey, Jones, what's up?" he shouted.

"Isabella," Fallon said. "She's in trouble."

The crack of thunder and the flash of lightning announced the rain.

By the time he reached Walker's cabin, he

was thoroughly soaked. He did not feel the cold. An icy psi fever was burning in him.

He went up the steps and pounded on the door.

"Isabella. Walker. Open the damn door."

There was no response. He was about to kick in the door when he discovered that it was unlocked.

The utter emptiness of the interior of the cabin gave off the ominous vibes of violence. He could feel it in his bones. He wanted to howl his rage into the teeth of the storm, but he made himself take a couple of minutes to search the cabin.

Footprints told part of the story. Isabella had entered the cabin. He could see her small, muddy prints on the floor. Two people in running shoes had entered through the back door, gone down the hall to the bathroom and then returned to the front room.

He went out through the kitchen into the backyard. Fresh tire tracks yielded more information. Walker did not own a car. The heavy tread belonged to an SUV.

He had missed something, he was sure of it. The fever searing his blood was making him careless. He had to stop and think or he would not stand a chance in hell of helping Isabella.

He went back into the cabin and stood quietly for a moment, opening his senses without trying to focus. The residue of some familiar currents of energy shivered in the atmosphere. He recognized them. One of the missing Victorian gadgets. That was how they had grabbed Isabella.

He saw the corner of the business card sticking out from under the rug. He picked it up. The name on the card confirmed his theory of the case.

"Son of a bitch," he whispered again.

He finally became aware of the small crowd forming on the front porch of the cabin. He looked through the open door and saw that half the town had followed him.

Henry stepped forward. "What's wrong, Jones? What happened to Isabella and Walker?"

"They've been kidnapped," Fallon said.

The knot of people stared at him, dumbfounded.

"Who would want to kidnap Walker and Isabella?" Marge demanded. "It's not like they're rich. There's no one to pay a ransom."

"This isn't about money," Fallon said. "It's about those damn Bridewell curiosities. Walker must have seen something he

416

wasn't supposed to see. I think Isabella was in the wrong place at the wrong time, so she was taken, too."

"It wasn't an accident that they took her," Patty said. "She had a feeling that Walker was in trouble. That's why she came here today to check on him. She thought maybe he was ill."

"What do we do now?" Violet asked. "Call the cops? It will take hours for them to get here, assuming they will even take a missing persons call seriously."

"I know who took Walker and Isabella," Fallon said. "Odds are they are still alive and will stay that way until nightfall. The person who is behind this has been very careful about not leaving any evidence. There's no reason she would change her pattern now. She's got a companion, someone to do the heavy lifting. They'll wait until dark and then they'll do what we plan to do with Lasher's skeleton."

"Dump them into the ocean?" Marge asked, horrified.

"Yes," Fallon said. "They won't want to drive far with a couple of kidnap victims in the back of an SUV. Too much risk of being pulled over by a cop. They'll stash Walker and Isabella somewhere until it's safe to get rid of them."

Marge looked at him, her face deeply shadowed with anxiety. "You keep saying she. You think that a woman took Isabella and Walker?"

"Her real name is Dr. Sylvia Tremont," Fallon said. "She's a curator at the Arcane museum in L.A. Everyone thinks she's on sabbatical in London. She's not. She's working real estate over in Willow Creek under the name Norma Spaulding."

33

Spaulding Properties was housed in a quaint, weathered commercial building on the main street of Willow Creek. The "Closed" sign showed in the window. Fallon walked past the entrance without pausing, as though he were headed to the drugstore on the corner.

When he reached the narrow strip of muddy grass that separated the premises of the real estate business from the restaurant next door, he turned quickly and went around to the back door of Spaulding Properties.

The rear door was locked, but that did not come as a surprise. Fallon reached inside his jacket and removed one of the electronic lock picks that he handed out like candy to J&J agents. It took less than three seconds to open the door. Whatever secrets Sylvia Tremont was hiding, she was not concealing them inside the office.

The back room of Spaulding Properties was remarkably uncluttered. There were no reams of paper, no stacks of printed brochures or any business machines. It had taken less than two minutes on the computer to discover that Norma Spaulding had not closed a sale in the four weeks that the office had been open.

He moved into the main room. The lack of sales had not stopped a few desperate homeowners from listing their properties with Spaulding Properties. Unappealing photos of a handful of aged cabins and the old Zander mansion adorned the wall.

He disregarded the mansion because, although it was no longer an active crime scene, it had become a grisly attraction for tourists and thrill seekers. It would not make a good place to hold Isabella and Walker.

He slipped into his other senses and studied the half-dozen featured listings with the cold-blooded logic of a killer. Swiftly he calculated distances from Walker's house, the degree of geographical isolation offered by the various properties and the proximity to the two locations in the area that provided the kind of powerful, reliable currents required to drag two bodies out to sea and make sure that the evidence disappeared.

Tremont would not use the Point, he concluded. It was too close to Scargill Cove. There was a serious risk that someone in town would see her and her companion, even in the midst of a storm. That left the second location, the blowhole site. The surf was violent there, and the currents were extreme. In the summer it was a popular tourist attraction. There was a convenient turnout.

In the end, one cabin stood out as the obvious choice. Certainty whispered through him.

He yanked the listing sheet off the wall and headed for the door. Although he was ninety-nine-point-two percent sure of his calculations, there was a small, but very real, possibility that he was wrong. He had to cover all the bases. Isabella's life was at stake. He opened his phone.

Henry answered halfway through the first ring.

"Six possible locations where she might be keeping Isabella and Walker," Fallon said. "I'm taking one. I'll read you the list of the other five properties. They're all empty cabins along the bluffs. You and the others check them. No one goes alone, understood?"

"Guns?" Henry asked.

"Oh, yeah," Fallon said. "Take guns. And the dogs. They know Isabella. If she's in one of those cabins, they'll tell you."

"Those dogs love Isabella. They'll rip out the throat of anyone who tries to hurt her."

34

Isabella dreamed . . .

She was waltzing with Fallon, wearing her lovely midnight-blue gown and her black crystal shoes. Fallon was resplendent in his black-and-white tux, the ultimate power suit.

They circled the glittering ballroom to the strains of the relentless beat. She should have been deliriously happy, but everything seemed wrong.

The ballroom was painfully bright, lit up with paranormal radiation from the most disturbing sectors of the spectrum. The senses-dazzling glare made it impossible to see the other dancers or the musicians. On top of that, the music was extremely annoying. She found herself wishing that it would stop.

And Fallon was not being at all lover-like. He looked at her with eyes that were hot and dangerous with psi fever.

"I'm on my way, Isabella. You do whatever

you have to do to stay alive until I get to you. Do you hear me?"

"Yes," she said. "I hear you. But what about the music?"

"Find the source and turn it off."

"How do I do that?"

"That's your problem. You're a J&J agent. You're supposed to figure these things out on your own."

She frowned, thinking. "But you're not really here with me, are you?"

"No."

"Then how can you be talking to me? There's no such thing as telepathy."

"True," Fallon said. "But you know me well enough to know what I'd be saying to you if I were there with you."

"Right."

She looked around, trying to bring the ballroom into focus, searching for the source of the music. She could do this. She had a talent for finding things.

She came awake to the muffled sound of pounding rain and booming surf. It took her a moment to realize that she was lying on a hardwood floor. She was cold and stiff. When she tried to move, she discovered that her hands and ankles were bound with duct tape. Mercifully, there was no tape across her mouth. Unfortunately, the obvious conclusion was that the kidnappers were not worried about her screaming. That, in turn, implied that the cabin was a long way from any source of help.

The music was still playing, but it was fainter now. She turned her head and saw the still shape of Walker lying beside her. He, too, was bound hand and foot.

She finally spotted the Victorian music box. It sat on a nearby table. The dancing figures were barely turning. The clockwork mechanism was winding down. Probably the reason she had awakened, she thought.

First things first. She rolled awkwardly across the floor until she reached the table. She levered herself onto her back, brought her knees up into a bent position, planted her feet against one leg of the table and pushed out with all of her strength.

The old table went over easily enough. The music box slid off and landed on the floor with a satisfying crack of glass and a clunk. The last notes of the waltz stopped abruptly. The dancing figures popped off and rattled across the floorboards until they fetched up against the wall.

To make certain the device was inoperable, she inchwormed her way to the broken artifact, turned her back to it and managed to grasp it in her bound hands. She slammed it against the floor a few times. Pieces of the mechanism fell out.

"That takes care of that problem," Isabella said softly. "Walker? Are you awake?"

There was no response.

She studied the shadowed interior of the cabin again, looking for anything she might be able to use to hack through the duct tape. She considered the small kitchenette. The place had obviously been uninhabited for a very long time, but with luck someone might have left a knife in one of the drawers. She started to work her way across the small room.

"Walker?"

This time she got a groan in response

"Walker, it's me, Isabella. Wake up."

Walker groaned again and stirred. His eyes opened. He looked straight at her.

"It's okay," she said gently. "Fallon will find us."

To her surprise there was no panic in Walker's eyes, just a bleak acceptance.

"She got p-past me, didn't she? I tried to s-stop her."

"I know, Walker. But she used a secret weapon on both of us."

"One of the alien weapons?"

"Yes, but don't worry, it's out of commission. I smashed it. Now we have to get free. I don't suppose you carry a pocketknife."

"Found a real n-nice one in the trash out behind Jones & Jones a few months ago," Walker said. "You wouldn't believe w-what people throw out."

"Do you have it on you?"

"In my new c-coat. Inside pocket. Can't imagine why anyone would throw away such a good coat."

"That's wonderful, Walker." She changed course and started to work her way toward him. "Turn onto your side. Maybe I can get the knife out of your coat."

He did as she instructed.

"Left pocket," he said hoarsely. "Hidden zipper."

It was tedious work trying to manipulate the interior zipper with her hands tied behind her back but she managed to get the pocket unzipped.

Footsteps sounded on the front porch just as she was probing for the knife. She froze, aware that Walker had done the same.

The door of the cabin opened. Norma Spaulding came into the room, a gun in her hand. A heavily bulked-up man who looked like he ate steroids for breakfast, lunch and dinner loomed behind her.

"Let me take a wild, flying leap here," Isabella said. "Your name isn't Norma Spaulding, and you're not in real estate."

"Good guess. I should introduce myself. Sylvia Tremont. I'm a curator at the Arcane museum in L.A."

"Well, that certainly explains a few things," Isabella said. She looked at the man. "Who's this?"

"His name is Vogel. Sort of an odd-jobs specialist. He was assigned to me a couple of days ago by my new associate when I said I was going to need a little assistance cleaning up a few loose ends."

"I s-saw you," Walker said urgently. "I s-saw you both last night. You were t-trying to sneak into the Cove."

Sylvia glanced at him. "I know you saw us. That's why you're going to take a very long swim this evening."

"What were you doing trying to sneak into the Cove?" Isabella asked.

"My new business associate concluded that you were going to be a problem because you are an unpredictable factor at Jones & Jones. She thought it would be best to neutralize you, as it were. She gave me a vial of a new experimental drug that affects the psychic senses in such a way as to make an individual behave in a dangerous and erratic manner. Jones would have assumed that you were going crazy. You would no longer have been any use to him. But when you showed up to check on this nutcase today, I realized that plan was no longer viable. Now I have no choice but to get rid of both of you."

"Killing us will be the biggest mistake you ever made," Isabella warned.

"It wasn't my first choice, believe me. I know Fallon Jones will search for you. That is not a good thing. But I've been very careful. I'm sure that, in the end, he will conclude that you just took off as you have been known to do in the past."

"He'll find you," Isabella promised. "He won't stop looking until he does."

"When this is over, I will disappear so completely that not even Fallon Jones can find me." Sylvia glanced at the pieces of the music box. "You would have to break it. I don't suppose you have any idea what that thing was worth in certain quarters?"

"Speaking of money, you owe Jones & Jones five hundred bucks," Isabella said.

Sylvia smiled. "And you're here to collect?"

"That's right."

"Good luck with that." Sylvia glanced at her watch. "It will be dark in a few hours. You and he will be going over the bluffs into

429

the sea as soon as night falls. I was planning to wait until midnight to make sure no one notices, but I don't think there's any need to hold off, not with this storm. No one will notice one more tourist stopping at the blowhole turnout to dump a couple of bags of trash."

"Since we've got all the time in the world," Isabella said, "mind telling me how you located the Bridewell curiosities?"

"I've been looking for them for years," Sylvia said. "To some extent, I was able to use the resources of the museum, but I had to be extremely discreet. I did not want to draw the attention of my colleagues or J&J. But after a certain point, I decided to fund my own search."

"And to do that, you needed money. A lot of it."

"More than I could afford on my salary from the museum, certainly."

"You set up a profitable little sideline selling off the odd paranormal weapon to Julian Garrett and Caitlin Phillips, using Orville Sloan as the broker."

"Sloan knew the world of paranormal arms dealing," Sylvia said. "It's a highly specialized field, as I'm sure you can imagine. He was the one who suggested that we work with Garrett and Phillips. The arrangement was quite successful for several months. Then I got a solid lead on a cache of curiosities."

"You found one of the two men who survived the explosion in the shelter, didn't you? Was it Kelso? That's the name of the family that used to own the lodge."

"His name was Jonathan Kelso. He was the last member of his family, and he was not mentally stable. By the time I tracked him down he was living in an institution. He told me a fascinating story about how he and two colleagues had discovered a number of Bridewell's clockwork curiosities. They wanted to find out exactly how they worked, but they knew the objects were dangerous. Kelso remembered the old bomb shelter behind the lodge and decided it would be a good place to run their experiments."

"They brought the curiosities here, tuned them up and then things went wrong."

"According to Kelso, there was an explosion. It killed one of the three outright. The second man's senses were severely affected by the heavy dose of radiation. He took his own life a few months later. Something about incessant nightmares. Kelso, himself, as I said, wound up in a psychiatric facility. But he was able to tell me about the commune that was going on in Scargill Cove at the time of the experiments. I started doing some research."

"You found Rachel Stewart."

"By the time I tracked her down she was dying of cancer and using serious pain meds. Her story was somewhat confused, but I was able to put the facts together into a coherent picture."

"She was a Seeker," Isabella said. "The woman everyone thought ran off with Gordon Lasher."

"Well, that was the plan. But Lasher was only interested in Rachel because it turned out she had a strong affinity for glass psi. Not only was she immune to the effects of the curiosities but she also intuitively understood how they worked. Furthermore, she could sense them at a distance."

"That was how she found the tunnel entrance to the bomb shelter."

"Yes," Sylvia said. "Lasher intended to use Rachel to remove the relics from the bomb shelter."

"She got one out for him, the clock."

"Yes. The idea was to store the devices temporarily in the Zander mansion until Lasher could figure out how to transport and sell them. When he and Rachel Stewart went back into the shelter to get another artifact, however, they quarreled. In the heat of the argument Rachel discovered that Lasher did not love her and was only using her. Surprise, surprise."

"So she crushed his skull with a tire iron."

"No," Sylvia said. "There was someone else there that night. Rachel said something about him not being right in the head."

"I hit him," Walker said. He rocked urgently, tears glistening in his eyes. "He hurt Rachel. He hit her and called her names. S-said he was going to take all the alien weapons. Rachel started to c-cry. So I hit him. Then she screamed and ran away through the tunnel and never came back."

"It's okay, Walker," Isabella said gently. She looked at Sylvia. "Thanks to Rachel Stewart, you knew the clock was somewhere in the Zander mansion and that the rest of the curiosities might still be in the shelter."

"Exactly. I set up as a real estate agent in Willow Creek and used my cover to search the mansion. I could sense the clock in the house but I couldn't find it."

"Because it was hidden beneath the new floor the killer had constructed in the basement," Isabella said. "He stored it there."

"I knew that even if I did locate the clock, there was no way I could get into the bomb shelter to get the rest of the curiosities. It was too well guarded by the good folk of Scargill Cove, not to mention a pack of dogs and a very serious lock. I could not find the tunnel entrance, either. I lacked Rachel's talent for sensing the glass psi at a distance."

"So you called in Jones & Jones," Isabella said. "You knew that Fallon would probably sense the clock if he went into the house and that he would tear the place apart to find it."

"Jones & Jones has a history with the Bridewell curiosities. I was quite sure that once Fallon Jones was on the trail, he would keep going until he turned up the rest of the artifacts in the shelter. I was prepared to drop a few hints about the events in the Cove twenty-two years ago if necessary, but as I expected, Jones was inside the shelter within twenty-four hours and the artifacts were trucked off to L.A. twenty-four after that. He's good."

"He wasn't working alone," Isabella said. This was hardly the time to get defensive, but an investigator had a professional reputation to consider, even when looking down the barrel of a gun.

"I'm well aware that you're a strong talent in your own right," Sylvia said. "Jones would never have hired you otherwise. If it's any consolation, I didn't know a serial killer was

434

using the house as a dumping ground."

"Thanks for that. It's a wonder he didn't catch you inside the mansion."

"I was only in the Zander house once."

"You plan to return from your sabbatical and join Rafanelli in his research on the curiosities," Isabella said. "After a discreet amount of time has passed, you will arrange for the gadgets to disappear from the museum vault."

"I'm afraid poor Dr. Rafanelli will get the blame when the Joneses discover that the artifacts are gone," Sylvia said. "Can't be helped, though. Someone has to take the fall. I will eventually resign in due course and disappear."

"Why on earth are you so obsessed with the curiosities?"

Sylvia blinked at the question. "Of course, I forgot, you have no idea, do you? I'm a direct descendant of Millicent Bridewell, and my talent is similar to hers. I can handle the psi in those artifacts."

"You mean you hope you can handle it. According to Fallon Jones, no one understands what Bridewell did with glass and psi."

Sylvia was clearly annoyed. "Now that I have access to a large number of her original creations, I can reverse-engineer them. My goal is to learn enough from them to be able to construct modern versions that will work even better than the originals. Instead of clock-work mechanisms, my curiosities will be powered by state-of-the-art technology."

"That kind of project would be a very expensive undertaking."

"Yes, it will be." Sylvia's expression tightened. "It is also an undertaking that Arcane would refuse to fund, given its ridiculous prohibition against weapons research. But my new associate has very deep pockets and is willing to finance a first-class lab for me."

"Where did you get the music box?"

"Family heirloom," Sylvia said. "Created by Millicent Bridewell herself."

"Why couldn't you just study that artifact to learn what you want to know?"

"It's not that simple," Sylvia said. Anger simmered in the words. "The music box was one of the more complicated examples of Bridewell's work. I've studied it for years and never figured out how she infused the energy into the glass."

"I'll bet you don't have any more luck with the other gadgets, either. How is your new business associate going to like it when she finds out you can't deliver?"

Outrage flashed across Sylvia's face. "All I need is time and a decent lab."

"Alien technology," Walker said. He rocked some more. "Too dangerous. Can't let the g-government have it."

Sylvia glanced at him, irritated. "Don't worry, the Feds will never get their hands on those curiosities."

For the first time Vogel spoke.

"Dogs," he said. He looked toward the window.

Sylvia frowned. "I don't hear anything."

Walker concentrated hard on Vogel.

"You're using a-alien drugs," Walker announced. "Poison."

"What the hell?" Vogel swung around, his face flushed a dark red with sudden fury. "Shut up."

"Yes, you are." Walker rocked fiercely. "You're on a-alien drugs."

"If you won't close your mouth, I'll do it for you," Vogel snarled. He pulled a roll of duct tape out of his pocket.

"Oh, wow," Isabella said. "Is this what they mean by 'roid rage? I've heard it's a major problem with guys who use steroids. No self-control whatsoever."

"Shut up, bitch." Vogel's voice rose. Face twisting, he changed course and went toward her.

"Vogel, stop right now," Sylvia said

sharply. "You take orders from me, remember."

Vogel ignored her. He reached down to grab Isabella's arms and started to yank her to her feet.

She got her focus and poured everything she had into an electrifying charge of energy.

"Get lost," she said softly.

Vogel froze. He released her, his expression going slack. He turned toward the door and started walking at a steady, deliberate pace.

"Vogel." Sylvia was alarmed now. "Come back here. Where are you going? What's wrong with you?"

Vogel did not respond. He opened the door, crossed the porch and went down the steps.

"Come back here," Sylvia shouted.

Vogel was in the yard. He disappeared from view, walking off into the driving rain. Somewhere in the distance dogs barked.

Sylvia spun back around to face Isabella. Fury contorted her features. "What did you do to him? You're just a finder-talent."

"I think he must have snapped," Isabella said. "Sorry about that. Maybe he's on drugs like Walker said."

Sylvia stared at Walker. "How did you know?"

Walker rocked.

Something went ping in Isabella's head. It sounded a lot like the ping on Fallon's computer.

"Oh, crap," she whispered. "You're right, Walker."

"Tell me how you know about the drugs," Sylvia hissed.

"Leave him alone," Isabella said.

Sylvia moved toward her. "What did you do to Vogel to turn him into a zombie?"

The storm was at nightmare pitch now. Lightning lit up the sky. It silhouetted the dark figure of Fallon. He came through the doorway on a floodtide of energy.

"No." Sylvia crouched directly behind Isabella and aimed the gun at Isabella's head.

"Make one more move and I'll kill her," Sylvia said. "I swear I will. Stay back."

Isabella sensed the rising heat in the atmosphere. She knew what Fallon was about to do. Sylvia must have sensed the threat as well.

"Stop it," she shouted. "I don't know what's going on here, but I swear I'll kill her before you can do anything to me. It only takes a fraction of a second to pull the trigger. She'll be dead before I will."

Isabella looked at Fallon. "It's okay. Trust me on this."

He stopped.

"That's right," Sylvia said. She seemed to pull herself together. "That's smart, Jones. Very smart. Isabella and I are going to leave now. She stays alive as long as no one follows us. Understood?"

"Understood," Fallon said. But in his eyes there was the promise of death.

"Good." Sylvia straightened slowly. "There's a knife on the floor, Jones. Use it to cut her ankles free."

The dogs were closer now. To Isabella's ears they sounded like a pack of hellhounds.

Fallon walked across the room, picked up the pocket knife and slashed the duct tape that bound Isabella's legs.

"You're sure you want to do it this way?" he said softly.

"I'm sure," she said.

"Shut up, both of you," Sylvia said. "On your feet, Isabella."

Isabella staggered awkwardly to her feet, aware of another kind of energy heightening the atmosphere. She knew then that Sylvia was going to try to kill Fallon.

"Can't stand," Isabella gasped. "My legs are numb."

Sylvia put a hand on her back and shoved her violently toward the door. *"Move."*

The physical contact gave Isabella the

focus she needed. She pulsed energy into Sylvia's aura, more energy than she had ever used in the past. She was suddenly on fire with power. It roared through her, filling the room.

The nexus energy, she thought. *I'm drawing on some of the natural power in the vicinity.*

"Run," she whispered. "Straight ahead."

Sylvia went absolutely still for an instant. The gun fell from her hand. Once again invisible lightning crackled in the atmosphere. Fallon had a fix.

"No," Isabella repeated.

Sylvia launched herself through the door and fled into the pounding rain.

The dogs were closer now, barking furiously.

Somewhere out in the storm a thin, high scream rose above the roaring wind and waves. It ended abruptly a few seconds later.

The dogs stopped barking.

Fallon pulled Isabella into his arms and held her as if he would never let her go.

A moment later Poppy and Clyde and the rest of the dogs rushed through the door of the cabin. They were delirious at the sight of Isabella. Henry and Vera and several other familiar faces raced up onto the porch and came through the door.

"Everybody okay here?" Henry asked.

Isabella raised her head from Fallon's shoulder and looked at her friends and neighbors.

"Yes," she said. "Everything is okay now."

35

Isabella and Fallon sat in the front of the black SUV. Walker rocked gently in the rear seat. They watched the sheriff and two deputies load Sylvia Tremont's body into a van.

In her mad flight from the cabin, Sylvia Tremont had fallen from the top of the bluffs onto the rocks below, breaking her neck.

"You knew she would run off the top of the bluffs," Fallon said quietly. It was not a question. "That's why you told me not to stop her."

"Yes." Isabella shivered. The full shock of what she had done was hitting her now. "I knew that would take her to the top of the bluffs."

Fallon took his right hand off the steering wheel and gripped her left hand very tightly.

"First time you've ever used your talent

like that," he said. Again, it was not a question.

"I told you, I've encountered my share of dead bodies."

"But you were never the one who made them dead."

"No," she agreed.

"You didn't want me to do it," he said.

"No."

"Because you thought I'd have a problem with killing a woman?"

"No." Isabella shivered. "Because it was my responsibility. I'm the one who brought her down on us. If I hadn't insisted on taking the Zander house case —"

"She would have found another way to get J&J involved in digging up the cache of curiosities," Fallon said. "The artifacts were highly volatile, unpredictable time bombs just waiting to go off. She needed us to get into the shelter, stabilize the objects and ship them safely back to the lab. Once they were well secured in L.A., she would have been able to arrange to steal them and let Rafanelli take the blame for the theft."

"Think so?"

"I know so," Fallon said. "Sylvia Tremont was a very determined woman. She killed Sloan in cold blood, and she was prepared to kill you and Walker, as well."

"Yes," Isabella said. "You're right."

"Should have let me handle it."

"No," Isabella said. Time to change the subject, she thought. "Any sign of the bodyguard?"

"Not yet."

"He's probably still walking," Isabella said. "I told him to get lost. He'll do just that."

"Alien drugs," Walker muttered. "Poison."

Fallon glanced at Walker in the rearview mirror. "What drugs?"

"I told you, *a-alien* drugs," Walker said urgently.

Isabella looked at Fallon. "The bodyguard looked like a steroid freak. Walker thinks Vogel was using drugs."

"I knew it." Fallon tightened his grip on the steering wheel. "Nightshade."

36

They sat side by side on the lumpy sofa, feet propped on the small coffee table, and drank some whiskey together.

"We're decompressing again," Fallon said.

"Yes."

"Twice in one week."

Isabella studied the contents of her glass. "It has been a very complicated week."

"It has," Fallon said.

"What are you thinking?"

"I'm thinking that one of the remaining Nightshade circles decided to try to acquire some para-weapons. When they got into that market they encountered the broker, Orville Stone."

"Who, in turn, led them to Sylvia Tremont," Isabella said, "who was busily selling off para-weapons from the Arcane museum basement. It must have been obvious that if she was already willing to risk stealing from Arcane, she was ripe for recruitment. Someone in Nightshade made her an offer."

Fallon turned the glass between his palms. "Tremont was thrilled because her new business associate promised her a lab of her own and unlimited funding for her experiments in glass psi."

"Yep."

"Operating a state-of-the-art lab costs money. Sounds like at least one of the Nightshade circles is still going strong. We need to find it fast."

"Any idea where to look?" Isabella asked.

"Maybe."

"You never say maybe."

"A connection to Portland, Oregon, came up not long ago when Jack Winters and Chloe Harper nearly got themselves killed in Seattle. One of the Nightshade people who died, a guy named John Stillwell Nash, was the CEO of a vitamin and health supplements company named Cascadia Dawn."

"A company that sells supplements and vitamins would make an excellent cover for an illicit drug lab. Did you check it out?"

"I've had people watching it. A new CEO took over shortly after Nash died. She used another name, but I think she might have been Victoria Knight. Before that I think she was Niki Plumer."

"Who was Niki Plumer?"

"A Nightshade operative. Figured in the case in which Zack and Raine were involved. She wound up in a psychiatric hospital. Supposedly she committed suicide but I've had my doubts."

"You think she became Victoria Knight."

"If I'm right, she's the para-hypnotist who showed up in Las Vegas in the Burning Lamp case a few weeks ago. My talent tells me she was the new CEO of Cascadia Dawn. But the first thing she did was sell the company and disappear again."

"Why sell it?"

"She probably realized that we were aware of the company. Also, she needs money. I think she sold a very profitable business, pocketed the cash and went somewhere else to fire up another circle. I've been waiting for her to pop up again. I believe she may have done just that."

"That fits. I told you that Sylvia mentioned that her new business associate was a woman who thought I should be neutralized."

"I realize it would have been very hard to poison you," Fallon said. "You would have detected the bad energy in the vicinity of the stuff. But I am very grateful to Walker. I owe him."

"We all do."

"We lost Knight's trail, but we know one thing for certain," Fallon continued. "Like everything else that has happened in the Nightshade case, the weapons procurement operation was centered here on the West Coast. For whatever reason, the organization, or what's left of it, appears to be based on this side of the country."

"Maybe because this is where Craigmore established it?"

"That could be it," Fallon said. "But I'm starting to wonder if perhaps it has something to do with the natural energy grids that run from Washington down through Oregon, California and Arizona. There aren't many nexus points as strong as the Cove, at least not that have been mapped, but there are a number of vortex sites like those in Sedona. Maybe there's one in Portland that hasn't been charted."

"You think Dr. Hulsey is trying to use the power of the grid to enhance the formula?"

"That's how it feels. If I'm right, it narrows the scope of the search somewhat."

"Lot of country between Washington and Arizona."

"True. But over the years several of the hot spots have been mapped. And there are talents who are good at sensing nexus and vortex points. We might be able to construct a map of the most likely locations for a Nightshade lab."

Isabella sipped some more whiskey and lowered the glass.

"Something happened today, when I put Tremont into the trance," she said. "I don't know how I did it, but I think that, just for a second, I tapped into the nexus energy in this area. I'm strong, but I've never felt anything like that before in my life. It was very strange."

"It wouldn't be the first time that a strong talent managed to pull some nexus energy. But it's a very high-risk pastime. It's like picking up a live electrical wire. The currents could short out your senses or even kill you. Promise me you won't make a habit of it."

A chill went through her at the memory. "You have my word on it," she said. "What's our next step?"

"If someone was running a research lab out of Cascadia Dawn, there has to be some trace of it left in the building. I'm going to send an agent inside to take a look around."

"Who?"

"The same one who helped clean up things in Seattle a while back. He's an illusion-talent. The guy's as cold as ice, but he gets the job done. I've learned not to ask for details afterward, though."

She glanced at him and smiled. In spite of the exhausting day, he looked energized. Sherlock Holmes with a bunch of new clues and leads to sort out.

"What do you think is going on inside Nightshade at this very moment?" she asked.

"My gut tells me that things have changed drastically at the top of the organization. The command structure fell apart after the founder died, and it has not yet had time to reconstitute itself. I'm not sure it can. I am finally beginning to perceive the outlines of the new version of the organization."

"I take it that you're not envisioning a kinder, gentler Nightshade?"

"No, I think that, for the time being, we're going to find ourselves dealing with a handful of mini-Nightshades, each one operating independently."

"Like a bunch of criminal gangs instead of one single mob?"

"Right." Fallon took his feet off the coffee table. He leaned forward, forearms braced on his thighs and cradled his glass in both hands. His eyes gleamed with a familiar intensity. "Which means that there is a high probability of outright warfare between some of the gangs. We're talking the usual corporate politics. There will be shifting alliances. There will be power grabs. Backstabbings. Betrayals."

"You look like a kid who just got a big stack of birthday presents."

His eyes heated with a little psi. She could almost hear the spark and snap of energy in the atmosphere.

"The infighting will work in our favor," he said. "It will give us lots of cracks and fissures to exploit."

"What about the formula? From what you've told me, whoever controls it, controls Nightshade."

"The formula was being produced in a number of different locations before Craigmore was killed. From what we can tell, each lab functioned independently, conducting its own research on the original version of the drug."

"All in an effort to deal with the side effects?"

"Yes. We took down five of the labs, but there are a few more out there that we haven't found. We have to assume that the research is continuing and that new variations on the drug are in the pipeline. Some versions are no doubt more effective than others. Each drug producer will fight to keep its formula secret while trying to steal other, more effective versions."

"So, in addition to the infighting, betrayals and backstabbings, we'll be seeing some corporate espionage among the remaining circles."

"We can work with that," Fallon said. "Where there is espionage work to be had, there are any number of job openings available for double agents, traitors, thieves and spies."

"And killers?"

"Yes," Fallon said. He looked satisfied. "I think the illusion-talent in Seattle will fit right in."

37

He woke up in Isabella's double bed, aware that it was nowhere near dawn. He checked the glowing dial of his watch. Two in the morning. Isabella was neatly tucked into the curve of his body. He was suddenly, fully aroused.

He eased one hand under the hem of her nightgown and moved his palm upward over her warm thigh. Levering himself up on his elbow, he kissed her shoulder.

"Are you awake?" he asked.

"No."

He slid his fingers between her legs. "Are you sure?"

"I'm sure."

"Okay," he said. "I just wondered."

He pressed himself against her soft rear, nibbled on her earlobe and started to tease her lightly with his fingers.

She sighed and turned onto her back. He felt energy heighten in the shadows. When he jacked up his senses, he saw the gentle heat in her eyes. She put her arms around his neck.

"I'm awake now," she said.

"So am I."

"I noticed."

He moved over her, capturing her beneath him, and kissed her. With a soft, languid whisper, she opened for him, inviting him into her warmth. He made love to her, slowly, deliberately, until she was hot and shivery in his arms, until he sensed the escalating tension deep inside her. Only then did he thrust into her.

"Fallon."

She came almost immediately and so did he.

When it was over, he withdrew reluctantly and fell back onto the pillow beside her. Reaching down between them he found her hand and clasped it. He waited until both of them were breathing normally again.

"Tomorrow we'll drive up the coast to Eclipse Bay and find your grandmother," he said.

"You're sure she's there?"

"Yes," he said. "It's all right to contact her now. You can call her in the morning. She's no longer in any danger."

"Thanks to J&J."

He looked up at the ceiling, intensely aware of her hand in his. "You're safe now, too."

"Yes."

"You can go anywhere," he said. "You don't have to hide out in Scargill Cove."

"I'm not hiding, not anymore. I've spent my entire life on the outside looking through the windows of people who actually have lives. Now I've got one of my own and I'm going to live it."

"Are you sure?"

"Scargill Cove feels like home," she said. "Interesting job. Nice neighbors. I think I was cut out for small-town living."

"You're sure you like the job?"

"I was born for it," she said.

"That's good because I need you to help me do this work."

"I agree."

"Marry me, Isabella."

She did not respond.

The unquenchable fires of chaos froze. Time stopped. Maybe his heart stopped, as well. He discovered he could not breathe, did not want to breathe, if he did not get the right answer.

"You don't have to marry me to keep me at my desk at J&J," Isabella said eventually. "I'll stay with you."

"I'm a Jones. In my family we get married. Ceremony, license, the whole works."

"Interesting customs in your family. We don't do the license thing in mine."

"I'm hoping you'll adopt my family traditions, but if you don't want to do that, I'll take you any way I can get you."

"I think I could adopt your customs if you think you can go along with one of my family traditions."

"I'll do anything for you," he said simply. "Name it."

"In my family we fall in love. Can you love me? Because I love you, Fallon Jones, with all of my heart."

The glorious fires of chaos flared high once more. Time went forward. His pulse restarted. He could breathe again.

"Isabella." He pulled her into his arms, crushing her to him. "I will love you for the rest of my life and whatever comes after."

"In that case," she said, "I will be happy to break a few old family traditions and marry you. In fact, to prove how much I love you, I'll even use my real name on the wedding license."

He laughed, the energy of joy pouring through him in a torrent. And then he was kissing her and she was kissing him and the night was on fire.

457

■ ■ ■ ■

The news of the death was in the Willow Creek paper the following morning. Fallon read it to Isabella over coffee.

> *The unidentified body of a man was found shot to death in a concealed marijuana plantation early this morning. Authorities believe the man either wandered into the plantation by accident or went there deliberately to steal some of the plants. It is believed that he was killed by guards hired to protect the crop.*
>
> *A representative of the sheriff's department said that the marijuana will be destroyed. The growers have been declared persons of interest. Anyone having any information about those responsible for the plantation is asked to contact the authorities.*

"I told him to get lost," Isabella said. "He blundered into someone's hidden marijuana plantation and got shot."

"If it's any consolation, he probably wouldn't have lasted long, anyway," Fallon said. "Not if he was on the drug. The latest information we have indicates that those who take it must take a dose twice a day, every day. Miss even a single dose and the senses start to deteriorate. Insanity and death usually follow within forty-eight hours."

"Yes, I know," Isabella said.

"But it doesn't make you feel any better."

"No," she said.

38

It had been a very bad week.

Victoria Knight took her glass of wine out onto the balcony of her condo to drink. The lights of Seattle glittered in the rain.

A very bad week.

Two well-conceived projects had floundered. It was true that the one involving Carolyn Austin had been chancy from the start. The odds had been stacked against success, Victoria thought, but when her new associate within Arcane had suggested the idea, she had thought it worth a shot. The opportunity to weaken J&J and, perhaps, loosen the grip of the Jones family on the Society had been irresistible. They had sought to harness the raw energy of a grieving mother driven by an obsessive desire for revenge and it had almost worked. Almost.

The second project had been far more elaborately designed and carried out. It definitely should have been successful. Victoria's fingers tightened on the delicate stem of the glass. The concept of developing a para-weapons lab based on Bridewell's inventions had been brilliant. *It should have worked.*

Both projects had floundered because of Isabella Valdez and, it seemed, the very town of Scargill Cove. Something about Isabella's energy made her formidable. It was a shame that Sylvia Tremont had been unsuccessful in the attempt to introduce the poison into Isabella's kitchen. But that had been another long shot.

As for the Cove, it was as if the small community was guarded by some kind of protective force field.

Two excellent projects in ruins. In the old days when Nightshade had been governed by Craigmore, that kind of track record would have meant a death sentence.

But Nightshade was different now. Following Craigmore's death, the executives of the Inner Circle had been unable to elect a new director. Instead, they had gone for one another's throats, literally in some cases. Two of the people at the top had recently been found dead. The official verdict in each instance was natural causes, but she was quite sure that was not the case. Someone was getting rid of the competition.

Meanwhile the surviving circles were on their own and operating independently. She had no way of knowing how many more were out there in addition to the one she controlled, but she had to assume that there were other cells that possessed a version of the formula.

But she had Humphrey Hulsey, the most talented of all the researchers, working on the drug. He was overseeing the construction of his new lab at that very moment. She had every confidence that the version of the formula that came out of his facility would be the most powerful and the most stable.

Whoever controlled the strongest variation of the drug, controlled Nightshade.

A bad week. But she had uncovered three traitors within Arcane, thereby proving that the fundamental strategy had potential. Carolyn Austin and Sylvia Tremont had failed, but they were proof that the Joneses had enemies who could be turned against them.

As for the third Jones enemy, he was now her new business associate. He was going to prove invaluable because he moved in the highest circles of the Society. The desire for vengeance was a powerful motivator. Her new associate hated the Joneses with a passion that had been seething in his bloodline for generations.

"More wine, Victoria?" he said behind her.

She looked down and saw that her glass was empty. She turned around. "Yes, thanks. It's been a difficult week."

Adrian Spangler smiled. Cold energy shivered in the atmosphere around him.

"Something tells me things will soon be looking up," he said. "Together, you and I are going to destroy the Joneses and everything they have created. We will take over Arcane."

He came forward with the bottle of wine. Before he filled her glass, he kissed her. She felt her blood heat.

Adrian was valuable because of his position within Arcane. He possessed a powerful talent and, like her, he was smart enough to stay off the formula until Hulsey had proven that it was stable. The sexual attraction between them had been instantaneous from the start.

Adrian Spangler was everything she needed to achieve her objectives, Victoria thought. But she was starting to wonder who was using whom.

Sometimes Adrian Spangler scared the hell out of her.

39

They drove into Eclipse Bay just after sundown. Like all small towns on the coast in winter, the community was quiet and mostly dark. The shops on the main street were closed.

Fallon followed the directions he had been given and pulled into the driveway of a weathered cabin. Light glowed in the windows. There was another vehicle in the drive, an SUV painted camouflage green and brown.

The door of the cabin opened before he got the engine shut down. Two women came out onto the porch. Both wore their tightly permed steel-gray hair cut short in the classic senior helmet. The taller of the two was dressed in military-style fatigues and heavy black boots. The shorter one wore a faded denim shirt, jeans and running shoes. In spite of their age, there was an air of wiry vigor about the women.

life," he said. "I've got one now, too."

"Feels good, doesn't it?" Isabella said.

"Yes," Fallon said. "It feels very good."

ABOUT THE AUTHOR

Jayne Ann Krentz is the author of more than fifty *New York Times* bestsellers. She has written contemporary romantic suspense novels under that name, as well as futuristic and historical romance novels under the pseudonyms Jayne Castle and Amanda Quick, respectively. She lives in Seattle.

We hope you have enjoyed this Large Print book. Other Thorndike, Wheeler, Kennebec, and Chivers Press Large Print books are available at your library or directly from the publishers.

For information about current and upcoming titles, please call or write, without obligation, to:

Publisher
Thorndike Press
295 Kennedy Memorial Drive
Waterville, ME 04901
Tel. (800) 223-1244

or visit our Web site at:

http://gale.cengage.com/thorndike

OR

Chivers Large Print
published by AudioGO Ltd
St James House, The Square
Lower Bristol Road
Bath BA2 3SB
England
Tel. +44(0) 800 136919
www.audiogo.co.uk

All our Large Print titles are designed for easy reading, and all our books are made to last.